MW01196331

THE
HOSPITAL

BOOKS BY LESLIE WOLFE

If I Go Missing

The Surgeon

The Girl You Killed

Stories Untold

Love, Lies and Murder

DETECTIVE KAY SHARP SERIES

The Girl from Silent Lake

Beneath Blackwater River

The Angel Creek Girls

The Girl on Wildfire Ridge

Missing Girl at Frozen Falls

TESS WINNETT SERIES

Dawn Girl

The Watson Girl

Glimpse of Death

Taker of Lives

Not Really Dead

Girl With a Rose

Mile High Death

The Girl They Took

The Girl Hunter

LESLIE WOLFE

THE HOSPITAL

GRAND CENTRAL

New York   Boston

This book is a work of fiction. Names, characters, businesses, organizations, places, and events, other than those clearly in the public domain, are either the product of the author's imagination or are used fictitiously. Any resemblance to actual persons, living or dead, events, or locales is entirely coincidental.

Copyright © 2024 by Leslie Wolfe

Cover design by Alexander Lozano. Cover photo by Spotmatik/Alamy stock photo. Cover copyright © 2025 by Hachette Book Group, Inc.

Hachette Book Group supports the right to free expression and the value of copyright. The purpose of copyright is to encourage writers and artists to produce the creative works that enrich our culture.

The scanning, uploading, and distribution of this book without permission is a theft of the author's intellectual property. If you would like permission to use material from the book (other than for review purposes), please contact permissions@hbgusa.com. Thank you for your support of the author's rights.

Grand Central Publishing
Hachette Book Group
1290 Avenue of the Americas, New York, NY 10104
grandcentralpublishing.com
@grandcentralpub

Originally published by Bookouture, an imprint of Storyfire Ltd., in 2024
First Grand Central Publishing edition: August 2025

Grand Central Publishing is a division of Hachette Book Group, Inc. The Grand Central Publishing name and logo is a registered trademark of Hachette Book Group, Inc.

The publisher is not responsible for websites (or their content) that are not owned by the publisher.

The Hachette Speakers Bureau provides a wide range of authors for speaking events. To find out more, go to hachettespeakersbureau.com or email HachetteSpeakers@hbgusa.com.

Grand Central Publishing books may be purchased in bulk for business, educational, or promotional use. For information, please contact your local bookseller or the Hachette Book Group Special Markets Department at special.markets@hbgusa.com.

Library of Congress Cataloging-in-Publication Data

Names: Wolfe, Leslie (Fiction writer), author
Title: The hospital / Leslie Wolfe.
Description: First Grand Central Publishing edition. | New York : Grand Central Publishing, 2025.
Identifiers: LCCN 2025009486 | ISBN 9781538772447 trade paperback
Subjects: LCGFT: Thrillers (Fiction) | Psychological fiction | Novels
Classification: LCC PS3623.O55298 H67 2025 | DDC 813/.6—dc23/eng/20250321
LC record available at https://lccn.loc.gov/2025009486

ISBN: 9781538772447 (trade paperback)

Printed in the United States of America

CCR

10 9 8 7 6 5 4 3 2 1

A special thank you to my New York City legal eagle and friend, Mark Freyberg, who expertly guided me through the intricacies of the judicial system.

An enthusiastic thank you to Dr. Deborah (Debbi) Joule for her friendship and thoughtful advice. She made my research into traumatic brain injury management and pharmacotherapy a far less daunting task. Her expertise and passion for precision and detail made writing this novel a fantastic experience.

ONE

Where am I?

The question rushes through my mind as my consciousness returns, hesitant and shattered, from a deep darkness. Slowly, accompanied by a throbbing headache that seeds nausea in the pit of my stomach, my awareness tries—and fails—to restore my understanding of where I am. Of what's happening to me.

Opening my eyes seems an impossibly difficult task. I battle the weakness in my muscles, yearning for the light to help me get my bearings. Yet, my eyelids remain stubbornly closed.

Fighting the frailty of my body, I try to raise my hand and touch my face but my hand doesn't move. It's as if it is too heavy to lift, to attempt the tiniest gesture.

Even my face feels like a stranger's. Distant. Cut off somehow. The sensory inputs are weak and remote, almost like something I would perceive secondhand, like watching an intense movie and sharing the character's emotions, sensations, and fears. Feeling real, but distant and disconnected.

As much as I struggle to open my eyes, not the faintest shred of light cuts through the deep, absolute blackness. My world has been swallowed by darkness.

Panic washes over me in a sweeping wave, each heartbeat thundering in my ears. My mind, a jumbled mess, grasps frantically at the frayed edges of my memory as I try to remember why I'm trapped in a paralyzed world. Every attempt to move is met with terrifying stillness where there should be motion.

What's happening to me?

A scream builds up in my chest and comes off my lips as barely a whimper, almost too quiet for me to hear.

A memory dashes through my frantic mind, fueling my all-consuming fear.

It isn't clear. It doesn't feature images and actions and people I recognize; merely a blurry recollection of emotions I've felt and things I've done. A dream more than a memory, a nightmare really, and just as terrifying.

In my vision, I am running for my life with frenzied footsteps that falter when I look over my shoulder, breathing shallow and fast between desperate shrieks. Instead of seeing who's after me, the space behind me is a void, filled with the same darkness that has overtaken every corner of my world now. I recall screaming, pleading, calling for help. I can still feel it in my body: the despair, the fear, the screams searing my throat. And running, faster and faster, with a sense that whatever is chasing me is gaining ground.

As I relive it in my mind, I feel the same fear gripping my throat and strangling it. The darkness grows suffocating, a relentless oppressor, ripping me from the ground and spinning me higher and higher, my thoughts spiraling into chaos.

From that torment, a single clear thought emerges.

Whatever I've been running from has caught up with me. And now I lie here, vulnerable and helpless, unable to move, unable to see where I am.

I breathe slowly, the effort to fill my lungs with air almost impossible, and urge my hectic mind to settle. It doesn't come quickly or easily. Flashes of the same memory, looping in my mind over and over, do nothing to calm my fears. But I keep at it, breath after excruciatingly slow breath, listening to the air entering my body then leaving it without apparent connection to the rapid rhythm of my heartbeats.

My mouth feels dry, my tongue sticky and swollen.

That tiny bit of sensory information is like unearthed treasure in the black emptiness in my mind. I take it and follow it like an unraveling thread, in search of a way out of the labyrinth. Soon enough, more such morsels start to collect and form an image I can read.

I'm thirsty. My lips are chapped, and the tip of my tongue does nothing to moisten and soothe them. I try to move my fingers one more time, slowly and mindfully, to no avail. Just as stubbornly, my eyes stay firmly closed, protecting the darkness within at the cost of my sanity.

Just as the irrational fear is starting to return, I hear the blaring yet muted siren of an ambulance in the distance, faint but approaching. I pay close attention to that and the other, almost indistinct, sounds I'm beginning to pick up, and images start taking shape in my mind.

A few moments after the siren stops, I'm aware of people chatting as they pass by, also distant somehow, but close enough. If I screamed, they would probably hear me. I draw breath as forcefully as I can and try to call out.

Only a whisper comes out of my mouth, and the people continue unperturbed, walking away with brisk steps.

Still, I'm not alone.

The whoosh of my own blood in my ears subsides a little as my panic wanes with that realization.

More sounds start filling my world, no longer dampened by my fear. A distant PA calls for a doctor to report somewhere I don't quite catch. Closer and a little louder, the subdued and rhythmic beeping of a machine, its sounds synced to perfection with my own heartbeats.

I'm in the hospital.

It's the only logical conclusion I can draw. And it means that I didn't escape from whomever I've been running from after all. I succumbed to their attack, and it landed me here, helpless and vulnerable and lost. Fear returns with that thought, but this time tinged with a fiery anger, swelling my mind with questions I can't answer, while the face of my attacker remains shrouded in obscurity.

I play that snippet of memory again, hoping I'll be able to catch a glimpse of the person I tried to run from. I can't visualize a face nor remember a name. I don't remember much at all; only that I'm not safe, and that next time, there will be no escape. I'm absolutely sure of that, as I'm sure of my own name.

I'm Emma Duncan, and I survived. I'm still alive.

It feels good to say it, even if it's only an unspoken thought.

My world has been silent for a while when the sound of approaching footsteps makes me hold my breath, while the thumping of my heart grows faster and faster, echoed by the increased beeping of the monitor.

Footsteps walk past, quickly and purposefully, then return. I can feel shifting air gently touching my cheeks, a sensation I've never been aware of before. Between the soft sound of rubber soles on the floor and the air moving inside the room, I can picture someone walking back and forth, close to me. Close enough to touch.

Perhaps close enough to kill.

My first instinct is to stay quiet and wait for them to be gone. It's senseless, irrational, only a short while after I tried my best to get attention by calling out. Maybe this person will have answers for me. Or perhaps they are here to finish the job they started when I was running, trying to escape.

A quiet sob leaves my chest before I can stop it. Tears emerge from the corners of my eyes, but they don't roll down my cheeks. Or I don't feel them if they do.

The rubber soles freeze for a dizzying moment, then approach quickly. A warm hand clasps mine and squeezes gently.

"You're awake," a woman's voice says cheerfully. "That's wonderful. I'll get the doctor."

TWO

Seeing Emma like that, lying motionless in a pool of her own blood, breaks my heart.

For a while, all I could do was stare. Her beautiful face, partly covered by loose strands of long, chestnut hair, blown gently by the cold wind, was turning pale under the moonlight. Her lips, slightly parted, seemed to be calling my name, only I knew they weren't. Her hand, twitching as it lay on the frozen ground, would never reach out for mine.

Not after what had happened tonight.

In front of me, the house stood shrouded in darkness, towering over her, her lifeless guardian. To the side, a grove of aspens softly whispered in the wind, their leaves rustling as they fell to the ground, forever defeated.

I drew closer, careful to not let anyone see me as I emerged from the shadows slowly, silently.

I didn't dare feel for a pulse, as if her skin could sear my trembling fingers. The vulnerability of that perfect body, the frailty of life itself, reminded me of my own troubled youth. My breaths turned fast and heavy remembering how powerless I used to be, at the mercy of others. Of my mother.

But that was many years ago. Let bygones be bygones.

The late November night had brought a layer of bitter cold air rolling off the mountain peaks, and I was soon shivering, my teeth chattering as I shoved my hands deep inside my pockets. The wind howled, and the tall aspens bent under its power, littering the asphalt with fallen leaves. A couple of wind-battered leaves, still green in places where the early frost hadn't bitten them yet, landed by Emma's head and floated on her blood, yellow and amber boats on dark red waters.

I touched my phone screen, considering the call I needed to make. Emma's fingers still twitched every now and then; she was still alive. I couldn't be sure how much time she had. The expanding pool of blood surrounding her head like a dark halo told me it was running out fast.

I dialed the numbers nine-one-one, but didn't connect. If I did, they would know who called, could access the phone's location history and know I'd been there, watching her, for hours. They would come after me with a vengeance, happy to have such a quick turnaround on a collar.

The alternative was to watch Emma die, right there at my feet. That couldn't happen. I couldn't bear it. Not with her. With anyone else, the decision would've been easy. I would've just walked away, not even blinking, not looking back once. Not making any calls, saving myself from any shred of trouble.

But Emma? My Emma? I couldn't just stand there and watch her die. No. Never. No matter the cost.

For a while, I paced near her, doing everything in my power to ignore the soft cries coming from her pale lips, wishing I could pick her up and comfort her, hold her tight in my arms, carry her inside to warmth and safety. Instead, I trod the driveway like a caged animal, considering my limited options. What if I called for help, then destroyed my phone before they could track it? I wasn't sure that would work. Then, what else could I do? What lie could I tell to explain my presence?

As I paced faster and faster, torn by my own indecision, I started to realize what I felt deep inside. How the metallic smell of her blood filled me with an unclear yearning. How deeply troubled I was by the vulnerable body lying at my feet, the power I had over her.

In that moment, on the serrated edge between life and death, she was completely and absolutely mine.

As I looked at her once more, still torn, I noticed her fingers falling still. The twitching had stopped; she was dying, or was already dead.

The time for indecision, for considering alternatives, had come and gone. Without any more hesitation, I chose the best of all the options, and made the call.

Now, as I stand in the shadow of the trees, staring at where her body used to lie, I know I made the right decision. Pristine, glimmering snow covers everything with a white layer of innocence. And Emma's still alive.

My sweet Emma.

THREE

The soft rubber soles walk away from the bed, then fade after a door is closed gently. I hold my breath, listening intently, while my mind fills with questions I have to ask. Distant sounds, barely perceptible, tell me there are people passing by outside my door, moving quickly, occasionally whispering. A metallic instrument clatters on a tray, and a beeping alert, much like a microwave's, makes me think of medical equipment I've seen in movies but can't name.

My nostrils flare a little, recognizing the smell of gauze, of sterile supplies, of disinfectants. It's faint yet fresh, as if a pack of it has just been unsealed. Yet I don't recall hearing the crinkling of torn packaging, not since I've been awake.

The door opens quietly, and I breathe in again; only the beeps coming from the heart monitor a giveaway of my anxious state of mind. Steps follow, heavier than the rubber soles I now recognize, but just as rushed. A faint scent of something citrusy, or perhaps hinting of herbs like sage or basil, reaches me. It is elegant and masculine, a cologne someone used sparingly. Then the approaching rustling of scrubs comes to a halt as the footfalls stop at my bedside.

"Hello, Ms. Duncan. I'm Dr. Sokolowski, your attending physician. Do you remember speaking with me before?"

His voice sounds muffled but is low, soothing, with a bit of a Slavic accent—perhaps Polish. And completely unknown to me. I've never heard that voice before. Why would he ask if I recognized him?

"N—no," I say, speaking with difficulty. The same weakness that has frozen my limbs is affecting my face, my cheeks, my tongue, but the panic that has been choking me is subsiding quickly. "I don't believe we've spoken before."

A brief moment of silence falls between us, then the sound of something on wheels being rolled over the floor, and more rustling of crisp fabrics as the doctor probably takes a seat by the bed. "You don't recognize my voice?" His voice is tinged with an undertone of concern that fills me with dread, and still sounds muffled, as if he's holding a handkerchief over his mouth. As if he's wearing a surgical mask.

I breathe out, relieved. Of course he is. It makes sense. "No. What's happening to me?"

He squeezes my hand gently. Distantly, through what feels like a nitrile glove, I feel his fingers searching for my pulse. "Don't worry, Ms. Duncan, I'll answer any questions you might have. You—"

"Emma." I swallow, my throat dry and constricted. "Please."

"All right, then, Emma." A hint of a smile colors his voice briefly, before it turns grim and concerned. "You were brought here after an accident. You've been admitted to Baldwin Memorial—"

I voice my protest, wishing I could put more strength into my words, and he stops speaking and listens to me.

"I was attacked. There was no accident." I breathe a little faster, agitated, scared even by the doctor's ignorance, desperate to set the record straight. I fight to lift myself off the pillow, but nothing moves, the stillness of my body dripping panic in my veins. "I was running and I—"

At a loss for words that could explain what happened, I stop mid-sentence, panting. I can't tell him what happened. I don't remember any of it.

The wheels roll on the floor briefly, and I realize he must be moving around on a wheeled chair, although I clearly heard him walking earlier. Then comes the sound of plastic hitting something lightly and papers rustling makes me picture the doctor reviewing notes in my chart, perhaps on a clipboard of sorts.

"It says here, accident, specifically a slip and fall. I'll correct it." Papers rustle some more. "Don't worry, you're absolutely safe here."

Despair swells my chest. "You don't understand," I cry weakly. "I don't think it's over. I know it's not over. I can feel it. And I can't see, I can't move—"

He squeezes my hand again, reassuringly this time. It feels just as distant as before. "We'll take good care of you. We have an excellent trauma team and none of us will let anything bad happen to you." His voice is serious, resolute.

I believe him, and allow myself to relax a little. "What happened to me? Why was your voice supposed to be familiar?"

"We've spoken twice before, but I'm going to explain what's going on. After that, I might have some questions too. If you need me to clarify something or slow down, please let me know."

"Just tell me what happened," I plead, terrified by the void in my memory. It isn't that I've forgotten some of the things the doctor has said; it's as if I've never met him before, as if nothing has existed since that moment when I was running for my life.

"Yes, let's do that," he says gently. "You've sustained a serious concussion, a traumatic brain injury caused by a blow to the head or a violent shaking of the head and body, that has impacted the visual cortex in your brain. I believe there was a blow, the kind we see when people fall down the stairs, rather than shaking, but we cannot completely exclude shaking. There was a laceration to the back of your head, and bruising, all indicative of a significant impact with a blunt object."

My blood freezes in my veins as I hear the words. Brain injury? It explains why I don't remember what happened. It means I might never know who hurt me. I might never see again or walk again.

Dr. Sokolowski pauses for a moment. "Due to the nature of your injury, you're experiencing significant symptoms. The most challenging right now is that you're unable to see, and have difficulty moving. There's significant swelling in the brain, compressing nerves and impairing their function."

It doesn't seem real, although it is. The thought of it chills my blood. "What will happen to me? Will I ever see again?"

"We're hoping this is what's causing your blindness and your paralysis, and that it will resolve as the edema does. That's the medical term for the swelling in your brain, by the way. We've conducted tests, a CT scan and an MRI, and we're not seeing anything irreversible on those scans."

"How long?" I demand, fighting back the tears that burn my eyes. I can't live like this . . . not for another minute. Terror seeps through my body like a wintry chill. "How long will I be like this? I'm scared."

The doctor draws breath and holds it for a moment. The simple sound of his hesitation unnerves me. He must be used to delivering bad news to patients by now. How bad is it, really? What is he not saying?

"I'll be honest with you, Emma. It's a serious injury, but it's important to note that the situation can change. The human brain has a remarkable ability to heal. While we can't predict the outcome with certainty, we are hopeful for improvements as we move forward with treatment."

"Hopeful?" I gasp, struggling to draw air, to fill my lungs, as if his words have burned all the oxygen in the room.

"Emma . . . I understand this can be terrifying, but you can't give up. Not now. Not ever." He squeezes my hand again, and that simple gesture instills a bit of courage in me. "We've started you on medication to reduce the swelling and manage the pain. The neurology team, led by Dr. Winslow, is still investigating. There could be damage to the spinal cord that hasn't shown on the scans. Sometimes swelling makes things hard to see. But I'm not overly concerned about that. The only visible injury you had was to the back of your skull, not your spine."

"You're saying my nerves are intact, but they just don't work?"

"Exactly. We think it's the reason behind the diminished muscle tone you're experiencing. Muscular tonus or tone is the amount of tension in the muscles, their readiness to perform their function with the expected strength. The fact that you can command your limbs, even if slightly, is why I strongly believe you'll walk away from this. But it might take a while." A pause, tense and heavy, while I hold my breath. His tone has taken a turn for the grim, contradicting his positive words. "It will take lots of work, and it won't be easy. Tests, treatment, and rehab. You'll have to learn to walk again, one step at a time. But first, you'll have to rest until the swelling in your brain comes down."

For a moment, the words seem distant, as disbelief becomes denial and intercedes between me and my new reality, refusing to accept it.

Then it hits me.

I'm not going anywhere.

It's not a dream I'm about to wake from, say thank you to everyone involved, then serenely drive home and resume my life. No . . . this is it.

The darkness, the paralysis, the fear.

"Oh, no." I can't help crying. The sobs roll off my trembling lips. I don't move, don't heave, just lie immobile on my back, as if the only thing alive in me is my pain, desperate to come out.

"I understand this is a lot to take in. We're here for you, and we'll take this one day at a time." He pauses for a moment, his soothing voice still sounding in my ears. "Let's talk about your memory. I'm a bit concerned that you've forgotten our previous interactions. We did this before, but I'm afraid I have to ask you again: what's the last thing you remember?"

Still clinging to the surreal hope that it's all a nightmare I will soon wake from, I struggle to gather my thoughts. "Um, I was running. I was scared . . . I was screaming, running for the door, I believe. I'm not sure."

"Who attacked you, Emma?"

I try to shake my head but don't feel as if it's moving much against the pillow. "I don't know. I—I just can't recall. It's all blank." I pause, the same flashback playing in my mind. "Will I be able to remember? I have to."

"I believe you will. Just give yourself some time."

Time. Something I don't have. Something I've already lost track of, squandered deep inside the darkness of my fractured mind.

"How long have I been here? Why can't I remember that?"

"A couple of days. But I'm less concerned with the apparent anterograde amnesia—that means the inability to form and access new memories—because you're heavily medicated."

"Okay," I whisper, wishing it would all go away. Everything. What happened. The darkness that has seized my world. My all-encompassing fear that this could be what the rest of my life is like.

"I'm more concerned with the post-traumatic retrograde amnesia you seem to be experiencing. That is, the loss of information acquired before the onset of amnesia, which, in your case, is probably the time of the assault. It's usually temporary, and partial—not a complete loss of memory. More like bits and pieces missing, or entire chunks, or perhaps remembered out of order." Another moment of silence, as if he's struggling to choose his words. "Except for what you described earlier, running and trying to escape the assailant, what else do you remember?"

My lips part, but no words come out. It's as if there's but a distorted blur where there used to be a life. Mine.

The heart monitor beeps faster and faster.

"It's okay," Dr. Sokolowski says. "I know you remember your name, so that's something, right?" I press my lips together. I can't bring myself to share his optimism. "Do you remember what year this is?" Another moment of silence, while inside I scream. "Who's president?" Another second of silence, then his voice comes again, brisk, upbeat, "Let's try this again in a day or two, once the swelling has gone down a little bit more. Then we'll dial back your meds and I'm sure you'll start remembering things. Your memory could return in scattered, incomplete flashes, or in larger, more cohesive chunks, complete with every detail." He gives my hand another squeeze. "Do you have any other questions I can address right now?"

Where do I start?

"I can't open my eyes," I whisper, feeling completely drained. "They feel strange."

"There's a dressing wrapped around your head, and it covers your eyes. Perhaps that's what you're sensing. You shouldn't try to open your eyes or strain them until we know what's causing your blindness."

I feel as if I'm fading away, and I fight it the best I can. "Thank you," I manage.

"Would you like me to call the police about your assault?"

"Yes, please." My weary mind grasps at the thought of that, hoping I'll feel safer once my assailant is found and arrested.

"All right, I'll do that right away." I hear the wheels roll on the floor, then his shoes moving in place as he stands. One of them makes a tiny squeaking noise.

"No," I say, changing my mind, feeling defeated. "We'd be wasting their time. I don't remember anything." I swallow with difficulty. "I'm sorry. It's just that . . . I'm so afraid."

"Nothing to be sorry about, but we do have to report it." The faint smell of herbs or citrusy suede seems to draw closer. "Here's a little something to drink. It's a straw," he says, as an object touches my lips.

Grateful, I draw in the cool liquid and swallow a few small sips. Water. Then the sound of a plastic cup being placed on a surface by my side.

"Thank you."

"Emma, you're safe here, I promise you that. Take as much time as you like, and when you're ready, we'll call the police for a statement. Meanwhile, I'll file the necessary forms with local law enforcement, but you won't have to speak with them until you're ready. All right?"

"Yes," I whisper, drifting away as I speak.

"For now, all you can do is rest. We'll take care of everything else, and it will work out, I promise." He touches my hand again, but I barely feel it.

Maybe tomorrow I'll remember who it was.

The thought swirls in my mind for a brief moment, then darkness and silence return to claim me.

FOUR

"It's George, isn't it? That's why—"

The distant, snickering voice loaded with innuendo wakes me with a start. Breathless, I listen intently until the light-hearted chatter of two young women passing by fades into the distance. The disappearing voices leave behind silence, heavy and dark, punctuated only by the heart monitor beeping.

Am I alone? Not knowing for sure drives me crazy. It's such a basic thing I've taken for granted all my life—knowing who else is in the room, if anyone at all. And there are so many other things, too. Getting a drink of water when I'm thirsty. Feeding myself. Going places.

"Hello?" I call weakly, the effort to speak making my headache worse for a moment before it subsides to a more stifled throb.

No one answers.

There's not the faintest sound to tell me if someone is watching me from the cloak of my blindness. At times, I think I hear someone breathing, but it must be in my imagination. Or my nightmares.

The doctor told me I was safe now. What was his name?

Ugh. I forgot. Something . . . maybe . . .

Frustration with my failing memory brings an unwanted groan to my lips. At least I remember his visit, and some of the things he said. This time. As for the previous visits he mentioned, a total blank.

I push my mind to go back and probe for anything to help me remember who hurt me. Who was I running from, when I was struck down?

Nothing. Only a heavy curtain of blackness behind my eyelids, where snippets of images used to appear like wisps of a dream, helping me imagine or remember things—like movie scenes played in the theater of my mind.

That was before the attack. At least I remember this much about myself; how my mind used to work.

"Please, help me," I whisper, the words not directed at anyone in particular. But it feels good to say them, as if out loud they are more powerful than thoughts somehow.

Faintly at first, then more clearly, a memory starts to form. Again, it's more a feeling than a memory. My face against a reddish-brown curtain imprinted with wavy streaks of light tan. How it smells: a faint, crisp scent of clean linen. Of laundry detergent and lavender softener.

And fear. It smells of fear.

My own.

My silent gasp threatens to shatter the fine filament of memory, but I hold on to it, unwilling to let it go, desperate to follow it wherever it leads. I see myself looking out the window from behind those curtains, my cheeks touching the fine fabric as I peek outside, where the stranger leans against a tree trunk, hands deep inside the black hoodie's pockets, staring at me. The light is fading quickly; the sun has already set. The backyard is deserted, the distant mountain peaks topped with snow towering over it like taciturn behemoths.

And that man is there, not moving, not taking his eyes off my window. Waiting.

For what?

The thread of my memory unspools in a different direction with a jolt. I see myself looking out the same window, but it's earlier, when the sun is just about to touch the snowy mountain peak, and aspen shadows are long and menacing. Was it earlier the same day? I can't tell. Instead, I remember my heart thumping in my chest when I saw that stranger lurking in my serene backyard. Grabbing hold of my phone, ready to call 911. My fingers trembling, hesitating as I doubted myself, my own sanity. Then I pulled the curtains shut, panting, shaking.

Yet the fear felt familiar somehow; I recall that clearly. But why, I don't know.

A noise coming from outside scares off the faint memory, rendering me painfully vigilant. The door opens gently, and the brisk, rubber-soled footfalls I recognize draw closer.

"You're awake, I see," a woman's voice says gently. "Good. Let's get you fed." Something rustles in the near distance, and objects clatter quietly. "Are you hungry at all?"

I allow the air trapped in my lungs to escape in a noiseless sigh. "What's your name?"

The steps are busy around me. "I'm Isabella," the woman replies. She sounds young. "And I want to know if you can swallow. It was all IV until now."

A frown attempts to crease my forehead, doing nothing but stirring my throbbing headache and yielding, defeated, against the bandages wrapped tightly around my head. "I believe I can," I say, hoping it's true. "I had some water earlier."

"Perfect," Isabella replies. "Just what I wanted to hear." Objects rattle in the direction her voice comes from. I hear a lid being twisted, then the container opening up with a soft pop. Something made of plastic clatters, then a moist, squelching sound as the nurse stirs something in a jar.

Applesauce.

The smell makes me crave the food I haven't touched since kindergarten. And the fact that I know that I haven't eaten it since then is refreshing—uplifting, even.

"Are you my nurse?"

Isabella moves things around quickly, and doesn't stop what she's doing to respond. "One of them, yes." She pops open another container and fills something with liquid. "I'm almost ready, hon."

"No rush," I reply, dreading the thought that I'm about to be spoon-fed. "Have you ever seen people like me recover?"

The clattering comes to a stop. Then Isabella approaches and sits on the edge of the bed. The surface tilts slightly under her weight, but I barely sense anything. "Try to squeeze my fingers as hard as you can," she asks, touching my hands.

I try my best, but my muscles refuse to obey. I try again and again, then stop when a sob threatens to escape.

"Yes, I've seen people like you recover. I see it every day," Isabella says. "You're able to move your extremities, ever so slightly, but it doesn't matter how little. All that matters is that you can. Didn't your doctor tell you all this?"

I can't bring myself to respond immediately. Isabella waits patiently. "I'm scared," I eventually say. "I can't—"

"You have to be brave. You have to believe you can recover, with all your heart. And don't worry too much. Just rest for now, give yourself time to heal." She pats my hand, and her touch is just as remote as the doctor's had been, as if she too is wearing gloves—I feel her skin brush against mine, the warmth of her hand, but it's all still distant. "Now, let's eat something, shall we?"

The first spoon of applesauce goes down with difficulty. My throat is sore, as if I'm coming down with a bad case of strep throat. I wince as I swallow, then ask for a bit of water.

"Let me take a look," Isabella says, after letting me drink

through a straw. The tray clatters when set on the table next to the bed. Then, an object clicks close to my face. I flinch. "It's just my flashlight. Nothing to worry about. Open your mouth."

I struggle to do so. My muscles don't obey me that well, although my jaw performs better than my hands.

Isabella touches my chin gently, probably getting my mouth open widely enough for a clear look. Then her fingers dance on the outside of my throat, feeling my glands and tracing the underside of my jaw.

"Your throat is irritated and a bit swollen. You'll need the doctor to check you out with a laryngoscope. I'll let him know." A click. She's probably turned off the flashlight. "Did you strain your voice or something?"

A flicker of a memory floods my mind so intensely, my breath catches. I see myself running again, my steps faltering. I recall the burn I felt in my throat as I screamed, desperate and angry at the same time.

Help! Someone, help me ... Let me go!

The shrieks resonate in my mind, piercing the stillness of my thoughts. The memory is so clear for a moment, then gone.

"I—I was screaming," I whisper. "Running ... I—uh, no one came."

"Oh, honey, that's terrible! Who were you running from?"

I don't reply. After a moment of silence, Isabella takes her seat by my side again, offering me another bit of applesauce by tapping gently on my lower lip with the spoon.

"No ... I can't."

"No worries," the nurse says gently. "I'll be around when you feel like eating a bit more. And if you need anything—"

"Will you please help me call my mom?"

FIVE

Oh, Mom . . .

Out of the fog of my mind, scattered memories of my mother collide together until it feels as if nothing is lost. The thought of my mother's warm hand stroking my cheek brings the sting of tears to my eyes. I wish I could run home to her, to sit on the floor by her side and lay my head in her lap. Rest, feeling safe, basking in her love.

The image begins to shift, as details start to find their way back from the abyss. The oxygen tube on a wheeled cart, always there by her side. The mask she keeps over her face at times, held in place with trembling, knotty fingers. The pallor of her face, the frailty of her body. The coughing and wheezing that make every breath she takes a battle for yet another moment of borrowed time, knowing there aren't many such moments left. Even if she's only just turned sixty.

But when was that? When did she turn sixty?

For a second, unspeakable fear slashes through my heart. What if she's already gone? What if my mom has died and I've forgotten all about it?

No . . . that can't be true. Please, don't let it be true.

Isabella is still fussing with the tray, putting stuff away probably, quietly humming a melody I recognize but can't name. Then she stops for a moment, long enough to squirt some hand sanitizer that smells of strawberries. Not real strawberries, but a chemical version of the scent. There's the sound of her rubbing her hands together energetically, while she resumes humming for a while.

Then rubber-soled footsteps approach me quickly. I feel the bed dip slightly, then sense a subtle change in the air, accompanied by a faint rustle of clothing.

Four faint beeps come from Isabella's direction; she's unlocking her phone, getting ready to place the call. "All right, I'm ready. What's your mom's number?"

A simple question I should've seen coming. No answer I can give. Just despair, filling my chest until I can't breathe.

"I—I don't know," I whisper, my voice shaking.

"It's okay, hon, we'll find it. Do you have a phone? I bet your mom's number is saved in there."

I remember holding my phone, ready to call 911, watching that stranger lurking in the deepening shadows of my backyard. I remember squeezing that phone so tightly, my knuckles whitened and hurt.

"No . . . I don't know. Maybe the police took it, after I—"

"All right, don't worry." I feel Isabella's hand give my forearm a gentle squeeze. "We'll figure it out. What's your mom's name?"

"Loreen Duncan," I say, grateful I can remember as much. "She lives in Lubbock, Texas."

"How about your dad? Maybe the phone is in his name?"

It rained the day they buried my father. I can still taste the dust-filled raindrops on my lips, mixed with the salt of my tears. The sound of moist earth crashing against the coffin reverberating in my heart. Going back home in stifling heat, while the sun happily cracked the clouds open, indifferent to my grief. The old farmhouse, badly needing new siding and a new roof too, its front door propped open as the small procession arrived. Our small family first—just me, my mother, and some distant cousins from Oklahoma—then a couple of neighbors, and some folks from the local church. The smell of burning candles and Texas summer dust, kissed by rain.

"No . . . it's just Mom now."

A moment of silence, while I hold my breath and Isabella's fingertips tap quickly on the screen of her phone.

"I found a Loreen Duncan listed. Let's give it a try, all right?"

I nod, but can't tell if my intention has become a motion Isabella noticed. "Yes . . . thank you." My voice trembles when I recall my mother's frailty. "Please, don't tell her what happened to me. She's not well, you know. I just want to hear her voice."

"Don't worry, I get it." Isabella sounds a bit choked. "I'll make the call, then put the phone next to your ear. If you recognize her voice, start talking and I'll step outside. Take as long as you want. If not, I'll keep searching for numbers to try."

I breathe in slowly, willing my tears gone and my voice strong. "Okay."

The phone lands on the pillow, slipping against my cheek just as a woman on the other end of the line says a weak, "Hello."

"Mom?"

"Emma? Baby?"

Tears flood my eyes as I gasp silently, unwilling to let my mother hear my pain.

"Are you there?"

"Uh-huh," I manage. "Yes, Mom, I'm here. How are you?"

"I'm so happy you called, baby. I miss you; you know that. I miss you all the time." She starts coughing but covers the phone with her hand, as her coughs are muted for a while, until they finally stop. "Sorry about that . . . you know how it is."

"I know," I reply, swallowing hard, trying to fight back my tears. "I miss you too. Maybe I'll come for a visit soon."

"Nah . . . there's nothing for you here but dust and horse flies. Live your life and be happy. You belong with Steve now, in a different world, not here, with a wheezing old woman."

Steve? Who's Steve?

The person who has the answer is the one I can't ask.

"I keep looking at the pictures you sent me. The ones from Cancun. You look so beautiful."

I can't think of anything to say. *I've been to Cancun? When?*

"Thank you," I eventually whisper. It's the best I can manage, while my mind swirls, desperate to find the tiniest trace of everything I've lost. What else don't I remember? And who is this Steve my mother is talking about?

"It's true, you know. You are beautiful. Your father wasn't wrong much in his life, may God rest his soul, but I'm happy he was wrong about Steve."

A beat of silence, while I listen, speechless. When I can trust my voice not to betray me, I ask, "What do you mean?"

"Oh, you know, when he said Steve was much too old for you. 'Nineteen years is too big an age difference,' he kept saying. But then, the pictures from your honeymoon made him stop bickering about that. You've never looked so happy, sweetie."

Oh, God . . . I'm married. To a man named Steve. To someone I can't remember.

A deep sense of panic returns as my mother's quiet chuckle turns into a short bout of coughing. I hear a hissing sound, as if my mother has turned on her oxygen and inhaled deeply.

What's happened to Steve? Why isn't he here, by my side, if he is my husband? Was he killed during the attack? But, most of all, where is the love? My heart should feel hollow, bereft, if someone so important is missing. Wouldn't my body, my heart, remember him before my mind? How could anyone lose so much and not know it? Not feel it?

I breathe shallowly, tense, dreading the hurt I fear is going to come. Rummaging for any recollection of the life I've lost, I find nothing. Just an ominous notion that something is indeed there, lurking, hiding, waiting.

I clear my voice quietly, then ask, as casually as I can manage, "What's your favorite of those pics, Mom? Describe it for me."

"Oh, that's not difficult to choose at all." Her voice is filled with joy, warming my heart. "It's the one on the beach, with the moon. Remember that one?"

"N—no, not really."

"Well, it's almost dark, the sky is an amazing shade of purple, edged with pink along the horizon. The moon is full, but just barely above the water. It's still, the ocean, and the moon is reflected in it, a long line of tiny glimmering ripples that almost touch the shore where you sit."

"Oh, I'm in that picture too?" I ask teasingly, already knowing the answer. Mom's favorite picture has to be one of me. I know that much.

"You and Steve both. He's sitting on a tree trunk, I believe, some chunk of driftwood from what I can tell, and you're curled up at his feet, in that sugar-white sand. His arms are wrapped around your shoulders and he's looking at you with so much love, baby. And you're shining. Your smile is infectious. You love him very much, don't you?"

Her words fade into the distance while my mind latches on to snippets of images her words evoke. The feeling of strong arms around my shoulders, keeping me safe, making me feel loved and protected. The warm, fine sand under my feet. A man's hand clasping my own and taking it to his lips. His breath searing my fingers and lighting a fire inside me that makes me crave his touch even more. Dimples in his cheek as he smiles. A touch of silver on his temples.

Then a voice, loud in my mind. "Cut! It's a wrap for today.

Brilliant performance, Emma! You are *becoming* Jane Watkins. It's compelling and authentic. Keep it up."

A chasm opens in my chest as shards of memories start forming a picture. A multidimensional one, with depths of emotions I'm starting to feel, sensations that seem so real now I can still feel them. My excitement to hear the director's words. The beaming smile I send his way. The familiarity of his touch when he walked me off the set, his hand on the small of my back. The way his lips felt under mine when I reached up and kissed him quickly, furtively, before anyone could notice.

"It's all you, Steve," I whispered, close to his ear.

Those words echo strangely now, in the darkness, filling it with colorful memories, quick fragments of action, pieces of a puzzle aching to be put together.

I am an actress. And Steve, a director. And we've worked together at least once.

Sifting through the images evoked by my mother's words, I relive that scene again and again, playing it in achingly slow motion, until I catch a glimpse of what I'm looking for.

On the hand Steve took to his lips that day, a gold band caught the light, reflecting a warm, radiant glow.

It's true. Steve is my husband and I love him.

"—keep watching over and over again—thank goodness for streaming." My mother's voice draws me back now, keeping the surging wave of pain at bay.

"Which one's your favorite?" I ask, my voice barely a whisper.

"*The Fall of Jane Watkins*, of course," she replies quickly. "That's your absolute best, by a long shot. I'm not really that fond of *Summer Love*." Her voice has turned a tad sad, almost disappointed. "I still can't understand why you agreed to do what you did. The movie could've been just as good without that scene. You could've said no."

"To what, Mom?" I ask, a bit distracted, or perhaps tired, yet afraid to end the call, the only thing standing between me and the surge of memories threatening to rip me apart.

"Oh . . . like you have to ask." A moment's reproachful silence. "Baring yourself for the entire world to see, what else? I couldn't show my face in church for months after that movie aired. Everyone here who knew you went to see it, and they wouldn't stop talking about it."

"That's how people are, Mom." My voice trembles a little. I feel sorry for putting my mother through that. It doesn't seem like it was worth it. I can't even recall having made a movie called *Summer Love*.

"Are you okay, baby?"

"Uh-huh," I manage, about to lose the battle with my tears. I wish I could tell her, but I can't burden her with this.

"You don't sound okay. Are you lying to me right now?" A beat of silence, while I search for the right words. "Is everything all right with Steve and you?"

Oh, Mom, if only you knew. I sigh, a pained effort to fill my lungs failing miserably. "Yeah, I'm just down with a bad cold, and medicated a bit too much. I have to go back to work tomorrow, so I might've overdone it." The layered lie rolls off my lips with unexpectedly familiar easiness.

My mother hesitates for a moment, probably not buying my story. "Whatever you say, sweetheart. Be well, all right? Drink some tea with honey and sleep some more. You'll feel much better!"

I make the promise I know I can't keep, then hold my breath until I hear the sound telling me the call has been disconnected.

Then I let myself go, inviting the lost memories in.

I remember Steve now, some of him, some of our moments together, but enough to carve into my chest with an overwhelming sense of loss. He's there now, inside my heart, retaking his rightful place as if he's been absent for a while, filling me with a hunger for his reassuring presence. I see myself in his arms, feeling safe and loved and cherished, believing everything will be all right and that we'll soon be working together on a new project, conquering the world again and lining the living room mantel with more golden statuettes.

Then the wishful daydreaming in my mind turns into a nightmare, chilling me to the bone. Was Steve the person I was running from when I was struck down? Was that the reason why he isn't here? The more I think about it, I feel the attacker was somehow familiar. How can I find out if it was Steve?

Oh, no . . . Please, no.

Tears burn my eyes, soaking my head dressing. The wail building in my chest chokes me as I desperately fight for air.

Rapid beeping from the machine by my bed matches my increasing anguish, then turns into a cacophony of continuous droning.

Isabella's panicked voice calls out, "She's crashing! Sats eighty-five and dropping. Need some help in here!"

Another, heavier set of hurried footfalls approaches. A man's voice announces in a tensely calm voice, "She's in v-tach. Amp of epi. Paddles."

That's the last thing I hear.

Then silence joins darkness and sinks me deep into nothingness.

SIX

Strangely, I somehow know I'm dreaming. Still, I can't wake up, as if darkness holds me hostage with long, sticky tentacles wrapped around my throat.

In my dream, I'm looking out the window, my face touching the cool fabric of the drape. The lights are off in the living room, the only glimmer of light coming from the phone I hold tightly in my hand. The display shows the digits 911, but my thumb hovers over the screen, trembling slightly, undecided.

My eyes squint in the dark, riveted, trying to see the face of the stranger leaning against the white trunk of the tall aspen. That silhouette has been haunting my nights since the first time I saw it.

I want to go out there and brace the biting cold, to see that stranger's face up close.

"Who are you?" The words, resounding in an altered version of my voice as dream-speak often does, never reach the man. Undisturbed, arms crossed at his chest, he waits, a black scarf covering his mouth, hood lowered over his face, shielding his eyes. As if he has an entire life to spend waiting. As if there is no place else he'd rather be.

The dream shifts, or perhaps a new one starts. I'm casually chatting with someone at the Village Center, two heavy shopping bags cutting into my fingers. The person I'm chatting with has no face, the way that only happens in dreams. But the backyard stranger is there, trailing my steps through the shopping center, dressed in the black hoodie and jeans again, yet at the same time leaning against the tree trunk.

"I know what I'm talking about." My own voice resounds in my mind, augmented by fear. "You have to believe me!" My hand is pointed where the stalker was until a moment ago, and the man smiling politely and yet derisively at me is a cop, badge and name tag affixed on his starched navy-blue shirt, and radio clipped to his left epaulet.

"Was it a man?" the cop asks, drawing his head weirdly close to mine. "A woman? Is there anything you can tell me about them?"

I shake my head, defeated. My shoulders hang low, and my breath catches in my chest when I lift my eyes to look at the cop again. "A man, I think. I—I don't know. But I swear, it's real. It's been happening for months." My voice sounds meek, powerless, and embarrassed.

The shopping center starts spinning around me as if I'm riding a carousel at increasing speed. Everything moves faster and faster, trailing colors and sparkles and sound bites from holiday carols and jingles. Only one thing stays put, moving with me, focused solely on me.

The stalker.

Staring right at me with fiery, fervent eyes.

Then I hear a voice, not my own, not anyone I recognize, whisper a name close to my ear. "Steve." With that word, a hint of breath touches my face, giving me goose bumps.

I startle awake, frightened, as a distant PA calls a Dr. Jones to ICU. The voice sounds artificial, an automated system of sorts, the kind they have in most large hospitals. Even if it isn't a real person behind that call, I relish hearing it. A bit of proof I'm still alive. And awake, the terrifying dream starting to dissipate.

I don't want it to.

I want to revisit it, to rewind it and watch it again somehow, although parts of it are gone forever now.

Buried in that dream is the face of my stalker.

Breathing slowly but as deeply as I can, I will myself back into the foggy depths of my subconscious. I look for glimpses of a face, of a hand, of something I can use. Yet the fragmented scenes remain hidden, unwilling to yield any useful bit of information.

Was it Steve?

Was that the reason I couldn't see the stalker's face in my memory? I've read someplace, probably when doing research for a part, that the mind withholds access to information that would be too painful to retrieve and process. As if the brain has its own parental guidance system, and until I become strong enough, I can't watch the most disturbing parts of the movie that is my own life, imprinted on the fickle fabric of memory.

Still lingering on the boundary between dream and wakefulness, I picture myself standing in my own backyard and approaching the stalker, fearlessly, half-knowing I'm safe. One step at a time, holding my mind's eye focused on the space where the face should be visible by now. Yet with every step, fear blooms in my chest, urging me to stop, to turn around, to run away.

I freeze in place, unable to take another step. I imagine myself calling him, as if I already know who it is, and watch carefully for the first thing that comes to mind, hoping it's a name. But only the sound of my own voice comes, shrieking, desperate, and scared.

Help! Someone, help me . . . Let me go!

Rattled, I pull myself out of that space, breathing heavily, still scared. I feel as if my dream has opened the door for that stranger to walk right in and finish what they started with another blow to the back of my head. It's absurd, yet feels so real it chills my blood.

A few minutes later, after my breathing has returned to normal, I imagine myself drawing a composite for the police. My complete ineptitude in all matters drawing aside, I try to visualize the silhouette again, as I recall seeing it from my living room window.

Was it Steve?

Were the stalker's shoulders broader than Steve's? Narrower? Were they bulky? No... athletic, rather, with lean legs like a biker's. Or a woman's. The arms, always crossed at the chest, weren't bulging like a weightlifter's; they were slender, yet strong somehow, although it wasn't the physical strength that had terrified me.

It was those eyes.

The intensity in them, burning with something I couldn't name. Perhaps it was loathing, or maybe something else. Yes... I recall how they made me feel. Like prey, petrified and filled with dread as the predator stared fixedly, getting ready to pounce. That's what I remember... not the color of the irises or the skin surrounding them. Not the thickness of the eyebrows or the shape of the nose. Just that chilling sensation that I was staring into the eyes of a dangerous hunter who ached for my blood.

A door opens nearby, and I lie still, listening. Familiar footsteps approach, and with them, a faint scent of basil and spice and suede. It's my doctor... I remember him, the slightly squeaky sound one of his shoes makes, the way his clothes, or perhaps scrubs, rustle when he moves. Even if I can't remember his name.

I breathe. I'm safe, at least for a little while longer.

"Hello, Emma. How are you feeling today?"

That's such a simple question, yet so complicated. "I'm

okay, I guess. As good as can be expected, with what's going on."

"You gave us quite the scare yesterday."

"I did?" As I ask, I faintly recall machines beeping and Isabella's voice raised in panic. "I thought I was dreaming. What happened?"

"So, you do remember?"

"Yes. Some of it. I couldn't breathe."

"Good that you remember. This is what we doctors like to call a remarkable improvement—you're forming new memories that stick." I can hear the smile in his voice, even if it's muffled by his mask. "However, you had difficulties breathing. That can sometimes happen with the medication you're on. I dialed back your pain meds just a little, to give you more strength to get back on your feet. If you experience any pain, we could always go back—"

"No. I need that strength. I need to get out of here. I—I just can't . . . live like this." My voice shatters. It seems hopeless, even as I speak the words. I still can't move. I still can't see. And I don't even remember the doctor's name.

"One day at a time, all right?" His voice draws near. His fingers touch mine. "Squeeze my hands, as hard as you can."

I try my best and feel a little movement in my fingers. Motivated, I push myself harder.

"Excellent," he replies. "Let's check reflexes next."

Sheets rustle and move around me. Something touches my left elbow, then touches it again. The doctor lets out a quiet sigh, barely perceptible, but I sense it and freeze. A few footsteps around the bed, then my right elbow receives a couple of taps.

"How am I doing?" I dread hearing the answer.

"Let's check your plantar reflexes first, then we'll discuss it." He pulls up the covers and exposes my feet, then runs something pointy and slightly unpleasant along the soles, from heel to toes.

Both feet are equally remote, as if they belong to someone else, but I can still feel what someone else does.

Something clatters at the foot of my bed after he covers my feet, then paper rustles as he flips through pages of my chart. "Your reflexes aren't where we'd like to see them yet, but there's still some swelling left in your brain putting pressure on those nerves. We'll keep you on Decadron until the brain swelling recedes completely. The neurologist, Dr. Winslow, is confident that it will happen in the next couple of days or so. I'll dial back the pain meds some more, but I'll keep you on Versed, to give you time to rest. That's a sedative. Sound good?"

He's about to leave, and I have a million more questions. "Wait, please, don't go just yet."

"Sure. I have a couple more minutes. What's on your mind?"

I can sense him standing by the bed, unwilling to take a seat, probably eager to leave. "I—I forgot your name . . . I'm so sorry."

"Nothing to be sorry about. I'm actually quite optimistic about your memory. You seem to remember more and more. And I'm Dr. Sokolowski—quite an easy name to forget, right?"

"Thank you," I say. "Can we check my eyesight? Maybe I can see now. If we could take this bandage off, I could try."

A moment of tense silence engulfs the room. "We did that," he replies, and my heart sinks. His voice is somber now, as if the earlier optimism has been erased. "This morning, when we changed your dressing. It was soaked with tears. You must've been crying."

"Oh," I manage to say calmly, although I'm falling apart. "I don't remember that. I don't understand how that can happen. I remember I have a husband named Steve, I remember what he looks like, and what happened when I couldn't breathe last night, what Isabella said, but I can't remember you testing my eyesight. Or changing my dressing."

Wheels roll and crisp scrubs rustle as Dr. Sokolowski sits

by my bed. "Emma, you shouldn't worry too much. Some of the medication we're giving you might cause delays in recovery—"

"Then why give those drugs to me in the first place? Let's just—"

"The biggest enemy right now is the swelling. That, we don't play games with. If left untreated, it could cause permanent cognitive and functional deficits. Your memory will most likely return after we stop your meds. Does that make sense?"

"Yeah . . . it's just that it feels as if I'm locked inside a dark, motionless world I can't escape, and I'm terrified."

"You're understandably anxious about your situation. We could add some—"

"Please, I don't want meds for that. I'll manage. It's just, I've never felt so vulnerable and so scared. I'm afraid of being attacked again. How will I know if someone's coming for me?"

There are the sounds of him standing and grabbing the chart, then scribbling something on it. "You are absolutely safe here, Emma. I promise you no one will lay a finger on you. Your case has been reported to the police, and they're looking into this. They'll find who did this to you, and they'll notify your next of kin."

I listen to his words, but they wash right past me, as if they're about someone else. As if I can't comprehend what he means. My mind is latched onto the same question, refusing to let go, and nothing else registers.

He sits again. "Tell me more about your life before the incident, what you're starting to remember. You mentioned a husband. Would you like us to call him?"

I lick my parched lips and swallow with difficulty. "I—I don't know where he is. Was he hurt in the attack? Why isn't he here, with me?" Fear fans out in my mind like a deck of cards being laid out on a table, each card a different nightmare, a new scenario I haven't thought of yet. "Why can't I remember? Isn't anyone out there missing me?"

"Let me look into it and see what we can find out. We have people who deal with this sort of issue. I'll ask them to make a few calls for you."

"Please, no," I whisper, irrational panic extinguishing the glimmer of hope I felt at the thought of being reunited with Steve. "What if it was him?"

"You mean, the man who hurt you? You have reason to believe it could've been your husband?"

"No." The word rolls off my lips in a tense whisper. "I just don't remember. And it's driving me insane. I don't know what's real anymore. And I've lost so much time . . . I don't know *when* we are, how much time has passed since the last thing I remember."

"Oh, I see." He stands and takes two steps toward the door. "Then we'll put a hold on looking for your husband until you're ready. All right?" His voice is pleasant and helpful, a beacon of hope, patience, and kindness in my permanent darkness.

"Yes." I pause for a moment, thinking of everything I still want to ask. "One more thing," I say quickly, afraid he's already gone. "What happened to the things I was brought in with? My clothes? Maybe I had my phone with me? His number would be in there."

Steps approach the foot of my bed, and the familiar plastic clipboard clatters. "I see we actually have some notes here about your personal items; I'll ask the nurse to get that sorted out for you." The clipboard clatters again as he puts it down. "I'll be back for evening rounds. If you change your mind about calling your husband, please let one of the nurses know. They'll take care of it for you. You said your husband's name is Steve?"

"Yes. Steven Wellington." *And I miss him immensely.*

My thoughts echo over the sound of the closing door, leaving nothing but beeps and silence behind.

I'm alone with my ghosts again.

SEVEN

My sweet Emma is still alive.

That makes everything all right. All the risks I took and I'm still taking, knowing that one day the police might find me and lock me up—all of that is worth it, just to know my Emma is alive. Instead of running to save myself, I chose to stay. By her side.

Last night, after everyone had left for the day, I snuck into her room. She was sound asleep; she didn't hear me opening the door or drawing close enough to touch her. All those meds have her out like a light.

I stood by the side of her bed and watched her, not moving, just standing still as hours passed. Moonlight cast a dim silver light inside the room through half-open blinds, giving everything long, menacing shadows. The green screen of the heart monitor with its constant beeping was the only thing seemingly alive. Because of that device, I didn't have to touch Emma's neck to feel for a pulse or bring my face close enough to her lips to feel breath leaving her lungs. I didn't have to touch her at all.

But I wanted to.

I still remember when I saw her for the first time. How I knew she was meant to be mine, the way one connects instantly with one's soulmate. She's my soulmate; there's no doubt in my mind. Even if she doesn't know it yet.

There's a frailty to my darling girl. On the outside, she seems fearless, driven and unstoppable, but I know all that is for show. A true artist, she never comes out of character, but I know better. Inside, she's just a scared little girl who needs love and nurturing to thrive, to become the best she can be. She's extremely fragile, and struggles to handle the stress of everyday life without me. I understand her; I know exactly what she needs.

She needs me.

Only she won't admit it, not even to herself.

She doesn't know the sacrifices I've made to keep watch over her, to be by her side, and make sure she's safe, despite some poor choices she's made. Because she's already had a few close calls, and if it weren't for me, she wouldn't be alive today.

I have the time and I love her enough to be patient, to give her the opportunity to understand who we really are to each other. And I'll be here, waiting, ready to hold her hand when she's willing to accept the truth.

We were meant to be together. Forever.

Before leaving the room, I touched her face gently, the tips of my fingers barely grazing her skin. She didn't feel it. Her breathing was low and steady and didn't falter. I leaned closer and whispered a few words in her ear, so quietly I couldn't hear them at all, just knew I was saying them.

"I'm right here, Emma. Always."

Then I kissed her lips softly, a feather-light brush, a whisper against her mouth that left her undisturbed. I lingered for just a minute longer, then snuck outside, my hands plunged deep into the front pockets of my hoodie. Missing her already.

I'll be back again tomorrow.

I can't stay away for too long.

EIGHT

Somewhere in the distance a phone rings, harsh and strident. It echoes in my head and then, all at once, it's like the doctor said it would be—a chunk of my past unlocking, all from that one sound.

Memories flood my mind as I lie still on my bed, the complete darkness becoming a canvas on which glimpses of my past start falling into place, forming images I recognize and cherish, as if seeing a loved one after too long an absence.

The phone call that changed my life came at seven thirty in the morning.

I was still asleep in the tiny one-bedroom apartment on Lexington Avenue. I shared that with the woman who became my best friend, Lisa Chen, a petite and slender Asian acting student. Behind her expressive eyes and delicate features was a powerhouse woman, talented and resourceful. I was lucky our roads crossed when they did. Together we went to auditions, laughed, and danced our way through life. When I took my first head shots, glossy, high-quality prints that did not come cheap and had cost me a small fortune—about a week's worth of waiting on tables at Taps On First—she was the one who helped me stuff envelopes with them, to send off to agents with hope in my heart.

I remember looking at my glossy head shots as if it were yesterday. My long, wavy brown hair shone with sun-fueled copper highlights, my blue eyes conveyed a sense of openness, and my lips promised a hint of a smile, perhaps a touch of amazement, of intrigue even. I wore a black top, simple and casual, and the photographer had stripped me of all my carefully chosen jewelry. All for good reason; without the bling, the woman looking back from those photos seemed self-confident and authentic.

And yet, rejection letters came one after another, not nearly as many as the letters I'd sent. Most agents didn't even bother to reply; it was as if those letters had fallen into an invisible abyss of shattered hopes and dreams. That abyss was called Hollywood, filled with young people like me who didn't believe they stood a chance.

In the meantime, there was Taps, a loud and always crowded sports bar with daily happy hours that lasted well into the evening. It smelled of molten cheddar and sizzling burgers, of spilled beer and boozy sweat. I worked there four nights a week, in between acting classes at UCLA, not because I liked sports or hollering drunks, but because I'd heard lots of Hollywood personalities hung out there.

In three long years, I didn't see a single one I recognized. With the wisdom of that defeat came the understanding that the bar's owner, a shrewd and rather short and bulky Armenian man in his late fifties, had enthusiastically spread the rumor, knowing too well it would bring him job applicants who looked good on camera, especially the pretty young women he loved to hire as wait staff. In his own words, "Sexy girls balancing beers and fries on loaded trays will never hurt a business." And his business thrived, although celebrities never came by.

But even though all I had was a lousy job, an apartment with mold on the walls, and a bed with a spring that poked my back every time I rolled over, I couldn't bear to give up on my dreams.

Growing up, my mom told me I was beautiful, many times, until I started believing it. I'd wanted to be an actress since I was fifteen, and all I talked about was Hollywood and movies. My parents didn't discourage me, although my father wasn't all that enthusiastic. But my mom secretly pushed me to make my way out of Lubbock, Texas, to be the best I could be. And if that road led to Hollywood, she was okay with it. But first, I had to graduate high school and ace my SATs. That was our agreement. If I studied hard and proved I could pass the admission tests, my mother would do her best to support my dream.

I held up my end of the bargain, and graduated valedictorian, with a beaming smile on my full lips, and my long, brown hair blowing in the wind under the graduation cap I wore proudly.

I couldn't let my parents down by returning home a failure.

I felt like one that morning, though, barely awake on my lumpy bed. I'd been up working until three, and I nearly let the call go to voicemail unanswered. But, since hope dies last, I decided to give the early morning caller a chance.

"Emma? This is Denise Hastings," the caller said with a smooth, sophisticated British accent. "With Hastings Talent Agency."

I jumped out of bed, my heart thumping against my ribs so hard it almost choked me.

"Yes, Ms. Hastings, I know," I spouted the words without thinking. "I mean, I know who you are, and wow, thank you for calling me!"

"You don't know why I'm calling," the woman said calmly. "What if it's nothing to thank me about?"

The question sucked the air out of my lungs. After a long moment that felt like a cold shower, I managed to speak a few words in a faint voice, "I, um, I don't believe that's the case. You see, when agents want to turn me down, they don't bother calling."

As soon as the words left my lips, I felt like kicking myself. Denise Hastings would know I'd tried every agent in town, and they'd all rejected me. Now she'd most likely do the same.

The silence on the call was unbearable, and it trailed on, but I resisted the urge to say anything else. It was beyond fixing. Then Denise laughed, not sarcastically, but with the understanding kindness of a parent.

"You get points for having a brain, Emma. And humility."

I breathed, feeling beads of sweat bursting at the roots of my hair. "Thank you, Ms. Hastings."

"As it happens, there's a casting call for a nice little flick called *Eternal Serenade*. Are you—"

"Yes," I blurted, pacing around my bedroom excitedly. "Absolutely!"

The gentle laughter returned, subdued and a bit more critical. "Emma, if we are going to be working together, you have to learn to let people finish what they have to say."

"I'm sorry, Ms. Hastings. So sorry . . . it's just that I'm so excited, and I—"

"Really? You could've fooled me." A moment of silence, while I bit my lip to keep quiet. "Call me Denise."

That was the day I became an actress. A real one, with an agent and all. Denise Hastings was coveted by many aspiring actors. A veteran agent, a retired actress herself with two Golden Globes and an Oscar nomination to her name, she was quite selective with the clients she took on. For reasons I never really understood, Denise took an interest in me.

It wasn't the first time I auditioned for a part, but that particular audition was terrifying. Too much was at stake. Denise hadn't signed a representation contract with me yet, which meant she could always walk away, no obligations, if I failed to secure the part. But I didn't allow myself to think of that as I entered the studio I'd been directed to, and leaned against the wall next to five or six other young women, all more beautiful than I was. High heels, long, blonde hair, perfect teeth, and bodies to die for—scantily clad in form-hugging dresses—were the norm on those hallways.

I hid my heightened emotional state as best I could, transferring all that baggage onto the character I gave a voice to moments later.

I didn't stare at any of the men and women seated across from me with jaded expressions and slouched postures. I made eye contact with each of them, smiling briefly and professionally, and treated the entire moment as a sales pitch with my performance the featured product. When I opened my mouth, I *became* Sarah, the best friend of a woman heartbroken by the discovery of her husband's infidelity.

The part was mine. When he thanked me, one of the producers called me Sarah by accident, then apologized. I beamed.

Three feverish weeks later, we started filming the small budget production on location, somewhere in La Jolla, under the direction of a rising star Hollywood was starting to take note of. I'd heard the name Steve Wellington before; I'd even met him during my audition, although he'd hardly spoken a word and had seemed quite uninterested in my reading. But I didn't let that stop me. I saw a few of his movies in those weeks I spent preparing, and watched a couple of short interviews I found on YouTube. I researched him online, but not obsessively, just enough to know what to expect.

But I hadn't expected the Steve I met on set.

As I let my mind sift through memories, I see Steve slipping a gold ring on my finger, his eyes filled with love, my heart swelling with joy. When he lifts my veil and we kiss, cheers and applause erupt somewhere behind us, close and yet a world away.

But that didn't happen until later. Much later.

There was a strength about him, an aura of power that surrounded him like a glow, commanding everyone's attention. Wearing a formal suit with a white shirt and a dark gray tie, he seemed ready to pitch a new project in front of top-notch financiers or show up on the stage at the Dolby Theatre to claim his statuette. With a chiseled face, prominent cheekbones, a strong jawline, deep-set blue eyes that remained intense even if he was checking the lunch menu, and a baritone voice that carried over the set in quick bursts of enthusiastic direction, Steven Wellington was more than intimidating. His first-day speech was testament to that.

"It's up to us, the people on this set, to make this movie successful. Own it! I'd like to believe you're here because you believe this movie deserves the best it can get, and that best is you. Let yourself shine! It's a story we believe in, a story we can easily relate to, a realm where human frailty and redemption are woven together into an inspiring experience." Steve paused for a beat, while everyone stood silently. For a brief moment, his eyes met mine, then moved on as he continued, "I want to express my gratitude to each one of you for bringing your passion and talents to this project. Let's get rolling!"

Eternal Serenade was my first real part in a multi-million-dollar project. I was both excited and terrified at the same time, knowing quite well all that hung in the balance. I knew, seconds after hearing Steven Wellington speak, that if I made the tiniest mistake, I'd be off the set faster than he could speed-dial his casting director for a replacement. If I forgot my lines or choked, he'd dismiss me without giving it much thought.

I started filming in that state of mind and nearly choked, twice, each falter making things worse. Steve stopped rolling and beckoned me over.

"Trust yourself," he told me in a low voice, meant for only me to hear. "You got this."

And just like that, with a few words, he helped me find my footing and shine.

Under his direction, I was learning and enjoying my work more than I'd thought possible. He pushed me to explore depths of the character that I hadn't considered, encouraging me to experiment. Which was terrifying at first, with so many people watching—an entire crew that could've been disappointed in me.

It took me less than a week to realize that, despite being motivating with everyone on set, Steven Wellington had taken a particular interest in my acting.

One evening, after having to shoot the same scene three times in a row because of the leading actress's poorly masked scorn at every line of dialogue I voiced, Steven spoke with her privately in one of the small, unfurnished bedrooms that served as an equipment storage room on set. She emerged scowling, slamming the door as she left.

I watched her go with a concerned frown. My first real part in a movie, and I had somehow managed to antagonize the lead. Hollywood is a small place; I couldn't afford to be blamed for dissensions on the team.

With that in mind, I almost turned down Steven Wellington's dinner invitation.

I was glad I didn't, when, hours after closing time, we were still chatting on the small, deserted patio, our table cleared except for two now-empty bottles of beer.

We found we had a lot in common, Steve and I. We were both fans of Scorsese's earlier work; Steve had studied him in detail, and I had seen most of his pictures. We both cited lines from *New*

York New York, in roars of laughter when I imitated Liza Minnelli's extravagant style and stretched my voice to sing a few notes of the title song. Then Steve turned into De Niro in *Goodfellas* with a few lines I immediately recognized. He was crazy good, convincing. He would've made one hell of an actor.

"I was there on the set, when they filmed that," Steve said. "Scorsese was saying, 'Remember, Jimmy's a charmer, but he's also calculating. He's got this surface charisma that draws people in, but underneath, he's always calculating, always planning and scheming.' Or something like that," he added, as our laughter resumed. "It was then I knew I wanted to be a director someday." His eyes glimmered when he spoke. "My work brings stories to life." He gestured enthusiastically. "Molding them as if made of clay, only they're made of emotions. People think stories are made of words, or facts, events, that sort of thing, but they're wrong. Emotions. That's what we resonate with."

"Were you an actor?" He was handsome enough to have been an A-lister if he'd chosen to.

He tilted his head just a little, a hint of a smile fluttering on his lips. "Nope. I never acted. I could never do it. Not well, anyway." His smile bloomed, putting a tiny dimple in his chin. "I was an intern . . . the unpaid kind. I dropped out of school and packed groceries on weekends to afford it. I was more of a runner than anything, although I was billed as production assistant. That's mostly what I did. Got everyone their coffees and learned from Scorsese himself."

"Oh?" I said, suddenly aware of how late it was, how deserted the streets were, and how our laughter had echoed just earlier.

What am I doing here? With my boss, no less?

But the time to think had come and quickly gone, between long days spent on set working, anxious, palm-sweating moments rereading my lines one more time just before my scene was up, and more late-night dinners with Steve.

In the still darkness of my world, I recall our wedding, and this time, I linger on the memory, basking in his love, missing it.

"You're not supposed to see me," I shouted, when he saw me in my wedding dress before the service started. But I wasn't really upset; the look in his eyes was enough to erase any superstition from my mind. I walked over, lifting the skirt just a little, and kissed him softly. "Now, get out. I'll be there in just a minute."

I looked in the mirror once more, while Mom rushed to arrange my veil and fluff my skirt. Denise watched me from her chair with a bit of melancholy in her eyes. I mouthed thank you to her as I ran my hands over my svelte waist clad in luscious silk. The dress was exquisite, with lace in patterns of delicate florals across the sheer sleeves, back, and neckline, cascading down to a flowing satin skirt that danced lightly with every step. Denise had helped me choose it, the only extravagance for an actually rather modest event. It was way over my budget, but the vendor had been suspiciously quick to knock a full 50 percent off the price tag—probably Denise's doing. A bouquet of white roses and trailing ivy was the final touch. It was perfect.

"You're so beautiful," Mom said, stroking my face with trembling fingers. Her eyes gleamed with tears. "Be happy, my little girl. That's my wish for you."

It was surreal.

I can't remember much of anything, other than being with Steve, walking toward him between two rows of smiling people. Looking in each other's eyes as we said our vows. Saying, "I do," then Steve whispering, "I love you," as he slipped the ring on my finger. My lips under his for a breathless, dizzying moment, a promise of more happiness yet to come.

. . .

"Dr. Parrish to the nurses' station," the PA system announces, startling me out of my reverie. The darkness of my world is overwhelming and scary.

I should call Steve. *What happened to him? Why isn't he here?*

The unwanted, inconceivable thought returns, chilling me to the bone. *Was it him? Was he the one who tried to kill me?*

A shift in the air draws my attention. I listen intently. The door has opened quietly, and silent footfalls approach on gum-soled shoes. A faint scent I am not familiar with finds my nostrils; it isn't Isabella.

I feel like screaming, yet lie there perfectly still and defenseless, not daring to breathe.

Has he come for me?

NINE

Terrified, I exhale quietly, as flashes of memories flood my mind like shards of a broken mirror. I see myself running, turning to look over my shoulder and faltering, almost falling, yet grasping at the wall for balance and racing for the door. I grab the door handle and pull with all my strength. I look over my shoulder again, only to see that raised arm coming down with a merciless blow.

And still my attacker's face stays hidden in the shadows of my mind, invisible.

The floor creaks almost imperceptibly. I'm not alone in the room. Not anymore.

"Are you here?" I ask, deciding to face whoever it is and fight for my life until the last breath has left my chest. "Where are you? What do you want?"

"Shhhh . . . you're okay," a raspy, gentle voice says. "It's Jasmine, your nurse. But you can call me Jas."

The relief I feel is so intense it fills my eyes with tears. "Hello, Jas," I manage. "You have no idea how happy I am to meet you." I pause, suddenly unsure. "Or have we met before?"

A light chuckle, sounding more like a gurgle, comes from the left of my bed. I envision Jasmine as a tall woman with a large bosom and a wide smile on her round face. "Well, depends on how you look at it. You might not remember me, but I've been assigned to your care for a few days now."

"You might not remember..." I repeat, my voice a tired whisper. "Of course, I might not. I'm sorry about that. I'll try to remember you tomorrow. Or have I said that before?"

"No, actually, it's the first time we've spoken." The bed tilts on the left side, and scrubs rustle when the nurse sits. A warm hand searches for my pulse on my wrist. "Can you feel this?"

"Vaguely."

A beat of silence, while Jasmine's hand gently presses my forearm. "What do you mean, vaguely?"

"Like it's not mine, that hand. My hand, I mean. I can feel it, but not really. Like I'm dreaming."

"How about now?" Jasmine clutches my fingers and squeezes a little tighter.

"About the same."

A moment of silence, then Jasmine lets go. "Interesting." She stands and the bed levels, but I don't hear her moving. "But it's okay. I'm sure it's a side effect from the sedatives and pain meds you're on. You're riding pretty high, you know?"

"The doctor said he dialed down my meds."

"And it's still the same? This feeling that your hand isn't yours?"

"Yeah." I wait for an answer, but Jasmine doesn't say anything else. She seems to have resumed her duties, walking quickly around the room, opening drawers, moving heavy objects on casters, the sound of wheels rolling on the floor unmistakable. "Is there anyone else in the room right now?"

The footsteps stop in place, a few feet away. "No. Why do you ask?"

"I just...want to know." I swallow hard, wishing I could

help myself to a drink of water to soothe my scorched throat. "I'm afraid," I admit simply. "I don't know if—"

"What happened to you, dearie?" The chart holder clatters when it bangs against the foot of the bed, plastic hitting plastic. "I see some notes here about police investigating, and a detective's name. Were you attacked?"

"Someone tried to kill me."

"Oh, my goodness," Jasmine says. "How awful! Who was it?"

I bite my lip, frustrated. It feels good to feel my teeth sinking into my flesh, one of the very few things I can actually do on my own. "That's exactly the problem. I can't remember, just like I can't remember meeting you before, or my doctor's name that I forgot a few times already, or lots of other things. I just can't remember!" My voice rises, still shaky, yet the pitch is increasingly forceful.

"Don't worry about it," Jasmine says, peeling the covers off my body. The chill in the air makes my skin prickle with goose bumps. "It's very common in cases like yours. You have a pretty serious concussion, and you're on enough meds to tranq a horse. It will come back to you."

"You don't understand," I insist, as Jasmine changes my sheet, rolling me gently. "I've forgotten lots of things—half my life, actually. I've forgotten who I was before this. I only remembered I'm married about an hour ago; it came back to me like a wave of emotions and details and images and sounds that only sometimes turns into a cohesive, solid memory, like I'm used to. And now I don't know where my husband is, or if he was the one who—"

"Shh . . . give yourself some time. It will come back. Posttraumatic amnesia almost always resolves without any issues."

"That's what he said," I reply. "Dr. um—"

"Sokolowski."

"Yes, him. Is he good?"

"The best." The response comes swiftly. "You were lucky to get him. He's a nice person too, not arrogant and entitled like some other docs I've seen, who look down their nose at patients and nurses both." She touches my face, cupping it in her palms. "Turn your head for me, gently, like this. Does it hurt?"

I wince. My skull is throbbing, and moving makes it worse. "Yes. But don't give me more meds. I need to remember. I have to."

"Okay. I just want to turn you on your side. It's not healthy to be on your back for so long. Would you like that?"

"I don't know . . . I guess."

"How did you like to sleep, before all this happened? On your left?"

"Yes." I smile a little. "How did you know?"

"Most people prefer sleeping on their left side." She rustles the sheets and touches my ankles briefly. "Your legs are warm enough; blood flow is just fine. Let's turn you now. We'll start with the shoulders and hips, and roll, just like this."

I allow Jasmine to shift my body and adjust my limbs as she talks, until I feel comfortable enough. I'm desperately trying not to think about what's going on. Not to visualize myself being handled and set in place like a broken doll.

The nurse moves gently, thoughtfully, and her voice keeps me anchored somehow, like something I can hold on to for balance. I thank her with a sad smile.

"If I don't remember, I'll die," I whisper, as Jasmine is pulling the covers over my body. "He will come after me again. I know that. I can feel it. I just—I need to be ready when that happens."

"He?" Jasmine asks, then silence falls heavy, suffocating, as I can't find an answer I can trust. "You know, these old fingers are dying to dial the cops and give them the name of whoever did this to you."

I sigh, the pained exhale leaving my body trembling. "I don't know who it was, Jas. And I'm terrified to find out, but I have to. Help me. Please."

"Shh . . . I'm right here," Jasmine says. "You need to get some rest now."

"How do I defend myself if they come? What can I do? I can't even move my hands." Despair colors my voice as I try to close my fists and fail, realizing I barely make my fingers twitch.

"Why don't I stay with you tonight?" Jasmine offers. "I'll sit right here, by your side, and make sure no one gets near you." She opens a drawer, then walks by the bed and does something to the IV bag feeding into my vein. I sense the IV tubing moving slightly, and the shift in the air when Jasmine comes and goes.

Drowsiness starts spilling throughout my body, warm and almost unbeatable, even if I want to stay awake as much as possible. I know she drugged me, against my explicit request, but I don't care that much anymore. "Thank you," I say, grateful and yet aware she has other patients to tend to. The moment I fall asleep, she'll probably rush out of there to catch up on her work.

The thought makes me realize how irrational my fears are. I'm safe here, surrounded by staff, in the middle of a hospital. Or perhaps I'm not that safe—the sheer size of the place allowing my attacker to sneak in and try again.

Because he will, if for no other reason than to keep me from testifying. How could he know I don't remember anything? And even if he did know, he wouldn't risk letting me live until my memory returns. I am nothing but a loose end, about to be tied up with a tight, deadly knot.

And this time, there will be no running away.

Something clatters loudly as it falls on the floor, startling me. An involuntary gasp comes off my lips.

"I'm so sorry," Jasmine mutters. "These old hands, they don't work as well as they used to."

I listen for other sounds, picturing the nurse going about her business. Tearing off some wrapping. Collecting some garbage, squashing it together, then opening a container and dropping the clumped-up stuff in there. Then closing the lid with a loud sound, metal hitting metal like in those foot-controlled trash cans. Or perhaps it's equipped with a motion sensor, its lid popping open when a hand waves in front of it. I find myself wondering if the container has the three interlocking circles of the biohazard symbol. In my mind's eye, it does. It's stainless-steel silver, and the circles are black. Not red, like I've seen in movies . . . black. I don't know why, but I'm sure of it.

My mind is playing games again.

"Ready," Jasmine announces, rolling a stool over by my bed and taking a seat with a satisfied sigh. "Now you rest, while I read some of this book."

"What are you reading?"

The stool groans a little under her weight. "James Patterson's latest. I love a good crime thriller." She laughs quietly and flips through the book's pages. I catch a whiff of the crisp scent of newly printed and cut paper. It's pleasant, almost like vanilla. It reminds me of cozy nights spent on the sofa with a book on my lap.

Silence lingers for a while, but then, as I'm about to doze off, a thought takes shape in my mind, chilling me. I wonder if she's still there, in the room with me.

"Jasmine, if you wanted to kill me, how would you go about it?"

TEN

The sound of an approaching ambulance siren wakes me with a start. I listen, the multitude of noises painting a picture I can see as easily as if I were leaning against the windowsill, looking out. The siren grows louder and louder, stopping abruptly as the vehicle stops. Its back doors swing open with a slight squeak, then the sound of the stretcher's wheels hitting the ground. The same doors, presumably, slam shut. The stretcher, rattling faintly on its wheels, and the moaning of a man, all interweave to tell a story I can't see with my own eyes, yet is still poignant. The sounds wane into the distance.

"Jasmine?" I call weakly, still drowsy after being asleep for a while—for an undetermined while; the grounding power of daylight's absence from my world leaving me prey to the maddening game of assumptions. I feel dizzy and lost, my mouth dry, my consciousness struggling to emerge from layers of medication, like a ship through thick ocean fog.

No one responds. The room feels eerily silent after the ambulance sounds. "Jas?" I call again, this time my voice strangled by tears.

I recall how upset my nurse was after my question, and how

coldly she'd replied, "I'm willing to overlook that question and blame it on the drugs you're on."

When I asked Jasmine how she would go about killing me, I'd wanted her ideas as a crime fiction fan, as a hospital employee, as someone who could see danger approaching. I did my best to explain all that. After a while, the nurse's voice warmed up again, and she apologized. But then she left the room after suggesting I get a psychiatric consult. She even wrote that recommendation in my chart.

I'm not crazy. I know I'm not. The throbbing pain in the back of my head isn't imaginary, and neither is the haunting memory of me running, pleading for my life. Now all I have are sounds and smells and a whole lot of time to try to piece together the memories that make up who I used to be.

For the first time in my life, I listen. I really listen, paying attention to sounds in a different, much richer way than I ever did before. In my permanently dark world, sounds have become three-dimensional, my awareness heightened by the lack of visual distractions. It's a prolific source of information, accurately drawing images for my mind's eye, images I can recognize and interpret. My hearing has sharpened, despite the cocktail of drugs that still makes me drowsy and weak. I can hear birds singing outside my window, and, at times, the hissing of wind, the light patter of raindrops, the creaking of the floor under the stealthiest of footsteps.

Maybe I won't be able to see my attacker coming, but I will definitely hear them. I can hope to have the upper hand for a second or two. But then, what will I do?

With that thought, I try moving my hand. At first, I feel for the blanket with the tips of my fingers, and relish the painfully slow crawl over the soft, fleecy surface. The sensation is just as strangely remote as before, but it's there, nevertheless. I try to make my hand crawl up the blanket and reach my face. After what seems like forever, I've maybe covered a couple of inches of that distance. My arm doesn't hurt, and neither do my fingers; they just refuse to obey my will to move. What used to come naturally is now an impossible struggle.

But today, I moved two inches more than I did yesterday. And the day is just starting.

In the distance, the lighthearted voices of two women engaged in conversation approach quickly, then fade in the distance as they walk past my room. "... you want to keep going there for lunch. I knew it," one woman says in a singsong voice, giggling.

"Shut up," the other one replies, laughing quietly. "Or you're not invited." I can tell the two women are good friends, the kind who confide in each other and gossip together. The almost-absent sound of their departing footsteps makes me think of the shoes Isabella and Jasmine both wear. Comfortable, sensible shoes that don't clack at every step, disturbing patients. The owners of the two young voices are probably nurses.

Meaningless chatter ... another one of life's little luxuries I no longer have. Nothing about my life is meaningless now. As my attention turns toward my stubbornly sluggish fingers, the memory of my screams invades my mind with a vengeance, forcing me to relive the moments before I was struck down. Those eyes ... such anger, such fierce rage, pinning me under that loaded glare, petrifying me. And something else I didn't remember before. Excitement. A glint of exhilaration, as if my falling down would be the grand finale of a grueling race.

Were those glinting eyes Steve's?

As if in a dream, I remember the look, how I felt under the daggers of that hateful scowl, the coldness of it. But not the actual eyes that seeped such rage. Were they blue, like Steve's?

I can't be sure.

All I recall is how I felt. How I ran, screaming until my throat burned raw.

The memory dissipates into nothingness, disappearing at the

precise moment when I was struck down and my entire world went dark in an explosion of green stars bursting behind my eyelids.

I have nothing. No answer to the question that keeps me from calling my husband, from having him near. From not feeling so desperately alone and vulnerable. And no idea why he isn't looking for me.

I've never known Steve to be a violent man, but there are lots of things I don't know about him. Until a day or so ago, I'd forgotten he existed. What else am I missing?

I breathe deeply as I keep flexing my fingers, determined to make them work again. Letting my mind wander, I rummage for bits and pieces of my past to put together into something coherent. For a while, I can't make much sense of the snippets flashing through my mind. But then, in a burst of clarity, it comes to me, crashing over me like a wave. Grateful, I let myself become immersed in discovering who we used to be, and Steve's voice reverberates in my mind.

"Oh, baby, we made it," he whispered excitedly, as the Golden Globes announcer called his name. He gave me a quick kiss on the lips, then walked toward the stage with a spring in his step and a smile that could've lit up the whole of Tinsel Town. I stood and applauded, happy for him and just a little bit sad for me. My own nomination for a Golden Globe, for the lead role in *The Fall of Jane Watkins,* hadn't materialized.

"This will change the direction of our careers," he said later, still excited after a long ceremony, followed by an after-party. We were having champagne for breakfast at one of the restaurants in the Beverly Hills Hotel. Champagne and pancakes. "You'll see. We're just getting started." His eyes glimmered with joy.

But that had come afterwards.

First, it was the excitement of filming *Jane Watkins*. I'd never seen Steve so feverishly excited before. He slept barely four hours a night, working all the time, losing weight from not eating, even if I chased him with sandwiches or snacks. It seemed his entire being had condensed into this inner, all-consuming fire, that found no reprieve until the last scene was filmed.

My relationship with Denise grew over that time, becoming more of a close friendship. She came by the day's location whenever she could, watching with proud eyes how I brought Jane Watkins to life. Between her coaching and Steve's direction, I blossomed into an actress who discovered her own voice. The script was brilliant, the story one that promised to have a memorable grip on viewers. And I loved Jane, the widowed mother of a seven-year-old boy, her multifaceted personality, the frailty that became her strength when she had to fight for her child.

To my horror, however, after the summer *Jane Watkins* was released, I started being referenced as a nepo actress, my success credited entirely to my husband. Everyone's mind was less on my performance and more on my marriage with the rising-star director everyone was talking about. That lasted for a few months, and culminated with the Globes in January and the People's Choice win for me about a month later.

And then some other movie was released, and another, and the dust of oblivion started falling thick on our careers.

For a while, Steve was picky about the projects he wanted to work on, concerned with the reputation he was only just starting to build. I was auditioning for everything Denise landed on my schedule, but producers shied away from me for some reason. One actually said to me, after an audition, "This is great, Emma, but you'll always be Jane Watkins, and we need someone entirely different. Someone more . . . fresh," while others probably assumed that I only got the Jane Watkins part because I was Steve's wife, and held no merit of my own. No, they said it was just the excellent script and the direction of Steve Wellington, who was oh so great.

One such day, a while after Steve's Golden Globe win, and after an audition that ended up with reassurances and well-wishing instead of a contract, I came home to find a housekey, tied with a red bow, waiting for me on the dining room table, placed upon two airline tickets.

"What's this?" I asked, looking into Steve's boyish eyes.

He grinned and took my hand. "You'll see."

We flew into Tahoe that afternoon, a short flight that didn't yield any answers to my barrage of questions. He sat next to me, looking at me with that sparkle in his eyes I loved and a hint of a smile that put dimples in his cheeks, and didn't say a word. He drove a rental car from the airport for about forty minutes on beautiful, winding mountain roads, and stopped in front of a large cottage-style single story built in the middle of four acres of woods. I had no idea who lived there. The lights were on inside, and in the landscaping outside. It was breathtakingly beautiful.

He cut the engine and looked at me. "Are you ready?"

"For what?" I wasn't dressed for a formal occasion. Not in a house like that. As for Steve, he always wore a suit.

"To be carried over the threshold, Mrs. Wellington."

"Aah," I squealed, looking at him, then at the house. I got out of the car and rushed into his arms. "You can't be serious!"

I was still squealing when he picked me up and carried me inside. He gave me the tour, and I was exhilarated and afraid at the same time. How would we be able to afford this? And why here, in Tahoe, when our lives were in LA? He wouldn't answer any of those questions; just waved off my concerns, reminding me our lives were just starting.

The house was amazing. Its angled, floor-to-ceiling living room window overlooked the distant lake and the towering snowy peaks beyond it. A rustic stone fireplace with a raised hearth acted as the centerpiece of the room, featuring a wood mantel and built-in shelves on both sides. The first object that was moved into the new house was Steve's Golden Globe, and it landed on that mantel, while I landed in his arms for a fiery kiss that made me forget my worry over our future.

It was fun to enjoy our fleeting success for a while. Steve's happiness colored our lives with fairy-tale glitter, while my gut churned, noticing how quickly the money went—soon after we closed on the Lake Tahoe house, Steve bought himself a new Beemer, an M4 Coupé in a stunning shade of metallic blue. Like a kid with a new toy, he never invited me to drive it, but he stashed a gift-wrapped box in the new convertible's glove compartment. He drove me to our favorite lakeshore vista point, then gave me the box.

"This is for you, my beautiful wife."

I smiled and got lost in Steve's loving blue eyes as I opened the package. The diamond bracelet was absolutely gorgeous.

For a while, we were blissfully happy. Then came the misery of not being able to repeat the success of *Jane Watkins*. No good scripts came his way. Producers seemed to prefer other directors. His phone rang with what he called "garbage ideas," and he refused them all for a while, saving himself for the next big blockbuster that never came.

Late at night, as disappointment layered our days with bitterness, we talked and talked, dissecting every aspect of every call we got or didn't get. Why so-and-so chose another director for their new psychological thriller. Well, of course, they did—they'd known that director for years, they were partying together, played poker on Friday nights and whatnot. Neither of us networked well with Hollywood's greatest; after a while, we started spending all our weekends in Tahoe, where not being invited anywhere seemed to hurt less.

But Steve was increasingly desperate. Two years passed, and his Golden Globe stood alone on the living room mantel.

I was less picky about work. Whatever Denise brought my way I auditioned for, and on occasion, I got reasonably good offers. Nothing at *Jane Watkins* level, but money was tight, and I knew my good years were numbered. Unlike Steve, time didn't work in my favor. *Summer Love,* a cheesy little flick where I bared my breasts for exactly one-point-five seconds, brought our first argument.

"—irresponsible, and that's an understatement." Steve's voice echoed in my mind, angry and cold and hurtful. "Have you considered what this will do? To you? To us?"

"I'm an actress, Steve. This role, it's . . . complex, it's real. I made a professional decision."

"'A professional decision'? Stripping down for the camera is now a professional decision?"

"It's not about the nudity. It's about the art, the story we're telling. I know you can see that. You do it so well with other actors. And it's just under two seconds of running time."

He laughed bitterly, shaking his head. "You call this art? I call it career suicide. And what about me, huh? What will I be—the husband of that actress who bared it all for everyone to see?"

"Oh, so this is about your ego, then? *Your* career?" In the heat of the moment, I forgot how much I wanted us to make up and be happy again. "What about *my* career? My choices? This is not the Dark Ages, you know."

He pointed an accusatory finger at me. "No. This is about respect. For yourself, and for me. You crossed a line. You should've spoken with me before signing that contract."

His raised voice made me take a step back. I didn't want to fight anymore, but he wasn't right about any of it. "I took this role because it challenges me. Not to defy or . . . or embarrass you."

"But at what cost, Emma? The whispers, the stares . . . Have you thought of that?"

"I won't live in fear. Not of the industry, and not of you." I crossed my arms and stared at him squarely, breathing away unwanted tears. He looked away, his shoulders lowered, his head hung a little low. "I want us to be happy, Steve. More than anything. But I do owe it to myself to try my best at building something for myself."

Thankfully, we made up the same night; I didn't know how to live without him anymore.

The second fight came when I took a waitressing job in Lake Tahoe, working weekends when I wasn't filming. Tourists made my job worthwhile, and I didn't care that the occasional one recognized me or catcalled at me with some lewd remark. I was getting some of the bills paid, and relieving a little of Steve's stress. Or so I thought.

He was so angry when I told him, but his anger fizzled out, quickly dissolved by my tears. He wasn't a man to stay angry at me for long; he loved me too much for that.

I recalled Steve as gentle and kind, almost fatherly, not someone who would've glared at me with rage-filled eyes, ready to strike me down.

As the PA system calls an emergency code, I wonder where he is. Why isn't he looking for me? Why isn't he sitting here, by my side, holding my hand?

He must be filming on location somewhere, I decide, after a moment of paralyzing, bone-chilling doubt. I should call his assistant to find out. What was his name? A young man with dark, curly hair and black eyes, probably not even twenty-two, who had a secret crush on my husband. He worshipped the ground Steve walked on, sometimes making me jealous, but Steve wasn't gay. I had nothing to worry about.

Maybe I should just call Steve instead. He's probably worried sick about me.

ELEVEN

"What's a code blue?" I ask as sort of an ice-breaker, before I dare to voice the more important questions on my mind.

I've been restless all day, consumed by too many fears to count, yet at the same time a little dazed, fighting off brain fog with little success. I recall bits and pieces of recent events, of yesterday, but it doesn't seem nearly enough. People were visiting with me the day before. Probably my doctor . . . but did he stop by once, or twice? Which one of the nurses fed me? Why don't I remember having three meals yesterday? I can barely recall one—a cream cheese of some sort. Was it Jasmine who came? I don't believe so. It's as if my brain fog has swallowed everything, leaving only traces in a twisted game of breadcrumbs I don't want to play anymore.

The doctor's shoes squeak quietly when he stops for a moment. He's tearing and rustling some wrappers over to the side of the bed, seemingly a few feet away. "Why do you ask?"

"Is that when someone—?"

He seems reluctant to answer. The rustling has stopped. He stands perfectly still, while I imagine he has plunged his hands into his pockets, the way I've seen doctors do, back when I could still see. "That's hospital speak for cardiac or respiratory arrest," he says after a while. "Nothing for you to worry about."

"Was I a code blue the other night?"

Another brief hesitation. "Technically, yes, you were. But there was no real code blue for you, because we were here, ready to help you breathe." A light chuckle, that sounds a bit dismissive to me, but perhaps I am being a bit childish. "You shouldn't worry about these things, Emma. Nothing is going to happen to you." The air shifts as he approaches the bed, bringing with him a faint smell of basil and fresh laundry—perhaps softener still clinging to his clothes. The bed tilts slightly under his weight when he sits, and something rustles close to my face. I hate that, not knowing when things or people get so close to me. But there's nothing I can do about it. I am instinctively anticipating something scary, although rationally I know he's not going to hurt me.

"How long have I been here?" I ask.

He pulls the covers off my upper body, then rolls up my loose sleeve to expose my left arm. His gloved fingers barely graze against my skin. "A few days," he replies, as he peels off a patch gently. His hands feel warm to the touch through the thin nitrile of his glove. The patch tugs at my skin as it comes off, making me wish I could scratch my arm right there, where the edges are peeling off. He takes it away, then applies a new one quickly, running his fingers over the edges to make sure it adheres well. The new one feels cold and moist. It makes me shiver.

"What's that?"

"The patch?" Dr. Sokolowski crumples something in his hands and stands. "It's your pain medicine. Slow-release fentanyl, so we can keep it low dose, just like you requested." I hear the sounds of him peeling off his gloves—a double snap—then he throws something into the trash. The can's lid comes down with the all-too familiar metal-on-metal grinding clatter. "How are you feeling? Does your head still hurt? One to ten, what's your pain level?"

"Um, about a four, but I can manage."

"All right, then you're all set. I'll be back tomorrow—"

"I keep remembering the same thing, over and over. But it's not a real memory; it's just bits and pieces of one. And it keeps coming back, all the time. It drives me crazy."

"That's called an intrusive memory," he replies. His voice is lower pitched, more empathetic. "It's quite common for post-traumatic amnesia." He pauses for a moment, then adds, "Think of memories as objects we place in drawers to retrieve when they're needed. Intrusive memories want to stand out, to come out of their drawers ahead of their turn. Sometimes that's relevant, a way for your subconscious mind to draw your attention to something you need to know. Other times, intrusive memories are just artifacts of a traumatized brain that is trying to make sense of what's in its drawers and how to access them in the right order."

"Why does it happen?" My voice has undertones of despair. "All I remember is running, screaming, and that look...filled with unspeakable rage. But I can't recall anything about their face. Not enough to remember who it was and tell the police about it."

"Post-traumatic amnesia is a defect in the consolidation and retrieval of memories. You probably remember how you *felt* about what happened, not the actual details." He pauses for a moment, but I don't speak. "Memory tends to come back in scrambled pieces, much like a puzzle. Your timeline can feel screwed up too. But as you figure out which piece goes where and glue them together, it will get better. Easier. And some of these memory fragments *will* be intrusive. They'll keep popping up in your mind until you decipher their message."

"When will I remember everything, Doctor? What can I do to make it happen faster?"

The bed tilts slightly under his weight. Warm, dry fingers squeeze mine. "To be perfectly honest, I was expecting it to have resolved by now. But it's like Dr. Winslow said yesterday morning—some of it might never come back. There could be some permanent deficits."

"What do you mean, yesterday morning?" Panic swells in my chest, leaving me breathless. "Was he here? Did he speak with me? I don't remember!"

"You don't recall the exam? Dr. Winslow discussing your CT scan with you yesterday morning?"

Desperate, I rack my brain, looking for the tiniest trace to back up what Dr. Sokolowski is saying. I have nothing. Just darkness, some shreds of dialogue and feelings and thoughts, all mangled together into an unrecognizable heap of dream-like memories. That annoying, repetitive snippet of my attempt to flee my attacker keeps resurfacing, and a vague feeling that some-one might've been there earlier, but I can't be sure. "No . . . I don't recall Dr. Winslow visiting yesterday morning. But I do remember you mentioning him before. How is that possible?"

He squeezes my hand again, and I wish I could pull away, although the doctor's gesture is meant to be reassuring and encouraging. I don't want solace. I want my life back. The beep-ing of the machine intensifies with the rhythm of my heart, mak-ing the silence of the room even more unbearable.

"It could be a residual effect from the Versed, making it harder for you to remember things in the first few hours after you wake up. That's the medication we're giving you to help you sleep at night." His fingers find my wrist pulse. "A new CT was done this morning, and the swelling is subsiding nicely. But there is scar tissue in the area where the injury was most severe, specif-ically in the visual cortex of the brain, extending into the hippo-campus, where memories are stored. That's why he—"

"I still can't see? He tested me?" Panic turns my voice high-pitched.

"Unfortunately, your vision hasn't returned yet. We're still hopeful, because the human brain has an amazing capacity for self-healing, for compensating losses of functionality. But there is a chance that some memories, and potentially your vision, might not return."

"No!" I cry, no longer able to hold back my tears. "This can't be happening to me."

"I can only imagine how overwhelmed you must be feeling right now." He must've said those words a thousand times. They sound rehearsed, automatic, and I barely acknowledge them.

What am I going to do? I've lost everything. My career is now gone; I'll never act again, never do the one thing I really loved. As for Steve... how can I offer him a good life, crippled and blind like this? He'd be better off without me. *Oh, Steve...* A suffocating sob chokes me, but I keep it locked inside my chest. *I need you.*

"Emma, we're here for you, and we'll do everything in our power to help you." I don't say anything; my head is still spinning, trying to process everything he's said. "Dr. Winslow ran some other tests, including a nerve conduction study, and he was very clear about the results. You *will* move again. It will take some rehab, but you will be able to function with minimal motor deficits. This abnormal muscle tone has us a little concerned, but we believe—"

"But I will be blind," I whisper, the words chilling me as I say them.

"We're not sure yet. There's a chance you will recover your eyesight completely. There's nothing on that scan to tell us decisively that you won't. But there is scar tissue, some of it in areas of your visual cortex and in the associative visual area."

"What's that? I don't understand."

"It's the area of the brain responsible for the interpretation and analysis of the information seen. Pattern recognition, analyzing color, form, and movement, spatial processing, and differentiating between past and present experiences."

"So, I could regain my eyesight and it could be completely useless? I would be able to see the letters, but not read? To see a car coming, and not remember I have to get out of the way?"

"We don't know that, but yes, that is the possibility I'm talking about. There's a strong chance it will recover completely, but it will take a little more time. And lots of patience. Perhaps I can give you—"

"No," I snap. "No more drugs. I'm groggy all the time. How can I remember anything if I'm zonked out of my mind? And I need to remember, Doctor, I really do. If I don't, I'll die." A sob escapes my lips in a shattered breath, despite my efforts not to cry. "I just want my life back. The things I used to do, the people I love. What am I going to do?"

"I promise, you will remember," the doctor says firmly. He stands, probably tired of all my questions and anxious to leave. "Then you'll give the police the name or description of the person who attacked you, and that will be the end of it. In the meantime, let's focus on your immediate recovery. Allow yourself to rest. And you should think of someone you could stay with, when you come out of hospital, just to be on the safe side." He pauses for a beat, seemingly hesitant. "Actually, there's a nice couple outside waiting to see you."

"I don't want to see anybody." The words blurt out of my mouth before I can check myself. I don't care who those people are. I'm not even curious. All I want is to be left alone.

"It wouldn't be a bad thing," the doctor insists. I can sense he's closer to the bed, perhaps leaning over me a little. "It will do you good. Trust me." There's an encouraging smile in his low voice, muffled by the mask.

Before I can refuse again, I hear the door open, and distant voices exchange words I can't follow. Cooler air rushes inside the room and, with it, a sickening, sweet perfume.

It fills me with dread. Forgotten memories rush to my mind from the depths of time, opening a chasm of pain in my chest. For an infinitesimal moment, I recall smelling that same perfume on my bedsheets one terrible summer night, maybe not so long ago.

Then, a familiar voice says, "Hello, Emma."

TWELVE

They say scent is the most powerful trigger of emotion and memory.

It's true.

Vivid recollections crash against my mind like furious waves against a rocky shore, eating away at it, piece by broken piece: that night, when I found a long strand of hair on the bathroom counter, and the fleeting thought that had crossed my mind with a twinge of fear. *Seems longer and darker than mine.* But I had chosen to shrug it off and go back to bed, where my husband was already asleep.

Then, not long after, another strand was coiled on my pillow when I returned from a few days spent filming on location. The bed looked poorly made, as if someone had just stretched the covers in a rush. It wasn't what Sofia, our housekeeper, would've called a made bed.

When I called her into the bedroom it wasn't to scold her, and she entered the room with her usual smile on her round face.

"Yes, Miss Emma?" Her words carried a strong Polish accent.

"Did you forget to make the bed?" I asked.

Her eyes had shifted toward the bed, her jaw slackening. She shook her head forcefully and seemed worried, if not scared.

"It's not a problem, Sofia. I'm just curious."

That was what I said to her, lying effortlessly, when I couldn't admit, not even to myself, that I needed to know what had happened. Why my home suddenly felt strange and unwelcoming. Why cold sweat was running down my spine as I stared at the white pillowcase, slightly smudged with a stranger's shade of lipstick, much darker than mine.

Sofia gave the bed one long, side look, and muttered something quickly in her mother tongue, then lowered her eyes. Her cheeks were on fire as she rushed to peel the sheets off. She was an older woman, about sixty at the time, with a maternal, overflowing bosom and kind, understanding eyes in a warm shade of hazel. Her jowls bounced as she hurried to remake the bed, still mumbling.

"No, stop," I said, interrupting the Polish words I didn't understand. "All I wanted was to ask if you know who—"

She froze in place, her head lowered, her hands clasped together in front of her body, seemingly ashamed. "I can't. Please, Miss Emma. I need this job."

My anger melted under her pleading gaze. She wasn't to blame for this. For any of it. I squeezed her shoulder gently, then walked away, struggling to keep myself from screaming.

Uncertainty is unbearable.

It's also stupid, the most pathetic form of self-deception there is. Not uncertainty in itself, but the way human beings cling to it, calling it hope and refusing to see the truth right in front of their eyes.

What, exactly, did I deem uncertain at the time? As I lie in bed, immersed in the unescapable darkness of my new reality, I realize it was all there, staring me in the face. Seeing my husband's hand touching the arm of a young actress, Mikela Murtagh, as he walked her off set on her first day of filming, not looking my way once. His fingers lingering on the small of her back, the way they used to linger on mine. His entire focus dedicated to coaching the new star, to improving her acting performance, just as he'd done for me on the set of *Eternal Serenade.*

It felt like a strange and ominous Groundhog Day, a warning I failed to see: my evenings alone, munching on room service dinners in front of the TV while his late hours were spent more and more being "still busy on the set," long after the day's call sheet had been wrapped. The strange sparkle in his eyes that wasn't meant for me, even when it was just the two of us, and which quickly disappeared when he saw me. His waning appetite, disappearing night after night when he finally returned to our hotel room, when all he wanted for dinner was a quick drink and some sleep, because tomorrow was a busy day.

After he'd met that barely legal skank, his tomorrows became routinely busy.

That's how my husband had dealt with the fickle gods of fortune. When we had both been faced with professional challenges—his Golden Globe and my People's Choice had remained the only two awards on a very wide mantel—I had taken any part that was offered to me. He had taken a mistress.

She was barely eighteen when he first cast her in one of his low-budget productions, the only kind of movie he seemed able to land. She was petite and seemed vulnerable and soft, with a gentle appearance and a nice smile, in dire contrast to her clothing—the bare minimum of fabric used for her ridiculously short skirts. Her hair, slightly darker and longer than mine, was styled in a side part and tied in a low ponytail she brought forward over her shoulder, with loose strands framing her face. Her eyes were contoured with eyeliner and mascara, discreetly, and a touch of subtle eyeshadow added dimension and depth to her expression. Her lips shone with a glossy, plum-toned lipstick.

But that expression of elegant, poised serenity was all an act, masterfully played for gullible people who wanted to believe in her charming innocence.

When they first landed on me, the girl's eyes had turned to steel, cold and spiteful. They had shifted from me to Steve and back, as if wondering what he saw in his wife. As if wondering whether she'd be a better deal for the rising-star director.

She introduced herself with a shy smile as "Miki," and gave my hand a cold and limp shake. That was my first encounter with Mikela. After a while, back in my dressing room, I recalled the sweet smell of her floral perfume, still clinging to where she'd touched me. I washed my hands furiously, the scent unnerving, like a bad omen of heartache to come.

Then, one weekend night, when I got to our Tahoe home after a long week spent filming a TV mini-series episode, I had showered and gone straight to bed, only to find traces of that sickeningly sweet smell embedded in the down of my pillow. The sheets were pristine, probably freshly changed by Sofia, but she hadn't known to air the pillow itself.

Steve was filming on location, north of LA, for a new project he seemed very excited about—a rom-com I was never invited to audition for. Miki got the leading role in that one. Not surprisingly, the movie flopped. Badly. I recall feeling almost grateful I didn't get to star in it. For a moment, I went so far as to assume Steve had kept me off the audition call for that one because he knew it wasn't going to be a blockbuster.

Yeah, right.

. . .

A bitter scoff expresses the opinion I have of myself, in retrospect, remembering those days that feel like a train wreck I am watching in slow motion, in the private dark room of my mind, unable to stop it and unable to run. By the time I was telling myself such deluded lies, I had become an expert in clinging to uncertainty as a way to survive.

Now I see it for what it really was. The beginning of the end.

With that newly found memory comes the heartache, acute and burning, as if everything happened yesterday. In a sense, that's true. The healing effect of time passing has been erased. The wounds are raw and bleeding, and there's nothing I can do but endure. Holding my breath as the flood continues, I recall what happened the following weekend.

It still makes me shudder when I recall the way he shouted my name.

"Emma! Are you insane?"

He'd walked in the door to find me standing by the table, pale, frozen, arms crossed at my chest, staring at the stack of papers I'd laid out neatly for him. The top sheet bore the logo of a divorce attorney in bold, unescapable lettering.

"No," I replied calmly, ready for the storm that was to come. "Just tired of your cheating, is all."

"What cheating?" he blurted, but his eyes veered away from mine.

"Steve . . . don't be a coward. Own it."

He paced furiously through the room, then into the living room, where he stopped and stared absent-mindedly at our two trophies standing pride of place on the mantel. I followed him, but stayed at a distance. "All right, I'll own it. Why are you still here?"

"What?" I asked, a chill rushing through my veins and filling me with dread. "Where else should I be? I don't have a secret lover to take me in while the divorce is pending. You could go to LA . . . we have a house there too, right?"

He stared at me unforgivingly. "*We* don't have anything much but a heap of papers waiting to be signed and a lot of bloody attitude." He stabbed the air next to my chest, but I didn't flinch. "This is *my* house. I want you gone. Is that clear?"

My lawyer had warned me of that possibility, and told me what I should do if it happened. Seemed it was quite common for cheating husbands to want to kick out their wives, so they could smoothly and seamlessly resume their lives with the mistress instead.

"Should we call the cops to settle this matter?"

My soft-spoken words lit up his eyes with instant rage. "I'll destroy you, Emma! To think I was ever in love with you . . . it makes me sick! You'll never amount to anything in this industry, you hear me? Why do you think I cheated in the first place?"

I held his gaze even if it hurt and hollowed me inside. He breathed heavily, panting, his eyes glinting with anger, while I held my breath, wishing it was all over. Eventually, he looked away, while his face colored an unhealthy shade of red.

On the way out, he grabbed the Golden Globe off the mantel. In eerie symmetry, the first object he'd brought into that house was the first he took away.

When he left, he slammed the door behind him so forcefully the wall cracked next to the frame, a fine line zigzagging all the way up to the ceiling.

The silence left in his wake was even more painful than the shouted insults and accusations. I relived our time together in my mind, all the things we said to one another, all the good times that the sweet-smelling homewrecker had stolen from me. I had been abandoned, replaced, thrown to the curb like a worn-out piece of furniture that no one wanted anymore. Or at least, that's how I felt at the time, and it killed me.

The divorce itself got turned into a tasteless, blazing circus. Lawyers on both sides were rubbing their hands, pitting us against one another—as if we needed any help in that area. At the center of our discord was the Lake Tahoe house. It was my only home, a place I loved dearly, but also the place Steve wanted to keep for himself. I didn't want his LA house or his high-rise condo in Santa Monica; I just didn't want to let go of the place where I'd been so happy, even if I could barely afford it.

The court sided with me on that, especially after proof of his cheating was brought to light by my lawyer. As for alimony, I didn't want any of it; I believed I could earn my own keep. I was surprised when the judge awarded me some money, but barely enough to cover the property taxes on the house. I was grateful for it, although the look in Steve's eyes as he handed me the keys sliced through my heart like a dagger. It felt like staring into the slit eyes of a deadly snake.

He walked away with everything else and his mistress, proudly showing her off the moment the judge's gavel fell.

It felt personal, like some sort of vendetta against me for humiliating him in court, for winning against him. It probably wasn't. It must've been infatuation, nothing else. As soon as he walked out of that courtroom, I stopped existing for him.

Then came the aftermath.

Denise worked tirelessly to resurrect my career, but work was scarce and ends just didn't meet. Sofia was long gone, although she'd cried and offered to stay for half the pay. I referred her to some of my well-off neighbors, as I still couldn't find work.

The only income I managed to secure came from waitressing.

I found a local place, Black Bear Bar and Grill, well-liked by the weekend crowds. The owner was a retired Silicon Valley executive with a keen sense of humor and a passion for film almost as consuming as his love for the ski slopes. He'd seen me as Jane Watkins and offered me the job with a wide grin on his boyish face, then immediately asked for an autograph on a napkin, to be signed right underneath the logo—the silhouette of the standing black bear.

That was the life I must've had right before the attack. That's all I can remember. After that point in time, everything is blank. I was the actress no one wanted to cast anymore. The waitress living in a Lake Tahoe house she couldn't afford. The divorcee no one missed.

And now, this. My entire life reduced to lying in bed, sinking into abysmal darkness.

Tears burn my closed eyes, but I breathe deeply and steel myself.

Hell, if I'm going to cry in front of that bitch.

One more breath of air and I am myself, and strong enough to speak. "Oh, Steve, I can smell her on you," I groan.

"*Her* is right here, staring at you." The fake-childish voice I learned to hate fills the room, emphasized by the approaching clack of stilettos.

For a moment, it slipped my mind that Dr. Sokolowski had mentioned a couple. I knew she was there, but I also didn't. That's how my brain works now, like a sputtering old engine making all sorts of weird noises.

It's irrational, because her sickening perfume fills the room and my mind with heartbreaking memories. But I'm not sorry for my words . . . the homewrecker deserves to hear it. I owe the woman who destroyed my life absolutely nothing. I still wish I could run and hide, not be forced to be looked upon by her, not when I'm so vulnerable. The thought of that makes me grind my teeth.

"Steve, please take your midlife crisis fling and go." My words make Mikela gasp and then there's a clacking of heels, approaching fast. I cringe.

"We need to talk," Steve says calmly. His baritone voice cuts through my heart. I miss hearing him, so unbelievably much, and yet, I realize, the sound of his voice scares me, as if now I'm hearing him speak for the first time, noticing inflections I don't recall hearing before. A certain warmth entwined with a distant, menacing chill, like the red and white of a candy cane. A hint of irritation, a note of embarrassment, probably on his mistress's behalf. And, worst of it all—pity. For me. That is the most heartbreaking.

The tuberose perfume becomes unbearable as Mikela stops by the bed. Horrified, I feel her cold fingers touching my hand, clasping it and holding it captive, forcing the tips of my fingers to touch something tapered. Wishing I could pull back, I force myself not to scream and pay attention to the sensation in my fingertips as Mikela rubs something against it.

It's the large stone of an engagement ring, the edges sharp, the surfaces smooth.

"Can you feel this? I'm no longer the fling, Emma. I'm the fiancée, while you're history. And nope, you're not invited," she adds, laughing coldly, letting go of my hand and walking away from the bed. "We won't have handicapped parking at the wedding." She pops a chewing gum balloon, adding a bit of peppermint flavor to the prevailing perfume scent in the air. "Guess where we're having it?" She pauses for a beat, as if I'm actually going to venture a guess. "Right here, in Tahoe, next month." I can hear the smug smile in her voice. It nauseates me. "I've always loved it here. It's where we made love for the first time," she adds, laughing ostentatiously. "In your bed."

"Jeez, Miki," Steve intervenes. "Stop this. You're not helping."

Steve is going to marry the conceited piece of trash who drove a wedge between us. For some reason, knowing that makes everything worse. As if until now, it wasn't real. As if I could turn back time somehow and erase the cheating, the divorce. The loss of Steve's love.

"Why are you here, Steve?" I ask quietly, feeling I can't stand the suffocating pain a moment longer. That moonrise in Cancun, his arms around my shoulders, none of it matters. All of it is gone, as if it never happened.

"Your mother called," he replies. "I wouldn't mind if you told her we're divorced. It's been a while now."

"How long, exactly?" I ask, desperate to feel grounded in time, but keeping my voice as casual as I can manage.

"What, you don't remember?" He scoffs and paces lightly, the sound of his footfalls going left and right at the foot of my bed unnerving me. "Two years and a half, almost three."

The shock traps air in my lungs. Almost three years, and I don't remember a thing. Then a chill spreads through my body in an instant. "Do we have kids?" I ask in a soft whisper.

Mikela laughs, her cackles sounding obscene in the tense silence. "Ha! You don't remember? What kind of mother—"

"Shut up, Miki." Steve's voice sounds tired. He's moving slowly. I can visualize him walking about mindlessly, his hands sunk in his pockets and his back hunched a little. "No, we don't have kids, Emma."

I breathe, relieved and devastated at the same time. Our love story left nothing behind but bits and pieces of scattered, faded memories dipped in sorrow.

"By the way, Denise called me, when you didn't show up for your audition. She asked me to check on you." The pacing stops and the bed moves slightly, as if he's leaning against the railing. "Listen, you're obviously incapacitated, and I'm really sorry about what happened. But you need assistance."

I hold my breath. Where is he going with this? Chills travel through my body as the voice I used to love now sounds menacing, the candy cane all white now, frozen like solid ice. "What are you saying, Steve?"

"I'm saying we'll take care of you. You have nothing to worry about, all right? I'll ask my attorney to draw up some papers, just to put us on the same page, and we'll take it from there."

Papers? My heartbeat pounds in my ears, almost drowning the beeps of the machine. Panic descends upon me, while the same question swirls in my mind, eager to get out.

Did you put me in here, Steve? Was it you?

Instead, I decide to say something else. "Please, get my doctor for me. I'm not feeling well. I can't breathe." I hold my breath until the machine's alarm, a continuous and loud beeping, goes off.

A long moment of hesitation before Steve walks out of the room, then returns with Dr. Sokolowski.

I breathe, filling my starved lungs with air, and the machine's alarm stops.

"Please, give us a moment," the doctor asks firmly. The air shifts as they walk past my bed. "What's happening? Your heart is racing," he says as soon as the door closes. The chest piece of his stethoscope feels cold even through the fabric of my gown.

"Please," I whisper, "I don't want to see them again. Don't let them come near me. He might be the one who—"

"You got it." He walks out of the room with a determined stride.

A heated dialogue erupts between the two men, right outside the open door. At first, I can't hear much of what's being said, but when the voices are raised, I catch a few words.

"—upsetting my patient. Is that clear?"

"I have important business to discuss with my ex-wife. She needs someone to take care of her, and I don't see anyone else lining up. Who's paying for all this, anyway? Insurance?"

"Mr. Wellington, don't make me call the police. Your ex-wife doesn't want you here." Dr. Sokolowski's voice is icy sharp. "Do we understand each other?"

Steve's rambling voice fades in the distance, mixed with Mikela's high-pitched replies. Then the door closes, and with it comes the sound of the doctor approaching the bed.

"They're gone. You can get some rest now. They won't be back to bother you again. I wrote a note for the nurses."

"Thank you." I breathe frantically, fighting the panic lighting my blood on fire. It will take me a while before I can feel safe again.

Because it isn't over.

During our time together, I can't recall a single time when Steve was violent—except perhaps the slammed door that left a crack in the wall—not beyond the occasional shouting match ripe with the usual invectives. Steve was too much of a coward for open violence. He was sneaky and conceited; that's how I remember him. But that was before he lost the Tahoe house to me. What if he's different now? What if he's changed since the divorce?

Am I remembering everything that's buried in my past? Or will tomorrow expose a new chapter of my life I've completely forgotten? And in this hypothetical new chapter, will I discover that Steve was the man who attacked me?

What does Steve really want? To finish the job?

THIRTEEN

It kills me when she cries.

My eyes shift from one screen to the next as I take in the scene. The image is a bit fuzzy; the cameras are small and low resolution, but it's better than the alternative. Like this, I can be with her all the time.

Six screens cover most of the areas I need eyes on. Three of the cameras are installed in Emma's room—one of them hidden in the carbon monoxide sensor above her bed. They're powerful enough to allow me to observe from a safe distance.

She's alone in her room now, and her self-control has given way to tears. It takes every bit of willpower I still have to not find that smug son of a bitch of an ex-husband and wring his damn neck. That wouldn't be smart. Not now, anyway. I have to be patient, but his time will come.

I turn my attention back to the screens, and lose myself in watching my darling Emma. Her lips are trembling, half-open in a silent, pained cry. I touch the screen with the tip of my finger caressing the grainy image of her cheek, pining for the moment I'll be touching her again.

She's not ready to accept me yet; I know it. But she will. Until then, I'm resigned to hating every minute those nurses spend with her, caring for her, feeding her, brushing her hair. Oh, how I wish that could be me!

The thought of touching her stirs me and I shift in my seat, my eyes glued to the screen. Her beauty's haunted me since the day I first saw her. I dream of her sometimes, and wake up aching for her, needing her like I need air.

She's mine.

Everyone'd better remember that.

I followed her one time she went out for errands, in LA. She stopped at a Starbucks; she likes a tall black coffee in the morning, with a touch of half-and-half. It was early, with long lines of caffeine addicts inside the store and at the drive-thru window. She chose to go inside, and circled the lot looking for a good space, while I waited in my car, parked by the entrance.

She pulled into a spot and got out of her Toyota. She wore tight jeans and a light sweater, and walked toward the entrance with a spring in her step, looking more beautiful than ever.

Two bikers rolled into the parking lot, their Harleys roaring right up next to me until they cut their engines. But the two bearded apes didn't notice me. Their eyes were glued to Emma's body.

"I could pound into that the whole damn night," one of them said as he dismounted. They burst into laughter. "Come on, haul some ass, man. I wanna be next in line."

"Yeah, it's quite the view," the other one replied, laughing, as he entered the coffee shop right after Emma.

I didn't feel the need to tell them how their attitude bothered me. There was no need for me to explain why their words made me sick with rage. I don't have such needs; once I've made up my mind, I act.

One of the Harleys bore a parking permit for a Riverside

address. We were on Sunset Boulevard, which meant they had driven Laurel Canyon or were about to. I had a fifty-fifty shot at it, which is always okay in my book. If I missed, there was always tomorrow.

All I had to do was open my car door just a bit, lean down, and nick the bastard's brake line with my pocketknife, in a place it wouldn't start draining fluid right away. Then I waited.

Emma came out of the store carrying her coffee. She rushed to her car and got in, seeming a little scared or perhaps upset. They might've said things to her, or worse, touched her. It was tough to say how upset she was with the sunglasses she wore and the sun in my face. She drove off fast, while I chose to stay behind.

I had something else to do that morning.

Both bikers wore black leather adorned with lots of studs, and gang colors on their backs. They were about forty-five or fifty, with salt-and-pepper beards and long hair, yellowed by grime, probably not washed since forever. One of them, my favorite of the two, spat next to my tire before mounting his Harley, and didn't even look to see if he'd bothered me.

I followed the Harleys to the bottom of Laurel Canyon, gritting my teeth because of the insufferable noise. Why do people put up with that?

Laurel Canyon was jammed, just as I had expected. I had to stop, slowed down by traffic, but the two bikers sped on, weaving recklessly, increasingly confident. The roaring of their exhaust faded in the distance, as I crawled along.

Then the traffic came to a complete halt. Cars stopped coming down on the southbound lane. About ten minutes later, a couple of police cars made their way past me with their sirens blaring, followed shortly by a fire truck and an ambulance.

I smiled, and rolled down my window to enjoy the sunshine on my face. When the first vehicle drove southbound after a while, I waved, and the driver slowed a little, lowering his window.

"Any idea what's going on?"

"Eh, two stupid bikers got creamed."

"Two?" I ask, *pleasantly surprised. I love it when karma agrees with me.*

"Yeah. Cops said one smashed into the other. It's a mess up there. Nothing's going through. I live down from where it happened, so I made it. Idiots, what can I say?" The man shook his head and took off.

After doing a three-point-turn, I drive south myself, back into Hollywood.

I had no business in Riverdale.

FOURTEEN

I wake suddenly. The sound of an ambulance pulling to a stop seems faint and distant, more so than before, as I fight the brain fog that clings to my mind, sticky and persistent. The siren is turned off while the vehicle's doors are slammed and a stretcher is lowered with a rattling thump, then rolled on its wheels in a rush. Then silence, nothing but my thoughts wondering if someone else is about to embark on a journey of pain and despair. Like mine. Or if they stand a chance of walking out of here made whole again, smiling, counting their blessings.

I push those thoughts away and clear my mind, determined to think about the past few days, to dig up any shred of information I can uncover from the depths of my struggling memory. About Dr. Winslow's visits, and his thoughts on my recovery. About Steve, and the two and a half years that were erased from my mind—all the time that has passed since my divorce. How could almost three years of my life vanish like that?

But yesterday or the day before, I didn't even remember Steve, and now my heart aches for the love I've lost. Anger still swells my chest at the thought of him cheating, of having replaced me so casually with someone else. The words spoken in anger still echo in my mind.

While some of my memories have returned, just like the doctor said they would, there have to be more buried in that scarred brain tissue, something that could explain why I was attacked. Why someone had such rage in their eyes when they raised their hand to strike me down.

I breathe slowly, wishing I could drink some water, but I can't manage even that simple, everyday gesture without help. No one is here with me. I listen intently, the way I do every time I wake up, and the silence is absolute. No other lungs breathing but mine. No one's shoes on the floor. Just the faint beeping of the machine in perfect sync with my heartbeat.

Not giving in to frustration nor despair, I let my mind wander as, once again, I force my fingers to work harder, to move my hand just a little bit further up, crawling infuriatingly slowly along the covers. It takes me about five long minutes, but I manage to reach the edge of the cover before I stop for a brief rest. A faint smile flutters on my cracked lips. A little bit more, and I'll be able to feel for that glass of water Jasmine keeps by the bed.

While my fingers resume their struggle, I recall telling someone about that stalker, and being comforted in a man's arms, the strong, protective embrace soothing, the man's voice now resonating in my shredded mind. Was it Steve? No... the voice was different, not as deep nor as commanding as Steve's. The emotions I recall feeling while being held in that man's arms were different. A little reticent or shy, perhaps, as if our relationship was new. It wasn't Steve. It was someone else, a man I can't remember.

I have almost dozed off again, when a sound outside my door startles me awake. Someone dropped some keys, then quickly picked them up and walked away. It sounds so familiar, reminding me of keys hitting the asphalt, in the dark . . . outside the Black Bear.

And I remember.

I see myself running toward the car, and the stalker emerging from the shadows. I hear his footfalls catching up with me, loud and menacing in the stillness of the night. The car keys dropping out of my trembling hands, hitting the ground with a loud jangle. Staring right at him, while I felt the gravel for my keys, afraid to turn my back to him for even a split second. Seeing him look at me, his face partly covered with a black scarf, his eyes shielded by the hood of his sweatshirt, terrifying me with that invisible stare.

I still hear the sound my tires made when I managed to climb behind the wheel and drive off, pedal to the floor, pebbles and dust thrown high in the air, while thinking, *Why did he let me go? I could've been such easy prey tonight.*

Then, stopping at a gas station on my way home, afraid he'd follow me there. Waiting for endless minutes before I thought it safe to go home. Not stopping until I pulled into my garage.

Thinking back, I can't figure out why I waited for a while before going inside, but I clearly remember I did, breathing deeply as soon as the garage door came to a close. Perhaps to steady myself before facing my boyfriend? It's a possibility.

My entire reality is woven out of shreds of memories I can't rely on, speculation, questions, and assumptions. And black holes in the fabric of time, where chunks of my past are still obliterated.

I must have walked into my house and found comfort in my boyfriend's arms. It must've been my boyfriend, my lover. Not a second husband . . . I'd like to believe I would've remembered if I'd been married a second time, at least now. Or perhaps Steve would've mentioned it. What was the man's name? A dark abyss gapes where that information should be stored. *Nothing.* I have no idea of his name, not even the letter it started with or a term of endearment I might've used, perhaps a nickname. Nothing.

Pieces of shattered memories start whirling in my mind, and his face is there, smiling at me. He was taller than me, with dark, tousled hair and fascinating hazel eyes. He opened his arms as I rushed to him, sobbing, still shaken after the encounter with that stalker in the Black Bear parking lot. I told him what happened in short bursts of panicked words. He held me for a moment or two, then decided to go after that stalker.

I said no, and my tears dried up that instant. How did he know it wasn't dangerous? He could've got killed. I could've lost him.

Then he turned on me, with pressures to quit my job and let him work to make ends meet. Our ensuing fight was a carbon copy of the one I'd had with Steve on the same topic, when I'd taken odd jobs after the Jane Watkins windfall had dried up.

Just as adamantly as before, I pushed back, refusing to become a man's ward in any meaningful way. I recall him shouting, throwing baseless accusations at me I didn't want to defend myself against. "It's irresponsible," he said, shouting loudly enough to make the large living room windows rattle, "to put your life at risk so you can hang out with the local drunks. I have a steady engagement with this series and I can take care of things. We could live a comfortable life if you just stopped being such a damn, reckless fool!"

I went to bed crying that night. He left, slamming the door loudly and not bothering to lock it. I did that myself, as soon as I heard him drive off. That stalker could've still been out there.

He must be an actor, because he spoke of a part he was playing in a TV series. I remember that much, and something else too. Later, when I got out of bed for a drink of water, I didn't turn on the lights in the kitchen. There was a full moon that night, and its silver light reflected brightly against the freshly fallen snow. I looked outside, leaning against the windowsill, to see the stunning view of the mountain peaks drawn in white against the starry sky.

He was there.

The stalker, leaning against the old aspen, was staring at my window.

I know I was cautious coming back from the bar but, still, I was followed all the way home.

It must've been that stalker who struck me down. But how did he get inside the house? I clearly recall running toward the door, reaching for the handle, struggling to get out. Screaming for help.

The door opens and startles me back into the present. My breath catches in my chest until I recognize the squeak in Dr. Sokolowski's shoes. He brings a scent of brown paper, and of heated microwave meals, as if he's just visited the cafeteria for a bite.

"Good morning," he says, pulling a chair on rollers close to my bed and rustling something loudly, really close. "I had one of the nurses pull your things from storage. Everything you came in with is in this paper bag, here, on the bed."

"Oh?" I'm thrilled at the thought of getting my phone back. "Thank you. Can you please look inside for me? I still can't move much, as you might've noticed." My fingers flinch slightly, but my hand rests on my abdomen. My attempt at humor sounds sad, a cry for help.

A brief hesitation, then the doctor says, "Okay." The paper bag rustles, and several items clatter. "Pocket contents, I guess. Mints. Keys on a chain, house and car keys. You have a Toyota, by the way. Do you remember that?"

A flash of a white sedan parked in front of my house lights up in my mind for a moment, then disappears. "I think I do. A white Corolla."

"Good." He sounds like he's smiling. "Loose change, two dollars and thirty-seven cents. A pair of jeans, socks, and running shoes. A phone, completely dead. Probably it just ran out of power." The bag rustles as it falls or is dropped to the floor. "Oh, and there's a note here. Some items were taken by the police as evidence. A sweater, stained with blood, and your underwear." He clears his voice quietly. "Let's plug this phone in and see if it works."

I smile weakly. I've thanked the man so many times it seems the words have lost their meaning. "How do you do it?" I ask instead. "How do you put up with all the suffering you see every day?"

The chair rolls away a little. "It's about helping people. It gives my life meaning. No matter how terrible the suffering, knowing I can make it just a little bit better makes me get out of bed each morning."

I turn my head away slightly, as if afraid he can read my thoughts, but my eyes are still covered with gauze, the windows to my soul obscured. I wonder what he looks like.

"What time is it?" I ask, not wanting him to leave just yet. Sometimes, the silence of my room can be unbearable.

"Oh, it's almost ten," he says, standing, seemingly ready to leave. "I have to go, but I'll check in on you later today." He walks over to the side of the room. The sound of vertical blinds being pulled, the clicking noise made by the chain, the swaying of slats hitting the glass pane sounds so familiar somehow. I must've heard it a few times since I've been here. "I pulled the shades open. It's sunny outside. You might feel the sunshine on your skin." He walks over to the door and turns the handle. "Get some rest," he says, then leaves. The door comes to a soft close.

Alone, I feel the sun touching my left cheek, warming my fingers. Encouraged, I resume my attempt to move my hands, to reach my face, inch by excruciating inch. Outside my door, two nurses chat cheerfully, something about the place they are going to for lunch, while my mind obsesses about the name of the man I used to live with. What did he look like? Tall, I remember, knowing how it felt to be in his arms. How my fingers ran along his jawline, his chin, his tousled hair, my own head tilted back.

Time stretches and weaves loosely between present and past, holding few answers to my questions. Indifferent to my concerns, the PA system summons Dr. Parrish to the nurses' station, just as I am beginning to feel the rumbling of hunger in my stomach. I wait for Jasmine to show up, patient at first, then increasingly tense.

How can I come to terms with living like this? With needing someone even for the most basic of human needs? Dr. Sokolowski has been encouraging and kind, but I don't feel I am improving that much. My head still throbs. I still can't remember much of my past, despite having little else to do but try. And no one seems to take my concerns seriously, not even Dr. Sokolowski.

Doctors never tell anyone when they're screwed. They are true believers in hope and its healing powers, but there are always limits to what hope can do. I desperately wish someone would tell me the truth, unvarnished, just as cold and unappealing as it could be. I am ready for it.

When Jasmine arrives, she finds me pushing my fingers to crawl one more inch further, and determined to find out the truth about myself. About what happened that night.

And for that, I need help.

FIFTEEN

"Ooh, that's something," Jasmine says, in her slightly raspy voice. "You're moving your hand quite well this morning."

I scoff. "You call this well?" There's bitterness in my voice. "Then I'm looking for bloody awesome, and quickly." My words are caustic, and my nurse doesn't deserve it. I breathe slowly, to steady myself, then say, "I'm sorry. I'm just losing my mind here."

"What's wrong? Is the pain worse today?" Her voice and footsteps draw closer, and a cool hand lands on my forehead with clinical interest. "You don't have a fever."

"The pain is . . . there. Not going away, just keeping me company." The self-pity I hear in my own voice is infuriating. That's not who I am, who I used to be. I'll never get anywhere with that attitude.

Snap the hell out of it, woman, I tell myself.

That phrase reminds me of the first movie scene I acted. The memories are crisp in my mind, as if that particular chapter in my story has survived intact, untainted.

My debut film was an indie production that paid me almost nothing, made while I was still taking acting classes at UCLA.

One of my professors encouraged students to audition, to act, to go out there and get used to being on set, to working with production teams, to following a director's lead. I responded to a casting call advertised in the local paper and got a five-line part—nothing to write home about.

Driving to the location at five thirty in the morning, I thought I was ready for it. For being on camera. I was excited, exhilarated even. But the first thing I did when I got out of my car was throw up, crouching down and holding on to the front tire for balance. I'd heard about stage fright, about the sudden urge to unload one's breakfast under the attack of overwhelming panic. I'd listened to other actors' stories about how they'd gone through it, and heard it all. How to breathe. How to become the character and just act naturally.

The same professor had a different approach to it. "Let fear rush through you, and put a timer on it. Give fear five minutes to do whatever it wants with you. Feel like throwing up? Do it. Wanna rush to the bathroom and pee for those entire five minutes? Do it. But when that time's up, fear will be gone. You will snap out of it. Accept your reality and shine through it. Walk on set with your head up high, like you've done it a million times."

I smile weakly, relishing the memory. "Accept your reality already," I whisper to myself.

"Huh?" Jasmine asks, her voice raised a little, above the sound of wrappers being torn and a tray clattering.

"Nothing, Jas," I reply. "Just talking to myself, I guess. And my head is throbbing."

"If you'd like, I could ask the doctor to—"

"No, please. No more meds. I need to move, to think, to remember. I have to." I will my hand to lift off the covers and only achieve a slight tremble. "See? This is all I can do. I can't raise my hand. Can't flex my fingers, can't grab that glass of water on the table. I have to wait for you to get a sip." My voice is level, clinical. No trace of self-pity left.

The nurse approaches and sits on the wheeled chair, by the bed, with a slight groan. She must be tired. "You're right, hon, and I'm sorry. I should've asked. Let me give you a bit of water." Her clothing rustles as she reaches for the glass. I can feel her breath touching my arm. "Straw coming your way."

I grab it with my lips and take a few thirsty gulps of water. "Thank you."

"Let's do this, see if it's any better," Jasmine says, taking my hand between hers and massaging it. It feels so good. "Try now," she says, after a while.

I try to flex my fingers. This time, I manage to touch my thumb with the tip of my index. "Look," I say, and Jasmine chuckles, sharing my enthusiasm. "And I can lift it a little. Maybe tomorrow I can get myself a drink of water. What do you say?"

Jas slaps her hands against her thighs with mock frustration. "Bye-bye, job security." She laughs. Then she stands and walks around the bed, and sits on its edge to give my right hand and arm a vigorous massage, all the way to the shoulder. "There you go. I want you clapping your hands by tomorrow, all right?"

"You got it," I reply. Flexing my right arm from the elbow gets me grinning widely—my right hand now rests on my abdomen, and I didn't have to crawl my way up there.

Then Jasmine works on something close to the bed on my left side—probably changing my IV bag—then switches sides and extends my right arm. "Let's draw some blood. Doctor's orders. Like we do every morning."

That comment puts a chill in my heart. Every morning? I've been poked for blood every morning and don't remember it? "Are you sure?" I ask, my voice shaky.

"Sure of what, hon?"

"That you drew blood every morning," I whisper. "I don't remember doing that."

"Eh," she says, sitting on the bed. "Don't read too much into it. Sometimes I do it before you wake up. And you're sedated. As we've discussed before, it could be a side effect from those meds, this short-term memory loss. I don't believe it has anything to do with your post-traumatic amnesia. It's a different thing altogether, and quite harmless." She ties a rubber tourniquet around my arm and squeezes it tightly until it pinches my skin.

Harmless? When my entire life is a puzzle with missing pieces, and my safety depends on my memory coming back to me?

In the distance, a car honks twice, while Jas lifts my elbow and slips what feels like a pillow underneath.

"I'm sure you recall the important things," she says. "Our brain usually does that. It discards the garbage, the fluff we don't need, like blood tests and being poked over and over." A moment of silence, followed by a prick in my right arm. Small objects, probably test tubes, move on a tray nearby. "For example, do you remember my name?"

"Yes. You're Jasmine."

"See? The important information is there," the nurse says, with a chuckle meant to reassure me. She pulls the needle out and I feel her applying a piece of gauze, sticking it in place with some tape.

"If you say so," I whisper. Again, the despair has returned, eating away at my strength, draining my courage.

"All right. Let's get you something to eat. I have some cottage cheese for you, a boiled egg with very little salt, and some red Jell-O. What do you say?"

"Do you think I can hold the spoon yet?" I ask, knowing the answer is going to be no.

"Let's try it together." Jasmine places the spoon in my hand, supporting it, then applies pressure on my fingers with hers, enough to keep the spoon steady. I feel it dipping into something, then Jasmine gently leads it to my mouth.

The cheese tastes wonderful. I eat more, each spoonful a struggle and a victory at the same time, while I force myself to not feel discouraged about how difficult it is. Tomorrow it will be easier. That's all that matters.

When I finish eating and Jasmine stands and takes the tray away, I start to flex my fingers, eager to exercise them until they feel normal again. I give my legs a try, but nothing happens. They feel like lead blocks, heavy and impossible to move. Frustrated, I let a long sigh escape my lips.

"Hang in there," Jasmine says, loading things on the tray and throwing stuff in the trash. "You'll be as good as new, I promise." Another object hits the trash can with a soft thud, then the lid falls with its usual clank. "Are you ready for your visitor now?"

A visitor? Is Steve back already? Or is it my stalker, here to finish the job? My heart starts pounding. "I—um, I don't want anyone to see me like this."

"Really? She seems like a nice lady. She says her name is Denise."

The adrenaline fades. "Oh. Yes! Please let her in."

SIXTEEN

Jasmine opens the door, bringing cooler air into the room. I hear her say something, then Denise says, "Yes, of course. I won't stay long." The door closes gently, and Denise's determined footsteps approach, then stop abruptly at a distance from the bed.

I think I hear a soft gasp, quickly muffled, perhaps by Denise's hand flying to cover her mouth. I can sense her standing there, looking down at the bed in horror. My lower lip starts trembling and a whimper escapes my strangled throat. I'm relieved to know she's there, but also reminded of what I've lost. "Denise? Is that you?"

Something rustles silently, then an object lands with a thud on a table nearby. Denise approaches the bed, her footfalls slower, softer, less determined. Then she squeezes my hand with her usual gusto. "Well, hello there," she says, her voice perfectly normal, even cheerful, her British accent sophisticated. She is one hell of an actress.

"Hi," I whisper, still struggling to hold it together. I force a deep breath into my lungs, though it does very little to help me get a grip.

"Usually, I drop clients who don't show up for their auditions. But out of all the excuses I've been handed in twenty years of representing talent, this takes the biscuit, so I'll make an exception." Denise sounds neutral, her fake indifference almost convincing.

I know what she's doing. She's acting like everything is fine, like things could be back to normal tomorrow or soon enough, in typical British style.

"You think I'll suddenly get out of here and walk straight onto a movie set, ready for action?" I scoff quietly, then sigh, feeling ashamed. Denise isn't to blame for any of this, including my lousy state of mind. She's only trying to lift my spirits. "I'm sorry I missed the audition," I add, my voice soft. "Honestly, I can't remember for what movie it was, or what part, and I'm sorry for that too." A tense silence for a moment, while Denise seems to be holding her breath, just as I am. "They say it's post-traumatic amnesia, and that it will go away soon. But I don't know anymore." I shake my head slightly, my muscles not obeying me, reducing my gesture to an imperceptible twitch, my throbbing head instantly punishing me for it. "I'm so scared, Denise."

"The girl I represent isn't scared of anything but failure." The chair rolls closer to the bed and Denise sits. "Well, unless they somehow changed your DNA. I have to remind you we have a contract. And I expect you to hold your end of it." Her interesting take on the talent representation agreement makes me smile. "That's more like it. That's the girl I remember—the cocky performing arts student from Texas who wouldn't let me get a word in on a phone conversation." She punctuates the last word with sarcastic humor.

Tears choke me again. "Thank you, Denise. You have no idea how—"

"It was the lead role in a feature film, *The Charade,*" she says casually, a hint of mock disappointment in her voice, and just enough humor to let me know she isn't actually upset with me. "I worked so hard to get you that audition. And do you know who got the part?"

A slight furrow tenses the bandages covering my brow. "Who?"

"Your best friend, Lisa Chen. She waltzed right in there, knew her lines, and did so well the producers didn't care the character wasn't Asian. She is now."

Lisa.

Thinking of her floods my mind with the echoes of her infectious laughter filling that small apartment on Lexington Avenue. I can almost taste the soup she used to make us in our only pot, where she boiled some canned chicken broth and some angel hair pasta, and finished it off with a touch of soy sauce. That recipe put us both through acting classes at UCLA. We used to have a hell of a time, carefree and hope-filled, as we knew we were going to make it in the movie industry without any other reason but our own determination and the strength in our young hearts. Brilliant and vivacious, Lisa brought joy to my life. I taught her all the American accents, and she picked them up with an amazing natural talent. She taught me how to learn my lines faster using the Chinese *loci* method, and to meditate, and how to breathe past stress and fear, although it was my professor's "Let fear conquer all for five minutes" technique that had proven most useful. We'd become so close, learning from each other's mistakes and achievements, opening doors for each other, teaming up to get ahead in life and in our careers. And just being young girls in Los Angeles, with endless ambition and dreams of Hollywood glory, having fun while we were at it.

"Has she come to see you yet?" Denise asks.

I don't answer. What if she's been here, and I've misplaced the memory like I have with recent doctor visits and blood draws and who knows what else? How can I ever be sure of anything again?

"She might be on location already," Denise says, seemingly rushing to find Lisa a good excuse. "They're shooting in South Texas—Galveston, I believe. Some other agent represents her. That short, sweaty guy who looks like Joe Pesci." A light chuckle. "I think Lyle—that's his name—actually channels Joe Pesci to make himself more interesting."

We laugh together, though mine is faltering. I don't quite know who Denise is talking about, although I feel I should. The man is my best friend's agent, right? I must know *of* him, at least.

Then the laughter fades, and silence returns.

"How can I come back from this?" I ask softly. "Everything I've built is gone now. It's over. I'm sorry, Denise, but your bet on me won't be paying off much."

"Oh, shut it."

I can visualize the sixty-year-old swatting my concern away with a quick, imperative gesture. Denise is straightforward and pleasantly blunt. Everything about her speaks of willpower and determination, and a limited tolerance for weakness. She wears her hair short, styled in a rather masculine "do," and never dyes the almost entirely white strands. On her, the look is classy and natural, paired with the dark business suits she usually prefers. I wonder what she's wearing today, for the hospital visit. Is black still appropriate in her mind? Or a bit too somber? Did she think about it? Or just put on whatever was handy, knowing her client was now blind?

What would she say if I asked her? She'd probably think I've lost my mind. It's most likely true.

The chair squeaks a little as Denise shifts in place, then she reaches out and takes my hand, holding on for a while. "Let me tell you how you come out of this. When you're ready, you give me a call. Not that I won't know when you're ready, because

I'll come see you every chance I get. Just to keep you in line." I can't help a smile. "Actors have taken breaks from acting before, you know. Most of them choose rehab for a sabbatical, sometimes prison, or maybe crash a Ferrari and spend months in traction, but if you had to go this way, I understand."

My smile blooms. Her optimism is irresistible. "Denise, I—"

"I'll get us a good publicist, and they'll sell your comeback like hot chocolate on a winter's day. I'm sure you're eager to get back on your feet again."

"Yeah, no kidding. I'm working on it." Sarcasm colors my voice just a little. Some self-pity too.

Perhaps sensing the awkwardness, Denise rushes to fill the silence. "Do you remember that time when Lyle—"

"Who's Lyle?"

A brief moment of silence. "Lisa Chen's agent. We just talked about him. The one who channels Joe Pesci?" Denise's voice sounds a bit less confident toward the end of her question, as if she's just starting to realize what's going on with me.

What should've been a fresh memory comes back to me, crumpled, slowly, as if emerging from a foggy and bottomless pit. "Oh, yes, I got it now."

"Well, do you remember that time we were together on location, the first day of filming *Summer Love*?"

"Um, a little," I reply. A glimpse of memory flashes through my mind. Denise and me walking over from the car, chatting, smiling, venti coffee cups in our hands, the sun just peeking over the horizon. The Californian sky a perfect and pristine shade of blue, untouched yet by midday smog. I'd dressed casually that day, in jeans and a black tank top, and recalled feeling a bit embarrassed walking next to Denise. My agent was elegantly fashionable in a black pant suit, the jacket an embroidered work of art with a mandarin collar—exquisite, without being over the top. She was classy, while I looked like her teenage daughter being dragged back to school.

A slight creak as Denise shifts position on the hospital chair. "You were a bit stressed out about that part and what it involved." She pauses for a moment, as if giving me time to remember. And I do. The prospect of baring my body on screen had terrified me, enough to ask Denise to hold my hand, so to speak, even if that scene wasn't on the call sheet for that first day. I had expected everyone on the set to instantly judge me, just for signing on the dotted line for a contract with lax nudity riders.

I was wrong. Everyone was professional and minded their own business.

Another memory wriggles its way to the forefront of my mind, about that day. I met someone on set. A man. It's important somehow, I can feel that, although I don't remember much about him.

"Yes, I know," I finally whisper. "You were there for me."

"I was, wasn't I?" Denise smiles. I can hear it in her voice. "That agent, Lyle, was something else. Hilarious, in a rather uncomfortable sort of way. He was shouting at that actor, stabbing him in the chest with his finger, huffing and puffing as if he were just about to have a coronary and drop dead. We stumbled upon a heated conversation between them. Oh, you have to remember this."

"N—no," I reply, although faint snippets of memory start dancing in my mind. A tall, handsome man with a strong jaw and mesmerizing eyes that lit up when he saw me. His dark hair, a little tousled, set quickly in order by his fingers, running through it like a comb and pushing it back. His voice, shouting, "I don't want to hear it, Lyle. I won't do it." Then the way his lips stretched into a smile when he saw me enter the set with Denise.

"Perhaps. A little," I venture.

"Adrian was his name, right?"

"Right," I reply, drawing out the word, unsure still. But, unlike the agent's, his name sounds familiar.

"And Lyle pacing around, chest pushed out, yelling, 'Take my advice, kid, sign here and the sky's the limit for Adrian Sera.'" Denise stops her imitation of the agent for a quick chuckle, then resumes. "'Hell, women will line all around this block for a night with Adrian Sera.' And some obscenities I'd rather not quote now," she adds, now laughing infectiously.

I laugh too. "Yes, that much I remember, now that you mention it. Adrian . . . that was his name, you're right."

"What was the poor fellow supposed to do, with rabid Lyle on his case like that? He just signed, staring right at you."

"Adrian—" I start to say, but stop, the words caught in my chest by the sudden feeling of loss that floods my heart. I can't say why; it's still a blur. I recall his interest in me, but I would have been married to Steve at the time, if it was during *Summer Love.* Happily, too, as it would have been before Mikela had insinuated herself into our lives. I remember smiling at him politely, then looking for the director, because he was about to give his first-day speech.

"I heard he made a career out of soaps." Denise sighs disapprovingly. "Those can be cash cows for young, talentless actors who can stomach over-the-top melodrama and endless, looping plotlines. Not exactly a steppingstone to an Academy Award. I mean, if you're okay with being on daytime TV and not being taken seriously as an actor, then sure. Why not?"

"Is he any good?" I ask, wondering why I can't remember.

"He did well in *Summer Love,*" she replies, as if reading my mind. "I can't speak to the soaps. He was stunning, though. Lyle Crespin had a point. He's some serious eye candy. I read somewhere he's dating a supermodel."

The agent's words resound in my mind, *"Women will line all around this block for a night with Adrian Sera,"* he said. The phrase, unburied from oblivion, starts haunting me. What else did he say, right after that?

What were Adrian and his agent arguing about? What was the thing he wouldn't do, but did anyway? Sign the representation contract? Why the hell not?

And why do I care? Why can't I just silence the echo of that memory, once and for all?

Long after Denise leaves, Lyle's insistent words stay with me, as if they're holding an important message I fail to understand. I let my mind wander and try to paint that scene. The location, how it looked. The people there. Denise. Adrian. Lyle. I start from him . . . I just picture Joe Pesci where my memory refuses to cooperate and draw his face.

Then, in my mind, I see him. Adrian Sera. The look on his face as our eyes met. The taste of his lips against mine when we kissed. The sound of his heart beating when I rested my head against his chest.

I realize it was Adrian Sera who comforted me after being stalked leaving the Black Bear that frightful night. He was the boyfriend, the lover I ran home to. His face appears clearly to me now, as does the sensation of his strong arms wrapped around my body, making me feel safe. His hand held mine when I filed a police report the following day.

Yes, Adrian Sera used to be my boyfriend. I recall caressing his face, looking into his eyes that could light up a room with the golden glimmer in his hazel irises.

My mind hungers to retrieve the missing pieces of our story together. I stumble through the fog of memory and find a thread to guide me.

SEVENTEEN

It felt strange to work without Steve seated in the director's chair, but I was thrilled to be back on a set, after surviving a long stretch of drought waiting for casting calls that hadn't come.

I had once been called a nepo actress, my fleeting success credited entirely to my husband. It never ceased to amaze me how, if a woman did something right, it had to be the man behind her who was the someone who, in fact, deserved the credit. That's what people usually chose to believe. But if she was wrong or made a mistake, the blame was always and entirely hers. Never the man's.

Merciless rumors had gnawed at me for a while, since news of our separation had gone out. I was a disappointment, they said. I never was that good to begin with, and if it weren't for my relationship with Steve Wellington, I would have never had a chance. I had committed the ultimate sin, divorcing the man credited with my success, a guy who knew other guys, in a man's world where men stuck together over thorny issues like ex-wives and divorces and other such nasty things. No one wanted Steve aggravated, because Steve knew people.

Producers didn't want to risk upsetting Steve Wellington—who might've been working his way through a relatively unglamorous list of projects, but faked glam like no one else.

And so, the casting calls stopped coming.

Denise tried her best to counteract what she called "the effects of the D-storm." Steve had made me sign an NDA forcing me to keep silent about the divorce, as if I were going to run to the tabloids and spill my guts. He probably made everyone sign such papers. And so, for a while, the divorce was kept a secret, although some industry insiders still knew. By the time the news leaked, it was no longer news, and the tabloids thankfully skipped it.

It meant Mom hadn't read about it in some checkout-aisle paper. With her breathing issues, she was better off not worrying about her daughter. I didn't tell her, although my heart still ached for Steve, for my destroyed marriage, for the love I still felt for him at times. I wished I could call her and just talk to her, but I couldn't. Not when I knew what that could do to my mother's ailing health. I kept wanting to go home for a visit, but work kept me tied to California.

More like looking for work, really. I had to be ready to audition for anything Denise could find, and there wasn't much.

When the grapevine started to carry rumors of how bad our divorce actually had been—and there was no doubt in my mind as to who had started that gossip—no one would touch me. Coincidentally, Mikela's name was prominently billed on many of the films I'd auditioned for, and only some of those films were directed by my ex.

At times, I thought of selling the Lake Tahoe house. It was mine to sell, and it made sense to move closer to Los Angeles, where I needed to be for auditions and casting calls. But the house was the first home I'd known since I'd left Lubbock almost ten years earlier, and all the good memories of my marriage were still lingering inside its walls.

Whether I admitted it to myself or not, I was still grieving, wandering from empty room to empty room, looking for what was forever lost.

That's who I was when I walked onto the set for day one of *Echoes of Tomorrow*. Thrilled to be working again, but still wounded, reeling from my divorce, and feeling a little lost on a set filled with so many unfamiliar faces.

Going through the motions without letting the smile on my face wane under the barrage of chaos that is the norm on first days, I followed my call sheet and used all my down time to sneak out and read my lines once more.

Returning after one such private rehearsal, I heard a commotion on set and approached with caution. The scene featured the male lead and a dog, provided by an animal wrangler I had worked with before. Her name was Miriam.

The director, a woman in her forties, dressed in ratty jeans and a worn-out tee-shirt, was shouting, "Adrian, the dog needs to come and sit next to you on the sofa. Miriam, please make that happen."

Adrian looked up and our eyes met. A flicker of recognition lit up his face and he smiled.

Smiling back, I approached, asking Miriam for permission with a gesture, then crouched down next to the dog and asked, "What's the pup's name?"

"Obi-Wan," Miriam replied, seeming a little impatient.

There were chuckles here and there, coming from the crew and other actors.

"Here, baby," I called, and the border collie approached quickly, his tail wagging low, cautiously at first, then happily. "I know what your problem is," I whispered, scratching the base of Obi-Wan's ears. "You're on the wrong set! You belong with the *Star Wars* crew, not here. I get it." Another round of chuckles erupted.

Miriam, tense at first, started to relax. "Emma, you got me going there for a moment. I almost checked my call sheet."

I smiled and looked at the director. She nodded and made a gesture, telling me to rush through whatever I was going to do. The schedule was tight.

I approached Adrian, who was seated on the sofa, as his scene called for. His legs were crossed at the knee, and he bounced his foot impatiently. The tension that knotted the muscles in his firm jaw dissipated as I drew closer.

He started to get up to meet me, but I stopped him. "No, just sit down, relax, and get ready to roll. You're stressing out Mr. Kenobi here. He's sensing your concern. Just breathe and let it play out." The dog was at my heel, and I leaned down to scratch his ears some more. "So what if the scene's not perfect? What if the dog sits at your feet instead of on the couch? That's what doubles are for. It will be fine."

He looked at me, slightly tilting his head, while his hazel eyes lit up with shimmers of gold, just as I remembered from the first time we'd met on *Summer Love*.

I hid my smile by looking at the dog for a moment, then nodded at the director.

Adrian held his thumb up.

"Roll sound, roll camera," the director called. "Marker!" she commanded, and an assistant clapped the slate.

Adrian's handsome face shifted to sadness, his gaze fixed on an empty space across the room, his shoulders slouched, his head hanging.

"Set?" The assistant director responded with a thumbs up. "And . . . action," the director said.

I patted the dog gently on his rump, and the collie padded softly into the room.

Adrian sat on the sofa, his legs no longer crossed. He seemed to emerge from his thoughts, his gaze focusing on the door. "She's gone, Buddy." The dog hopped onto the sofa. Adrian's hand automatically found the dog's fur and stroked it, the movement rhythmic and soothing, while his brimming gaze shifted away.

Miriam directed Obi-Wan with hand gestures until the collie rested his head on Adrian's thigh with a faint whimper.

"It's just you and me now, boy. She left us both. And she's not coming back." Adrian, in character, put his hand on the dog's head and closed his eyes.

"Cut!"

The dog, released from position by his handler, sprang off the sofa and stopped by my feet, wagging his tail happily. And when Adrian offered me a cup of coffee I didn't refuse, although I'd just abandoned a full one on a catering table by Miriam's chair.

Later that night, he took me to dinner at Angelini's. The restaurant was intimate, lit by candles that flickered on each table. The hostess led us to the patio, where a table had been set a little farther from the rest, our own private island in the fast-flowing river of Los Angeles tourists. A single delicate orchid decorated the table. Little white bulbs hung at the edges of the umbrella open above our heads. Soft music played in the background—old Italian songs that made me sway.

It was perfect.

He was perfect. He didn't seem to notice the dreamy glance the hostess had thrown his way, nor the way women's eyes lingered on his handsome face and taut, athletic body. His focus was entirely on me, as if I were his entire world.

Halfway through the meal, he disappeared from the table, leaving me insecure for a minute or two. I resisted the urge to look over my shoulder every five seconds, wondering when he'd return. Slowly, like the early promise of a nightmare at nightfall, my fears returned. Perhaps I wasn't ready for another relationship. Or maybe Adrian Sera was too good to be true. Or, even worse, what if I wasn't good enough?

I was about to finish my glass of wine, wondering how much longer I should wait before leaving, when he returned, his voice startling me. "I hope you like roses, Emma," he said.

I turned and gasped. Adrian stood there smiling, charming and confident, holding a beautiful red rose. Speechless, I took the rose, our fingers brushing. There was an undeniable spark between us, unexpected, almost overwhelming.

"Your smile could light up this whole town," he said, as he retook his seat. "I trust the lady is pleased?"

My cheeks flushed with heat. I lowered my eyes, batting my eyelashes just a little bit, and inhaled the fresh scent of rose petals in the summer breeze. "It's beautiful, thank you." I looked at him, letting my smile bloom. His eyes reflected the candlelight, the warmth of the moment. "No one's ever given me a rose on a first date before. You're full of surprises."

He topped both our glasses. "Only the best for a night like this."

I raised my glass and met his over the table. "To new beginnings," I whispered, blushing again, afraid I was being too direct.

"To a night of firsts, and many more," he replied, looking straight at me as he tasted the wine, his lips sensual, his smile heady, intoxicating.

Later that night, when he walked me home to Lisa's apartment, where I still crashed when I was in town, his kiss stirred up wants in my body I didn't think possible, not after Steve. But that's all there was that first night. A first kiss that left me wanting more. Much more.

"Dr. Whitting to the emergency room," the PA called, yanking me into the present so abruptly it leaves me feeling dizzy.

I hold on to the shreds of cherished memories of a time I was happy, grappling with the shadows of forgotten events, looking for more nuggets of happiness buried in my mind. But the thread of my romance with Adrian stops there, frayed, the rest in darkness, perhaps forever lost.

With a sickening déjà vu, I wonder what happened to Adrian and me. Did we grow apart somehow? Are we still together? I remember our fight, the day that stalker followed me from the Black Bear, but was that it for the two of us? I don't think so, recalling how I'd held his hand the next morning, at the police station, where I tried my best to provide a physical description for the precinct's sketch artist.

Then, where is he? Has he found someone new, on the set of a new production? Someone who felt really good in his arms while he kissed her because the script called for it, but left him with a yearning for an off-set, repeat performance? It happened with actors, more often than not.

The game of pretend is a dangerous one.

A quiet, familiar beep draws my attention. After a moment of hesitation, I figure out it is my phone. It's charged, ready to use. Only I can't use it. I wish I could grab it and flip through the messages I last sent, the photos I last took, until I find a lead, something to tell me what happened the night I was attacked. If it was someone I'd invited into my home, my phone might have a record of it. If Adrian is still a part of my life, my phone holds all the answers. And his number is probably saved in my contacts list.

"Code Blue, room 1204," the PA announces, startling me again. I hate how vulnerable and scared these sudden announcements make me feel. Any strange noise, in the split second before I can identify it, has nightmarish proportions in my wounded mind. Because, one day soon, that strange noise might be the villain's arm, raised above my head and ready to strike, to finish what was started at my house that night.

I won't see it coming. I'll only hear it, for a brief moment, before my life comes to an end.

My only chance is that phone, and I can't reach it, can't read through its messages or see the photos stored in there.

A knock on the door makes me flinch again. The machine starts beeping furiously by the side of my bed. Then the door swings open, and a familiar voice shatters the silence.

"Hello, girlfriend."

EIGHTEEN

"Lisa," I whisper, relieved. "You know, considering I'm the lead in a real-life horror show . . . could be worse." My voice is weak, despite my efforts to sound upbeat.

Lisa chuckles. "That's the spirit, Em. You're gonna get through this. You're the strongest person I know."

Something rustles in the air above my head. Then it moves away slowly and silently. I try to picture the source of that sound and fail.

"What's that?" I ask, hating myself for having to. For feeling so scared of every little sound. "I heard it before. Yesterday, or it could've been the day before."

"This?" The rustling intensifies for a moment. "I've brought you a red balloon, made of foil. It's got a nice message written on it and all. Says, 'Nice try. Now get back to work.'" Lisa chuckles while reading the message.

It's funny, I have to admit. In a rather sad kind of way.

The rustling comes to a stop somewhere at the far-left corner of the room, still above my head. "You're amazing, you know that? You're right, you heard the sound before. You have another balloon bouncing against the ceiling, kinda like mine, but not as pretty," Lisa adds, squeezing in one of her usual jokes. Her voice trembles, though. "There's a flower vase that came with it. Lilies, carnations, baby's breath, and a couple of roses."

"What does it say on the balloon?" I remember when I first heard the rustling sound. When Denise entered the room. The vase must've been the other sound I'd picked up on, the thump of a heavy object being placed on a table.

"Um, I'll give you a guess," Lisa laughs. " 'Get well soon.' Very original. It's blue, and starting to deflate. Pretty soon it'll fall from up there and land on something—scare the living shit out of you. If you like, I can take it with me when I leave."

"Yes, please." Lisa's thoughtfulness is heartwarming. "I heard you snagged the lead in a new movie. Congratulations," I add, smiling. I'm happy for her, while at the same time envying her freedom to move, to work, to live.

"I kinda feel bad about it." She shifts her weight from one foot to the other, seemingly undecided where to sit. Or if. "I'm gulping down your leftovers, I know. You and I both know the part would've been yours if—"

"Ifs and maybes don't belong between friends, Lisa. The part is rightfully yours. Make the most of it. Denise told me you're doing great."

Lisa clears her throat and sits on the edge of the bed. I wait for the hand squeeze that everyone seems to want to give me, but it doesn't happen.

"Speaking of Denise, I was wondering, um, if it's not too much to ask, and it's not the wrong moment either, because I kinda feel that it is—"

"Ask already," I say. "Under all this gauze it's still me. You can ask me anything."

"I—I wanted your permission to try to get on Denise's list. I know she has a closed book and hasn't taken new clients in ages, but she knows all the right people, and, uh, I need that like I need air. Lyle Crespin, my agent, is a lazy son of a bitch who thinks he's Joe Pesci."

"That's it? That's all you need?"

"She's one of the best agents in the business, Em. And no, that's not it. I actually wanted to ask you if I could use your name to get to her."

"Sure thing," I reply, biting my lip to keep myself from saying more. My friend's request isn't that unusual, but the timing of it, and perhaps the selfishness of it, upsets me to the verge of tears. I feel left behind, the remnants of my life picked apart like roadkill shredded by vultures on the side of the road.

"Really? Thank you so much," Lisa says cheerfully. There's a movement near my head, then her lips touch my cheek with a quick and enthusiastic peck. "You're awesome, even now, when you could've told me to go straight to hell and not let the door hit me on the ass on the way there."

It's true. Her comment soothes me a little. Lisa could've approached Denise directly. She didn't need my permission. With me out of the way, incapacitated as I am, Lisa could've easily used my name to get to my agent, and I would've never been any the wiser. It just feels strange, though, the timing of it. First, I was almost killed. Then, Lisa got the part I was supposed to audition for, and it's a lead role in a multi-million-dollar project, a career-maker.

The exposure and residuals would be worth killing for.

The chilling thought makes me wonder for a moment, before I scratch it off as my persistent paranoia.

It can't be true. Lisa has been my best friend since our early days at UCLA. She's always been kind, reliable, and honest. I feel ashamed for doubting her, for being so suspicious of a girl who wants nothing more than what I wanted for myself—and still do.

"I'm sorry I didn't come to see you sooner," Lisa says, her voice broken. "I didn't think I could control my emotions. You know me, crying at movies like an old lady." She tries to laugh, but it comes out hoarse. "I still can't handle it." She stands by my bedside, restlessly stepping in place, her heels clacking softly against the floor. Then she starts weeping, trying her best to hide the sound, but she can't fool me.

"It's okay, Lili," I say, using a nickname I gave her a long time ago. "I'm sure it's not that easy for you to see me like this."

"I'm supposed to encourage you," Lisa replies, barely able to stifle her sobs. "What the hell, girlfriend, you don't do this to me. I'm a wreck now, and my makeup will need twenty minutes of work." She manages a laugh, and I laugh with her, wishing I had her problems. "I never expected... Shit like this doesn't happen to people like us. It can't."

"Until it does. And I'm seriously screwed, Lisa. I don't remember any of it, only that someone tried to kill me."

"Who?" Her voice pitches higher in surprise.

I sigh bitterly, fighting back fresh tears of frustration. "I don't even know for sure if it was a man or a woman, and don't imagine I'm not trying to remember. All I do all day is lie here, in this bed, straining to force the past to show itself again. I'm going insane."

Lisa sniffles and unzips something—perhaps her purse—then with a faint rustle pulls a tissue and blows her nose discreetly. "Did you call the cops?"

"To tell them what?" For a moment, silence floods the room. "The hospital did... But you could help me remember. Was I having issues with anyone? Did I mention anything to you? Could it have been Steve?"

"Steve?" Her voice sounds genuinely surprised. "You haven't mentioned Steve in at least a year. Not since he got engaged to that piece of trash, Mikela."

The reminder hits me in the chest like a fist, trapping the air in my lungs. I somehow forgot about Steve's engagement and Mikela's oversized gem, the one she made sure I knew about.

The sense of loss for the love I once knew slices through my heart.

"Oh, hon, you didn't know?" Lisa returns to the bed and sits on its edge. Her voice is brittle with compassion. "Yes, you did know. You and I talked about it. At length, drinking wine, until you got entirely shitfaced and finally went to bed. Cursing his name so loudly the neighbors called."

"But that was before I—"

A sigh. "Yeah. How much do you remember now?"

Such a straightforward question. "That's exactly it. I don't know. Some of it, I guess. Bits and pieces, that's all that's left. It comes back in bursts, then nothing, or just some feelings, some flashes of what used to be my reality. And I'm not sure that the things I remember actually happened. But you could set me straight. You know everything that was going on in my life, don't you?"

"Yeah." Another sniffle. "Ask away."

"Have I ever mentioned being afraid of anyone?"

"You had a stalker. I was worried about that. You've gone to the police a few times, but they didn't do anything about it."

"When was the last time I mentioned that stalker?"

"About a month ago," Lisa replies. Her voice is unsure. "You thought you saw him again when you went shopping, here in Tahoe." Faint memories of me speaking with a cop at the shopping center fill my mind. Or was that a fragment ripped from a nightmare I had?

"Did I ever see him in LA?"

"Yes. You and I were walking home one night, and you pointed someone out to me. I couldn't see much—just how creepy it all was. That hoodie, the face shrouded in darkness . . . Like a horror-movie trailer."

"What did the cops say? Were there any suspects?"

"Um, they said that no laws had been broken. It was just

someone on the street. I wasn't there when you talked with the cops. I'm telling you what you told me at the time."

"So, it happened here *and* in LA?"

Lisa's hand touches mine with cold, hesitant fingers that immediately pull away, as if my condition is somehow contagious. "Yes."

A beat of silence, while I try to think. How could someone stalk me in both places? They'd have to know my schedule or follow me when I drove myself to the airport, then hop on the same flight. Or the next.

My brain fog refuses to lift, held in place by medication and the throbbing headache that isn't letting go.

"I guess your *Summer Love* boobs made quite the impression," Lisa quips.

"Ah, if only I could hit you now," I reply, smiling for a moment that feels just like old times, when such exchanges ended in roaring laughter.

"Your boyfriend was becoming a little obsessed with that stalker of yours. He wanted to follow him, to lure the creep out of hiding and pull a gun on him. You didn't let him."

"Adrian is something else, isn't he?" There's love in my voice.

A moment of uncomfortable silence makes the beeping of the heart monitor sound louder than usual. "Bryan, not Adrian," Lisa says gently. "As far as I know, you and Adrian have been over for months."

My lower lip quivers. "No . . . not again. I can't go through this again." First Steve, now Adrian. I'd be better off not remembering them at all.

"What are you talking about?" Lisa's fingers stroke my face briefly with a gentle, soothing touch. "Don't cry, Em. It breaks my heart."

"I've only just started remembering Adrian, and how I feel for him. How much I love him. And now . . . you're telling me he's gone? I have to live through that all over again, with no recollection of having done it before. I just . . . feel the loss."

Lisa struggles to stifle a sigh. "It's Bryan now. Two weeks ago, when we last talked, you two were still a thing. You like him a lot, I know that much, and I have to agree. He's a hunk."

Tears flood my closed eyes, soaking my bandages. It's a sickening déjà vu, the Groundhog Day from hell. "Who's Bryan?"

"Ooh, he's hot, your Bryan," Lisa says, instilling a bit too much cheer into her voice. "Do you remember working at the Black Bear Bar and Grill? On weekends?"

I remember that much. But Lisa's question prods my memory into giving up a few more visual tidbits: the exterior of the establishment, a rugged log cabin, with a large, carved wooden sign featuring a standing black bear. The interior, expansive and somehow still not large enough to accommodate the weekend rush of tourists, drowned in the rich scent of grilled cheeseburgers and the inviting buzz of conversation, occasionally interrupted by hollering bouts of laughter. The wood-paneled walls, adorned with hunting-themed paintings and the occasional bear-themed trophy, like mounted stuffed heads or claws turned into pendants and hanging from long, thin strips of leather, in the Native American style of making huntsman jewelry.

I see myself chatting with someone across the tacky bar counter that has been sliced and carved out of the trunk of a massive redwood. A bearded man in his mid-thirties with a kind expression on his face, who grinned widely as he filled a row of glasses with liquor in one artful pass. The bottle, tilted just so, let the amber liquid cascade smoothly into the glasses without spilling a single drop, filling them one after the other, then loading them on black, glossy trays that I picked up to deliver. A drunk's hand on my butt, and me swaying out of his reach while expertly balancing the heavy tray above his head. Then, later, the silence of the deserted bar after closing, and the tiredness I felt when I finally took a seat at the counter. And a voice, sounding clearly in my memory, asking if I wanted a drink for myself.

"Bryan is—"

"—the bartender at the Black Bear," I whisper.

"Yeah. That's where you met, isn't it?"

I recall the man, but my feelings for him are still buried somewhere, in a drawer of my memory I'm afraid to open. "Was it him?" I ask quietly. "The stalker, was it Bryan?"

"I don't know, Em." Lisa stands and starts pacing the room slowly. "You could drive yourself crazy like this." She stops and groans loudly. "I don't think so. Bryan wanted to track down the stalker, remember? To do a—what was it? Yeah, a citizen's arrest. I just told you."

Stubbornly, I refuse to accept the answer. People lie about things more often than not, and so could this Bryan have. He feels like a complete stranger to me. "You say you were there with me, Lil, and saw this person yourself, but claim you didn't see much. Was it Bryan?"

"I don't know, all right?" Her foot angrily stomps the floor. After a moment, Lisa draws closer, hesitantly. "I'm sorry, Em. I shouldn't have raised my voice—"

Her reaction gives her away. She's hiding something, and knowing that fills my heart with fear. There's only one reason why she'd do that. "Are you lying about being with me that night? Was that stalker you?"

NINETEEN

As Lisa storms out of the room, crying, I call after her, weakly at first then as strongly as I can manage.

"Lisa, please come back." I listen for a while, and hear nothing. No footsteps, nor doors opening or closing. Nothing, as if Lisa is frozen in place, to watch me unseen and listen to me squirm, drowning in my guilt. "Lisa?" I call again, raising my voice. "I didn't mean it, I swear."

I stifle a frustrated scream. I would be just as mad in my friend's place. There's no basis for my accusations, only that I'm losing my mind, unsure of what really happened and when.

In the distance, a toilet flushes, and the tank starts refilling with a muted, multi-tonal whistle. It sounds oddly familiar, like a tune can sound familiar after hearing it on the radio a few times. I must've heard it . . . who knows how many times since I've been here. My memories are not mine anymore, and even those I manage to snatch in my daily tug of war with oblivion, I could lose by the next time I wake up from my troubled sleep.

Perhaps that's why Lisa didn't answer my call; she must've already locked herself in the bathroom, probably still crying. My accusations have sliced through a dear, loyal friend's heart, and I cannot forgive myself for it.

Still angry with myself and deciding to make amends, I wait, minute after long minute, for Lisa to come out of the bathroom. She mentioned her makeup needed lots of work, and I know my friend is nothing if not meticulous about her appearance. In my world, I have no way to tell time, no sense of its passage, no real connection with the hues of daylight or dusk people see outside their windows, helping them get grounded in reality. *Sensory deprivation,* one of the doctors called it. At the time, I thought it meant the loss of my eyesight. I never thought I'd miss sensing time just as badly.

I'm sure there must be some solutions available. Perhaps a specialized timepiece that could read the time to me or something like that. I don't know Braille, and don't believe I could ever learn it.

Not until I lose all hope of ever regaining my eyesight.

The bathroom door opens with a recognizable squeak, then is closed quietly.

"Lisa?" I call, then listen. In the distance, I can hear Lisa speaking with someone, but I can't catch what she's saying, not at first.

It's Jasmine, my nurse. When she speaks, her words carry over better. "I will let you know, I promise," she replies. "I have your number." She sounds unexpectedly chummy speaking with my best friend.

"Perfect, thank you. I have to go now. She'll understand." A pause, as Jasmine's reply comes too low to decipher.

Lisa's voice again, a little harsh, colder than before, dismissive. "Please, apologize for me, all right?"

Then another door opens, and the light clacking of her heels fades in the distance, leaving nothing but silence behind.

And more questions.

How does Lisa know Jasmine? They seem familiar with

one another, Jasmine quick to take orders from my best friend, although they've only just met. What am I missing? Why does Jasmine have Lisa's number? My paranoia returns in full force, eating away all the guilt over making hurtful accusations earlier.

When Jasmine shows up later with my meal, making apologies for Lisa's rather abrupt departure, I am monosyllabic. I don't care to try to hold the plastic spoon myself; just endure the humiliation of being fed some rubber-tasting chicken with squishy, overcooked peas, wishing it was over already. I feel like throwing up. Not even the Jell-O makes me smile like Jasmine says it usually does.

As if I can trust another word from Jasmine again. Until I can be sure I can trust her, I only have one question.

"When's the doctor coming?" I ask, as she clears the tray into the trash can, the one with a metallic lid that opens by itself, grinding against the edges. The stainless-steel one that I feel sure has a black logo on it. Not red, like I've seen in doctors' offices.

"He comes every evening at about six," the nurse replies, sounding a little clipped. "Are you feeling ill?"

"I'm just swell," I snap. "Really enjoying my time at this luxury spa."

A moment of tense silence. "Sorry, hon. I meant, if you're not feeling well, if there's anything I can do for you, just let me know, all right?"

It's pointless. And perhaps completely wrong to suspect Jasmine of anything. She could've killed me fifty times already. She has access, while I'm asleep, to stick me with whatever chemicals she sees fit. "No . . . I'm sorry. I've been edgy all day, I'm losing my mind here. Even Lisa . . . I accused her of something, and I should've known it was wrong."

The heavy footsteps draw closer to the bed. I hear the chart clipboard rattling against the bedframe, then papers rustling as its pages are thumbed through.

"I see Dr. Sokolowski dialed back your sedatives and your pain medication. It's lower than what I usually see in my other brain injury patients. Perhaps he went a bit too far? I could adjust the dose for you, to make you a little more comfortable."

Tears burn my eyes under my closed eyelids. Those are my options: losing my mind in a whirlwind of fear and anxiety while waiting to be killed, or being drugged out of my mind, a neat little vegetable resting in a pickle jar, locked in a dark closet somewhere.

"No . . . I'd rather stay awake as much as possible. And the pain isn't as bad anymore," I lie, wondering how convincing I sound.

"As you wish," the nurse replies, and the clipboard clatters as it's placed in its usual spot. "I'm here if you change your mind."

"Thanks," I whisper, wishing she'd leave already so I can be alone with my exhausting thoughts; to rummage through them until one finally makes some sense and points me in the direction of my stalker.

As Jasmine leaves the room, an unwelcome thought slices through my mind. What if the person who tried to kill me and my stalker are two different people? What if I've been wrong the entire time?

When Dr. Sokolowski finally comes, he finds me worked up into a motionless frenzy, all my angst turned inwards, driving me insane. As soon as I hear the familiar footsteps, I call his name, my voice desperate. "Dr. Sokolowski? You have to help me, please. This has to stop," I plead, well aware I'm making little sense.

"What's wrong, Emma?" The chair is moved closer to the bed, then squeaks when the doctor sits. Then he lowers the bed rail; it makes its own unique rattling sound.

"This memory thing. I keep discovering things I forgot from my life before, and things I learned since I've been here, but then forgot again, as if I can't form new memories anymore. It can't go on like this. Please, do something."

"Let's talk about your memory," the doctor replies, after a long moment. "I believe I explained post-traumatic amnesia. Do you still recall that?"

"Yes, a little. Something about the memories being there, but I can't access them? Not until I'm ready?"

"Exactly. It's a defect in the consolidation and retrieval of memories, and it's as simple as it sounds. In the sorting system of your memory, drawers are all still full of stuff, but your brain, as it heals, still can't remember where you keep the socks and where you keep the tee-shirts. And sometimes, it does recall, but it just doesn't want to open certain drawers, afraid of what could lie in there, of how painful it could be. Your subconscious mind is protecting you."

"I get that. But then, if I manage to finally remember something, why do I forget it all over again? Just the other day I learned my ex got engaged about a year ago. Today, I didn't remember any of it. I had to discover it all over again."

"You still have swelling in your brain, some residual inflammation. If you fell and twisted your ankle, how long would you not put weight on it?"

"Um, about three, four weeks?"

"That's about right. Until then, until it's healed at least to some reasonable degree, your ankle cannot function properly. Sure, it holds the foot in place. The joint is still there, and it could technically function, only it can't. It's too swollen. The tendons are overstretched, perhaps even torn. They need time to heal."

"I see," I reply, starting to understand where he's going with his orthopedic metaphor.

"So, then, why would you give your ankle, a relatively simple, almost mechanical system of poles and ropes and pulleys, so much time to heal, and be so impatient when it comes to the most complex organ of the human body?"

I sigh. "So, what you're saying is, wait some more? But what if something happens to me? And you said I should be able to form new memories, only I still can't. Not all the time. Not normally, anyway. It doesn't feel normal."

The doctor chuckles quietly. "There's something you can't understand, Emma, because you don't see what we doctors see every day—even this conversation we're having, the arguments you're making, the way you challenge me, is an amazing story of healing. All this, coming from a person who was found unconscious, lying in a pool of her own blood, with a five-inch head laceration. It's a thing of wonder. Your cognitive abilities are almost entirely intact. And what's not there yet will come in due time."

I breathe slowly, trying to find the power to believe and hope, to draw some inner peace from his encouraging words. "Then I need you to help me call the cops."

"You remember who attacked you?" His voice, steady and soothing, is still muffled by the mask he's wearing. No one else wears masks; not Jasmine, and not Isabella. Where is Isabella, anyway? Why can't I recall talking with her recently? How come I remember Jasmine, but not Isabella? Only I do remember her . . . sort of. At least, I remember she exists.

"I—no," I reluctantly admit. "I still don't remember who wants me dead. But there are things they should know about what happened. I do remember something, not much, but it could get them started. Or perhaps there's something on my phone worth looking at." Silence fills the room, spreading dread inside my body.

"So, it's the same as yesterday. I thought, perhaps—"

"Yesterday? What happened yesterday?" My voice hits the high pitch of sheer panic.

A stifled sigh leaves the doctor's chest, shifting the air just a little and bringing the smell of starched scrubs and soap, breath mints, and a hint of exotic basil on suede. I shudder, waiting for him to speak.

"The cops were here yesterday evening. You asked me to call them, and I did. A Detective Burton spoke with you. Don't you remember any of this?" His voice takes the color of concern.

I'm not sure of anything anymore. "N—no. What did I tell him?"

"Her. Detective Burton is a woman," the doctor clarifies. "You told her what you remembered about the attack, what you've told me a few times. You were running, looking behind you, seeing only someone who struck you down, no physical description other than white and relatively slim, athletic. Then I gave them the injury specifics, the diagnosis, and my assessment of what weapon could've been used. A blunt object, perhaps the grip of a gun, a baseball bat, or something similar. Does any of that sound familiar?"

"So, the cops were here," I whisper, feeling defeated and immensely tired, like a swimmer about to drown from the effort of staying alive, of taking oneself to shore. To safety. "Did she look at my phone?"

"She did, yes, but didn't have the code to unlock it. She might come back for it. She said there wasn't much to go on, but they're investigating. They're looking at footprints around the house and traffic cameras in the area. Oh, and they took the security tapes from your home surveillance system. She was sure the attack happened at your house, because you were found on the driveway, by the door."

Somehow, I made it out of the house that night. I don't remember how; I must've managed to open the door after all.

I listen to all the details of the conversation I've been involved in, stunned that I don't remember a single thing. At least with that neurologist, Dr. Winslow—I know his name now, even as I recall I've kept forgetting him—I have some idea of what he told me. But this Detective Burton? I'm drawing a complete blank. Although the dark emptiness that is my mind shouldn't be referred to as blank. To me, blank is white nothingness, not this black abyss.

"What else am I forgetting, Doctor? Is she going to call me? What happens next?"

"She took some notes, and said she'd be in touch, yes." A brief silence, while the doctor stands and walks over to the side table by my bed. "She left her business card. Here you go." He puts it under my fingertips. I feel the raised ink and a rather large, circular logo. "I'm going to leave it on your bedside table again. If you remember anything and want to speak with her, just let me know and I'll help you make the call. Her mobile number is on the back of the card.'"

I lie there spent, unable to think, immersed in my merciless reality. "Thank you," I eventually say. "And I'm sorry . . . it's just so terrifying to not remember much of anything that happens to you."

"I'm going to call Dr. Winslow for another consult," the doctor says, sounding a little concerned but apparently trying to mask it. "Do you remember him?"

"The neurologist?"

"Yes, the expert who's been treating your brain injury," Dr. Sokolowski replies, sounding as though he's smiling. "Some things actually stick, and that's a good sign. But let's hear what he has to say anyway. I'll try to get you on his schedule for tomorrow morning, unless he's in surgery."

"Thanks," I whisper. "Do you have a few more minutes? Could you help me figure out what's in my phone? I, um, don't trust anyone else."

He doesn't reply right away. He's already taken a few steps toward the door, probably eager to resume his rounds. "If someone came to my house, I'm sure there must be some trace of that in my phone. Please."

Hesitant steps return to my bedside. "All right, but I only have a couple of minutes." There's a small clatter as he takes the phone off the table, and the power cord falls to the ground with a light tap. "What are we looking for?"

The door opens and someone walks in, pushing something on wheels that rattles. The smell of food tells me it's probably a meal cart. "I'll come back later," Jasmine hastens to say, sounding a bit tense, apologetic.

"No, that's fine. I have to run anyway." Dr. Sokolowski puts the phone back on the table. "Let's continue this tomorrow, all right?"

TWENTY

I let my mind wander freely, not making any effort to focus my attention on anything in particular. So far, it has proven the best way I can trick my brain into releasing more of the memories it holds hostage. Since Dr. Sokolowski left, and Jasmine finished feeding me and changing my dressings, and all the humiliating tasks she calls her nightly routine, I've been dozing off, again losing track of time. Of myself.

How much time has slipped by since Dr. Sokolowski came to visit? Has Dr. Winslow come to see me yet? I can't handle another "be patient" speech without screaming. Something must be wrong with my memory. There is no rational explanation for the way some things come back to me only to disappear again, as if everything is swirled in a tornado of snippets and glimpses and insanity. I want clear answers, even though I know they aren't always possible with brain injuries.

And that's only the mental part of my ordeal. The fact that I've only marginally improved my ability to move is another terrifying thing no one seems to care too much about. Yes, I understand the throbbing in my head marks where I was hit, centered on the visual cortex area of my occipital lobe and the cerebellum—responsible for skill memory and movement coordination. The doctor explained at length how I need to be patient, and how inflammation recedes, slowly reducing pressure on those areas of the brain as it resolves.

Well, screw that. I can't take it anymore.

Stubborn and desperate, I resume my hand exercises, a program I devised for myself. The elevated position of my head is going to help increase the difficulty of the exercises. This time, I want to force my hands to move up my body until I can touch my chin with the tips of my fingers.

Planning to ask Jasmine for another hand and arm massage, I start the slow crawl of my left fingers up my thigh until I reach the flat of my stomach, then, at an angle, up my chest, infuriatingly slowly. At times, my entire arm trembles with the effort to hold on, to keep dragging itself up. When I reach the edge of my blanket I am covered in sweat, but grinning, satisfied with that modicum of success. If I keep going, soon I'll be able to scratch my own chin.

After a little longer, my left arm gets a well-deserved break while I focus my efforts on my right. It works better, faster, completing the entire exercise in what feels like twenty minutes or so, but I can't be sure.

The PA calls for Dr. Parrish to report to the nurses' station, tearing through my focus for a brief moment. My mind wanders off while my hands work out the challenge of climbing up my body and back down again without slipping.

Obsessively, I wonder if Lisa would harm me. If the sweet face I know so well could've scrunched in rage, spewing hatred through fiery eyes. No...not my Lisa, not those glistening eyes that have laughed with me during the happiest days of my life and have cried with me when my heart was broken. Not the sister I always wished for but never had.

But do I really know her? What do I know about Lisa that I can be sure of? Yes, she was a little too eager to get on Denise's list, but such zeal isn't beyond comprehension in our line of work. As friends, we've gladly shared all the opportunities that have crossed our paths.

So why does it feel different this time?

Could it only be because I'm stuck here, in my own endlessly dark hell, while life carries on without me? *Has* Lisa done anything wrong, or is it the perception of my own loss that makes everything look amiss? With an agent like Denise, doors would open for Lisa in a big way, because she's a talented, bright, and beautiful actor. *The Oscar goes to . . .*

The thought echoes in my mind. An Oscar used to be my dream, most likely still is Lisa's. It isn't her fault that she wants to pursue it to the best of her abilities. She's immensely talented, an actor who can sell any line, any emotion, play any part she wants. Be anyone she wants.

Including a stalker.

The thought chills my blood.

Trying to recall the prowler, the menacing silhouette leaning against the aspen in the moonlight, the image comes effortlessly to my mind. I overlap Lisa's features, trying them for size and fit as if I would a garment, imagining my friend wearing a hoodie, hands plunged deeply in its pockets, face obscured by the shadows.

Could it have been her? How tall was that stalker, anyway? I should've looked at that aspen trunk, found a knot or some other mark where the top of the hooded head touched the bark to figure out the stalker's height. I could've learned something about that creep.

Yes, it could've been Lisa, even if I always thought that stalker was a man. Was he? He looked like one, but what did I really see? Lisa's own account of the story colors my spotty memory of that night. I'm not even sure it happened; she could've made it all up.

That stalker could've been anyone.

Damn.

My hands shake badly, from fear and the effort made to move them. Forgetting what I can't do, I instinctively interlace my fingers on top of my stomach and breathe deeply. The posture feels good, more normal—although touching my own fingers is still surreal, as if my hands are numb. Only I know they aren't.

A light knock on the door makes me jump out of my skin.

The door opens slowly, and light footsteps mark someone's furtive approach. I want to scream, but know it won't matter. Where is the nurse? It has been a while since I've heard anyone chatting in the corridor.

The stranger draws close slowly, tiptoeing until coming to a stop by the bed.

Cringing inside, I wait for the blow to come, but it doesn't. A quiet cry leaves my lips, fear getting the best of me.

"Hey," a man's voice says gently. "It's me, Bryan."

I breathe, filling my starved lungs with air. I'm still alive. For now. And there is no murderous undertone in his voice.

"Bryan?" I ask tentatively, my voice a little shaky. I don't remember much, despite my conversation with Lisa. This guy is supposed to be my boyfriend, but even his voice sounds unfamiliar.

The man takes my hand. "That's me." A moment of silence, while I struggle to pull my hand out of his, unwilling to be touched. "I was worried, you know. You just vanished. Didn't take my calls, my texts went unanswered. I thought you'd totally ghosted me." There is a trace of a smile in his voice. "I managed to save your job. Three days of no call, no show, and you're out. You know the big man's policy, right? But he'll take you back, now that he knows what happened."

Bryan keeps on chatting, seemingly undisturbed by my silence. But all I can think is, *What if he isn't real? What if Lisa just said there was a Bryan so that a man could gain access and kill me?*

In my frantic mind, Lisa has become the ultimate criminal mastermind, more ruthless than Al Capone himself. Complete nonsense. It makes more sense to accept I might've dated the Black Bear bartender for a while. Who knows how breaking up with Adrian made me feel, if I don't remember any of it? Heartache creeps up on me and chokes me. I miss Adrian's strong arms, his warm embrace, how he made all my fears go away.

"—and I just cut him off. I should've done it after the third drink, but he was a big guy with a lot of sorrows to drown."

"Why? What happened?"

"I just told you," he says, sounding a little confused. "Never mind," he adds, while his hand finds mine again. This time, I don't pull away. "His wife left him."

"Ah, yeah, that will do it." I smile with sadness, remembering how I felt after my divorce.

"Anyway, so he didn't take a cab. He drove himself straight into the lamppost in our parking lot. Bang, and the damn thing fell on the ground like timber. Now it's all dark, until the big man gets it fixed. Boozers don't seem to care."

His idle chatter brings back more flashes of memories. Beers shared at the bar counter after the last few drunks had been sent on their way, the floors swept of all the crap they left behind. Leaning toward each other, whispering all sorts of nothing, the music's volume lowered so we could actually hear each other speak; the big TV above the bar muted, the flicker of its screen the only light around us.

Glimpses of the past continue to unfold in my mind, triggered by Bryan's voice. I see myself laughing at his jokes, most of them about drunks and bars, husbands and wives, or rednecks, his favorite three topics. Clinking beer bottles above the shiny counter, and wishing him a happy birthday.

"Oh, almost forgot," he says, "Tom wanted me to say get well soon. He said something about your promise to teach him how to make crepes? Is that true? Old Tom wants to make crepes?"

"Yeah, he wants to surprise his wife. For their anniversary." The reply comes effortlessly. I know who Tom is and what we've talked about. I pause for a while, slowly relaxing, knowing that at least for now, I'm safe. Bryan talks about things I remember clearly, and that almost makes him family. "Did I tell you about the stalker?"

"What stalker?" Bryan asks.

His words send a chill through my veins. I clearly recall Lisa saying that Bryan wanted to lure the creep out and pull a gun on him. Someone is lying.

"Oh, I thought—never mind."

"You mean that son of a bitch I wanted to beat senseless last month?"

My breath catches in my lungs. "What son of a bitch?"

"You told me he was following you after work. I pulled the security tapes at the bar and showed them to the boss. He said I should work that punk over a bit, then do a citizen's arrest and call the cops."

"And? What happened?"

"Nothing. He never showed up again."

I exhale. Is it true? He just went away? Or did Bryan just serve me a good lie on a platter? How can I believe anything? How can I tell the truth from the lies?

"Was it you?" I ask calmly, steeling myself.

"Was it me, what?"

"Who put me here."

He slaps his hand against his thighs, or so I think when I hear the sound he makes. The faint smell of barroom grime fills my nostrils. "Jeez, Emma, are you crazy? I'm not going to hold this against you, because you're, um, you know, injured and all. But man, that hurts. I'd never lay a finger on you, and you know it."

The beeping of the heart monitor speeds up gradually.

If not him, and not Lisa, then who? Who wanted me dead so badly? And why?

It doesn't feel like a month ago, the time when the stalker lurked in the Black Bear parking lot, staring at me. It feels like ages. And Lisa said that I was seeing Bryan for a few months, and that I'd broken up with Adrian a while ago. Time has stopped making sense, swirling instead of being the linear, taut thread that anchors life to reality.

I'm choking, breathless, while my heart thumps desperately in my chest. The beeping turns into a steady alarm tone.

"Em? Are you all right?" Bryan shouts. His hands are on my shoulders, shaking me. I can smell the stale tobacco on him, shrouding him like a cloud.

"Sir, you need to step away." Jasmine's voice is uncompromising, but only the sound of her footsteps comes to my ears. Not his.

Bryan isn't budging from my bedside. "Emma, I'm right here, baby."

"Sir, please leave."

My mind goes slowly dark, fading away like a burned-out candle. Before I slip away, I hear Jasmine's voice shouting, "Some help in here!"

TWENTY-ONE

I don't mind killing people.

I have no guilt about it—no tormenting, second-guessing thoughts. To me, it's like taking the trash out. No need to obsess over what the trash might think or feel. If it's trash, it needs taking out, because otherwise it would soil my life and taint everything I care about.

I don't particularly enjoy it either. It's a chore; nothing more, nothing less. Something that needs to be done to maintain the kind of perfect life I envision for myself and my dear Emma.

I can think of a few other pieces of trash that deserve a permanent visit to the landfill. I'm not taking care of it today, though it's not because I don't feel like it. It's mostly because they're not the root cause of some evil, like those two bikers were. Those particular issues are a symptom of a bigger, more disturbing problem I don't know how to fix.

Emma Duncan has terrible taste in men.

What is it with these beautiful, successful women that makes them willing to accept the company of such disappointing men? It's as if she's looking to be around losers and bums of all sorts.

For years, she's been willing to work in bars, waiting on drunks, *putting up with their lustful looks and lewd comments and butt-grabs, and for what? There are other things she could've done for money between films; more elegant, even ladylike if I may call it the old-fashioned way. But she had to go looking for work in those sordid places, and smile at those people for tips.*

Then to date one of them? Aren't there any better men out there? Men like me, for instance?

This Bryan fellow, what a sorry-ass loser. His ratty jeans look as if he's fished them out of a trash can. His beard is unkempt and looks as if he'd been on that island with Tom Hanks in Cast-away. And a plaid shirt? Come on. I bet he smells of stale booze and piss, just like the dubious establishment he calls his place of employment.

Don't even get me started on Mr. Steven Wellington himself. He's got some attractive features; I'll give him that. His face is memorable, with that high forehead and cheekbones, and defined jawline. Blue eyes never hurt anyone in the movie industry. I can see why she fell for him. But his ego is oversized to the point where I don't understand how any of his films are released. Nothing seems good enough for that man. Being married to him must've been hell in a cage.

I saw them interacting, after their divorce. It irked me to see how badly he treated Emma because of that bimbo, Mikela Murtagh. Now that's a weird association. Mr. Highbrow him-self, with his Oscar dreams and making classic films, and that nineteen-year-old floozy, with her red-soled Louboutin stilettos and designer-brand skirts that barely cover her ass. I can venture a guess who pays for all that stuff.

I saw them there, in Emma's room, saw them show their true colors, even if my camera system is in black and white and the sound isn't that great. I missed some of what was being said, but I could still see more than enough. I wonder what they really want from her. That Mikela is after something. She doesn't say much, but I'm willing to bet all of my tomorrows that she's driving all this. Wellington's just a puppet she's playing. I wonder why she destroyed Emma's marriage—for which I'm grateful, by the way.

She's wearing that monstrous ring; she's landed herself a five-star meal ticket. What else does she want?

No idea, but I know trash when I see it.

Regardless how disappointing these people are, Emma chose these men. I'd love to be able to blame it on them and them alone; then my decision would be an easy one. Simply a chore I'd have to do. But nothing would be accomplished. She'd waltz away, pass right by me, and pick another loser. That's infuriating.

If she were mine, she wouldn't do any more stupid things. I'd make sure of it.

And I wouldn't have to endure seeing someone like this lowlife Bryan put hands on her.

It takes every bit of willpower I have to not find him and wring his damn neck.

TWENTY-TWO

In my dream, someone's breath hits my cheek, giving me goose bumps. Then, a voice whispers in my ear, calling my name, "Emma." I wake with a start, gasping for air until my breathing normalizes, soothed by the noise of objects being placed on a tray. The usual sound of my mornings.

"Ah, you're awake," Jasmine says from a few feet away. The noise doesn't stop. A foil lid crackles as it's peeled off, then the trash can opens its lid with the familiar creak. An intrusive, infuriatingly pointless thought tugs at my mind relentlessly. *Does that trash can have a black biohazard logo?* For a moment, I think of asking Jasmine, but then decide not to interrupt the comforting sound of the song she hums over and over while working.

"Good morning," I say, then pause briefly. "I guess."

"You guess right," the nurse replies cheerfully, approaching the bed with the rustling of scrubs and the smell of lavender dryer sheets. "It's morning, and the sun is shining. How are you feeling today? Any pain?"

"Just a bit of a headache. And my muscles still don't work."

"They will," she replies, then resumes her humming when I remain silent, lost in my thoughts.

In the distance somewhere, a fly stubbornly bangs against the glass, its buzzing faltering each time. It seems eager to break free, to get the hell out of here. For a moment, I reflect on my goals, not much loftier than an insect's. It seems the fly has better chances of seeing its dreams of freedom come true. One open window, one door that doesn't slide closed fast enough, and it will soar to the sky.

If only I could see the light of day again, I think, imagining bright sunshine splashing against the windowpanes, luring the fly with its promise of warmth and life and joy. *If only I could be free again.*

I won't break open the floodgates of my despair. I've tried to be strong thus far, refusing to be defeated, clinging to every shred of hope the doctors and nurses offer. But sometimes the realization of my condition leaves me breathless, dangerously close to admitting defeat.

How much longer will it take to get out of here?

My breath shatters. *What if that never happens? How can I live like this?*

"What's wrong, hon?" Jasmine asks, rushing over to the bed.

I push the tears away, refusing to give in. While there's still life coursing through my veins, I *will* fight. "Just wondering, how do hospitals keep flies out? Those doors are open all the time."

A moment of silence, while Jasmine probably stares at me, unseen. Then she laughs heartily, and starts adjusting my bed and propping up my pillows. "I don't know all the secrets. Probably that's above my pay grade. A question for the hospital admin, wouldn't you say? Definitely for someone making more money than me." Arranging the covers, she adds, "I believe they have strong fans at the entrance, pushing the air out. It's called a positive pressure environment. Won't let anything get in—bacteria, dust, insects, all the tiny creepy crawlies."

It makes sense. "I understand."

Jasmine punches a pillow a couple of times, then lifts my shoulders gently and slips it behind my nape. "Is that nasty little thing bothering you? I could zap it in a jiffy. One spray of disinfectant and it will drop like a fly." The laughter returns, Jasmine clearly thrilled with her pun.

"N—no, please. It just wants to get out of here. Doesn't deserve to die for that reason." My voice falters.

The bed shifts and groans under Jasmine's weight. Then, her warm fingers stroke my cheek. "Oh, hon, you'll get out of here, I promise. Let's get you something to eat. We have yogurt for today, with whole wheat crackers, some toast with cheese, and a cookie. Do you want to try and hold the spoon?"

"Yes," I say, ready to find out if all my work will show any results.

It doesn't.

I struggle just as much as before to hold the spoon, to bring it to my mouth, and if it weren't for Jasmine's hand guiding mine, I'd drop it.

I'm unable to feed myself, to perform even the simplest of tasks, those that everyone takes for granted. Until they're gone.

A slightly turned head makes my message clear, as I struggle to swallow the bit of yogurt left in my mouth.

"Oh, honey." Jasmine sets the food aside—the tray lands noisily next to the bed, probably set on the chair. "What's on your mind?"

I struggle for a moment with words I don't want to hear myself say out loud. "I—I don't think I can live like this, Jas. I wish I was dead." I sob with my mouth open, my wails hoarse and dissonant.

"Shh . . . it will be all right," Jasmine says after a while. "Do you know why?"

My curiosity defeats my tears. "No. Why?"

She doesn't respond immediately. "Are you still afraid you'll be attacked again? By the same person, coming to finish what they started?"

"Yes."

A light chuckle. "That means you want to live. Deep inside, that's what you want. Otherwise, you'd have me leave the door wide open and you'd welcome that son of a bitch, ready to go to the other side."

I mull over her words for a moment. "Yes. I suppose."

"Then accept you want to live, make peace with it, and let's work on getting better." There's a rattle and her weight shifts as she leans to get the tray and sets it on the bed. "The only thing you want to escape is your current situation. And that, I promise you, is not worth your life. This will pass."

"It better," I reply, feeling ashamed of my moment of weakness. "I'm ready to get the hell out of here. Just like that fly."

I finish eating, then Jasmine cleans everything up and wipes my face gently with a moist towel. It feels refreshing. My mind drifts away to Adrian, to our love affair, a story with an ending still hidden in the murky haze of time and memory.

The nurse works on my IV, quickly, silently. I can feel the gentle shifting of the tubing. Then she rolls up my left sleeve and checks the patch I wear on my arm.

"You're not in pain anymore, are you?"

"Not really."

"Some pain is good for you," Jasmine says, tugging lightly at the corner of my patch. I can feel it starting to come off my skin, but Jasmine stops and rolls my sleeve down. "It reminds you you're alive and have something to fight for."

I shudder, recalling how friendly Jasmine was when chatting with Lisa, how she knew my friend's phone number. Does it matter? Can I trust her?

The door swings open, and Jasmine freezes. Her hands stop

for a brief moment, holding the edge of my blanket, then she brings it back down to finish arranging it neatly. "Good morning, Doctor," she says, just as I recognize the slight squeak in the doctor's shoe.

"Good morning," he replies tersely. "I'll take it from here."

In silence, Jasmine moves to collect her things, the tray, some other items on the table, then leaves, closing the door behind her.

I turn my head in the doctor's direction, wishing I could see the expression on his face. He seems unusually tense. I hope it isn't about me, but fear that it is.

The chair rolls on its wheels and stops by the bed, and Dr. Sokolowski takes a seat. "I have about ten minutes until I have to get back to the ER. Would you like us to look at your phone now?"

TWENTY-THREE

In the brief moment between Dr. Sokolowski's question and my answer, the frayed fabric of a memory started coming together in my mind. Like snippets from a movie, outtakes dropped on the editing room's floor, fragments of my past life started rolling at the front of my consciousness, luring me to explore their secrets.

I was at my Tahoe home, on the back porch, looking at the wintry mountain peaks, white against the purple dusk sky. Adrian was by my side, laughing, touching my arm as he talked. We were both swaddled in warm blankets, lounging on chaises by the firepit. Tall flames burned cheerfully, scaring away the biting cold of the late fall evening.

I texted someone on my phone, then took a sip of wine from the glass I'd left on the firepit tabletop, far enough from the flames to keep it chilled. Watching a few scattered snowflakes touch the ground, I wondered where they came from. Not a single cloud floated in the perfectly clear sky. In the distance, the lake was an ominous, metallic blue.

It felt good to be out there, to live in the moment next to the man I loved, taking it slow for a well-deserved weekend break after the rush of auditioning and filming had left us both exhausted.

The night before I had caved to Adrian's insistence and called in sick, skipping my Friday shift at the Black Bear with very little notice. I felt bad about it; the owner deserved better from me, especially at the start of the season, when hordes of tourists were about to invade with the first snowfall, more of them than a full complement of staff could handle. Friday nights were quite lucrative for me and made a difference, especially when I was out of acting work. But Adrian had insisted, and I had my own reasons to give in to his wish.

The week that was just ending had been challenging for me, with back-to-back auditions and no contracts signed, and evenings spent alone at Lisa's apartment, while she was shooting on location somewhere in Mexico. Adrian was working on a TV pilot, shooting the outdoor scenes in Arizona somewhere, with a plan to be locked inside a soundstage for the following six weeks at a Universal studio leased out to Netflix. At least he'd be home, in Tahoe, for the weekends. If they didn't fall behind with their schedule.

Worries about my struggle to land roles started seeping into my mind, but I pushed the grim thoughts away and focused on Adrian's charming smile. He lounged on the chaise and leaned into his elbow to face me, telling me a funny story about a conflict between their executive producer and one of the makeup artists on the show. He had a way with words, turning any story, no matter how banal, into an adventure I could imagine as if I were there, witnessing it in person.

His eyes sparked, and his smile was intoxicating. For a moment, I thought of taking his hand and dragging him inside, into the warmth of our bedroom, but I lingered, the evening too beautiful to end so soon. My wineglass was almost empty, but

I didn't draw Adrian's attention to it, knowing he'd stop talking and do something about it, perhaps get another bottle. I didn't want that. I wanted everything to stay exactly the way it was for as long as possible, his soft, melodious voice carrying me away, the look in his eyes lighting a slow-burning fire in my body.

It was bliss.

The first time my phone chimed with a new message, I ignored it, hoping it was muffled enough in my pocket for Adrian to have missed. He didn't stop talking, telling me about his new project, his future plans, all layered with generous servings of juicy Hollywood gossip.

"Everyone knows what they did. And she's half his age, or less, just some floozy no one wants to be seen with. Can you believe it? After their photo was splattered all over the tabloids, he had the gall to say he didn't—"

Adrian's story was touching a nerve, with its painfully familiar notes of Steve and Mikela. My smile started waning as my mind drifted inwards, where the wound still ached.

When my phone chimed again, I welcomed the distraction and fished the device out of my pocket to read the message.

"The Bernards invited us to spend next weekend at their LA home," I say cheerfully, interrupting his story. "Next Friday is Mike's birthday."

When I raised my eyes from the phone's screen to look at Adrian, he was looking away. Tension clenched his jaw.

"What do you say, huh?" I was excited to go, to see people, to be seen as someone who still mattered.

"I'm sick and tired of people invading our world, Em. It's hurtful, really, how you prioritize everyone over me. I thought you liked being here with me, right now, the way we were up until those stupid motherfuckers ruined it for us with their text invite."

My happiness withered and blew away in the gusty, cold wind. The Bernards were nice people, dear friends of mine. I reeled from the unwarranted insult. "I'm sorry, I didn't know you felt this way. Of course I like being here with you."

"You don't, Em, not really. At least be honest. With yourself, if not with me." He started tugging at the edge of the blanket and got angry when it got caught in the chaise's leg, trapping him for a split moment. He quickly freed himself and stood, eager to get out of there. To not look at me anymore.

The slamming of the French door closing behind him resonated in the silence of the late evening for a while, its echoes opening a chasm in my chest.

That's all I remember.

Was that the end of Adrian and me? It doesn't seem possible; what I felt and still do seems too strong to wilt and die from a minor disagreement. Yet the memory stops there, leaving me aching for more, for answers. The anguish I felt that night is strong, unaltered, as if it happened yesterday and I'm still waiting for him to come back, to forgive me, although I did nothing wrong.

"What's the access code?" Dr. Sokolowski asks.

For a brief moment, I'm disoriented. *What access code? Oh, yes, we were going to look at my phone.*

To my surprise, the four digits I give him unlock the phone.

"It worked." The smile in the doctor's voice is clear. "Your memory is getting better, isn't it?"

Exhilaration swells my chest. "Yes. I'm starting to remember more and more of what happened before—" I can't bring myself to say the words. I'm afraid the intrusive memory will pop up again, the way it's been doing every day. And I can't stand hearing my own voice screaming for help inside the chasm of my own mind.

"Where do you want to start?"

I hear the phone beeping faintly as he touches the screen,

probably browsing through the device. It's an unspeakable invasion of privacy, yet I have no other choice than allowing it to happen. I cringe, thinking of my photos, wondering if there are any he shouldn't lay eyes on. It's too late now. If I have any chance of figuring out who wants to kill me, it's in that phone.

"Let's look at text messages first, please." My cheeks warm with embarrassment. "What are the most recent?"

"One message came yesterday, from an attorney, Perry Sheldon." He whistles in amazement. "This man heard you're incapacitated, yet sends you a text. People's stupidity is limitless," he mutters, more to himself.

His voice is unforgiving, and that chill rubs off on me, when I think of lawyers. Steve mentioned drawing up papers. That's probably it. The name sounds unfamiliar.

"Then some messages from Bryan. Do you remember Bryan? His number is in your contacts list, just the first name."

"Yes." I hold my breath, wondering what we messaged about, because I don't remember much about us, not even after he visited with me.

"Good. There are some older messages that point to a romantic relationship between the two of you. Then a few messages where Bryan asks if he was dumped, ghosted by you. He's, um, sad and concerned he's not hearing back from you. Then a warning that you might lose your job for not showing up and not calling."

"Yeah, he told me about it."

"He came to see you? That's great."

"Not really." A moment of silence, while I find my words. "I don't remember him much."

"The most recent message from him reads, 'Maybe when you'll be able to read this, you'll also remember who we were to each other.' Sounds like a decent man."

I press my lips together as tightly as I can. "He probably is. I wish I knew. Anyone else recent?"

"Is this Bryan someone who could take care of you?"

Panic rips through my chest. "No. I don't have anyone." The beeping of the machine quickens.

What am I going to do?

I've pushed the thought aside for as long as I can. I didn't want to think about what would happen when they release me from the hospital. How I would take care of myself, how I would pay the bills. But the moment to deal with this is now, and there's no escaping it. As soon as we're done with the phone, I'll have to think of options. Find one where there are none.

"What else?" I ask impatiently. "Did I invite anyone to my house on the day of the attack?"

His fingers must dance on the screen, accompanied by faint sounds. "N—no, not that I can see. There are some messages from Denise Hastings, she's also in your contacts list. She was concerned you missed an audition and kept asking you to text her back after that. And then . . . A couple of confirmations, an invitation from a producer to audition for some role, and that's about it. Oh, and Lisa Chen, also in your contacts list. Do you remember her?"

"Yes, she's my best friend."

"Seems that way. She was concerned with you missing an audition, then says here she feels bad for landing the role in your place, then a number of pings, asking if you're okay." A moment of unbearable silence. "Nothing else in your texts, I'm afraid."

"How about emails?"

It takes him a while to reply. "Nothing I can spot without reading them word for word. I'm looking at those that were sent or received right before you were attacked, and I don't see much. Some shopping confirmations, a couple of emails from Denise, a link to an Instagram photo sent by Lisa, forwarded from someone else, that kind of stuff."

"And calls?"

"Let's see." I hold my breath, knowing this is my last chance. "Just Bryan, Denise . . . oh, and the Lake Tahoe Police Department. They called you a couple of days before the attack, and you spoke with them for almost five minutes. Do you remember that?"

It must've been about the stalker. Why else would the cops be calling me? "No." My voice trembles. *I have nothing.* "What's going to happen to me?" I ask. "I'm not getting better fast enough, I don't have anyone to care for me, I have no place to go, and no money to pay my bills if I'm not working."

The phone clatters when he sets it on the table. A moment later, a familiar beep tells me he's plugged it in. "Emma, I know it's hard for you to believe, but these things have a way of sorting themselves out."

How? By landing me broke and homeless, a ward of the state buried alive in some hellish place?

My heart races, and the heart monitor's beeping betrays me. Moments later, I feel something cold touching my chest through the fabric of my gown. It makes me wince from the unexpected contact.

"Shh, just my stethoscope, Emma. Taking a quick listen. Your breathing is fine, but your heart is struggling a little. Nothing to worry about. Just try to relax."

"How could I possibly relax?" I snap, feeling I'm drowning. Then, another thought lights my mind like a bolt of lightning. "Please, don't up my meds to help me relax. I need to get better, to move. I need to see."

"All right," Dr. Sokolowski replies, with a poorly restrained sigh. "I won't up your meds. I'll just add a little something for your heart. Let's try to get Dr. Winslow in here tomorrow, first thing, for another exam, and take it from there."

He squeezes my hand and I'm grateful, yet afraid to count on him. I'm nobody to him, just a barcode on a patient bracelet.

He could be reassigned to another department and forget I ever existed.

"I need to know when I'm going to be able to walk out of here."

He pushes the chair to the side. "You're right, we need better answers and a good action plan. Then we'll start you on rehab with one of the best physical therapists in the state."

His phone chimes, and he lets go of my hand. "I'm afraid I have to go, but I'll be back later to check on you."

I wish he'd stay a moment longer, but the door coming to a soft close behind him leaves me with the silence of unanswered questions.

Why did Lake Tahoe Police call me?

TWENTY-FOUR

My eyes feel squishy when I try to blink under the gauze, and my lids are heavy. I understand that's to keep them from getting dry, or something like that, since I'm not able to blink with the gauze wrapped tightly over my eyes. As much as I strain to peek, all I see is complete and absolute blackness, the perfect image of nothing. Even with the gauze on, I should at least see some hint of blurry daylight.

It's not there. I'm still blind.

Disappointment chokes me for a moment, until I will it gone. I can't think of a single case when self-pity helped anyone, and I know for sure I'm not going to make history this way. Denise was right; there's no room in my life for failure. If there's any shred of possibility I might one day get up from this damn bed and walk out of here, I will do that. It's a solemn promise to myself, unwavering, renewed with every breath.

I lie on my back, my hands taking turns to move up and down my body, all the way to my chin and back. Every few minutes, I try to lift them off the bed. By the time I start feeling pangs of hunger, I'm actually able to lift them high enough to break contact with the fleecy cover.

It's a win.

I give myself a break, letting myself rummage through misplaced memories for traces of what happened to Adrian after that night. For answers to the many questions swirling inside. Unnervingly slowly, an answer comes to me in the form of flashes, broken imagery I can put together into something that makes sense, an episode of my past life I can relive.

Adrian and I didn't break up that night. Our romance didn't end with the slammed French door and his angry words thrown my way. The evening was bleak, spent with him giving me the silent treatment while I walked on eggshells around him, trying to bring back the bliss so brutally dissipated by the Bernards' invite.

He spent that night in the guest bedroom, sleeping fully dressed on top of the covers, while I tossed and turned, waiting for him to come to bed. To me. Then he flew out early the next morning, heading into LA and blaming it on a tight production schedule.

On Sunday night, the doorbell startled me out of my spaced-out TV binging. I must've gone through an entire season of *Yellowstone* but couldn't recall much of it. I answered the door reluctantly, only after the second chime.

A dozen red roses waited in the arms of a young, freckled delivery courier. I signed for them quickly and closed the door, not before a gust of wind brought scattered snowflakes inside. My heart swelling, I set the vase down on the table and reached for the card.

I hope you still like roses, my love.

I sunk my face into the velvety blooms and filled my lungs with the scent of rose petals. Then I called him, and we chatted until two in the morning. I was so in love with him it seemed scary; the loss of control, the reckless willingness to abandon all that I was for a moment of happiness in my lover's arms.

Adrian was undeniably handsome, in an intensely charismatic way that reminded me of the day he and I first met, when his agent was foretelling women lining up for a date with him. Although he hadn't used the word "date"; he'd been way more explicit than that. And right about it, too.

Adrian would've been insanely successful as a fashion model, with his chiseled features and always tousled dark hair. The golden sparks in his hazel eyes every time he looked at me made me feel I was the luckiest woman alive. Men like him usually dated models, A-list actresses, and socialites, not women like me. I never thought of myself as special from any point of view, not until he made me feel that way. His love was strong enough to make him indifferent to the incessant advances of almost every woman he met, while I basked in the envious looks they threw my way whenever we went out together. I enjoyed it just like some people enjoy walking on a wire hundreds of feet above ground; it was exhilarating and addictive, while at the same time intensely scary. The fear of losing him grew at the same pace as my love for him.

Looking back, I can say he was the only good thing that came out of my divorce. After that trauma, I was understandably shy to enter a new relationship. I'd resisted for a while, but he swept me off my feet and took me to a place I'd never envisioned. We were happy. Not in a domestic, almost boring style, but in a constantly thrilling, one-hell-of-a-ride-through-life kind of way.

The Saturday evening of our first fight marked the beginning of a new era for Adrian and me. We spent the following weekend at home, together, snubbing the Bernards' invite. It was what he wanted, and he didn't concede, even if I was visibly upset about not going.

On Saturday afternoon, he found me sitting sadly out on the

porch, precisely where, one week earlier, our crisis had started. He was dismayed, seemingly shocked to discover how much I'd wanted to go. I was surprised myself, in no small measure, at how little he understood me.

I decided to explain. Sitting down on the sofa in front of a lively fire, I stared for a moment at my People's Choice award, standing solitary as the only trophy on the mantel. Then I bared my deepest fears to him.

"For you, it's different," I said, looking straight into his eyes. "You're working, and offers are piling up. But women actors have a very short shelf life. Acting is a relationship business more than anything. I need to be out there, seeing people, being seen by people, even if, at first, no one will invite us to the really glitzy parties."

He listened to every word I said with keen intensity, a hint of a frown lining his brow. I gave him a moment, encouraging him to interrupt, but he simply nodded.

"We can't afford to live in isolation, Adrian, no matter how much we both like it and think we need it. And it's not good for the soul, either. We're around people all week, I get that, but that's work. Just . . . open your heart and let some of these people in. I promise you won't regret it."

Without a word, he pulled his hand from mine and checked the time on his phone. Then he sprang to his feet, a look of excitement and determination in his eyes. "You're right. Do you think the Bernards would still welcome us now? We can still make the 4 p.m. flight."

On the short and almost empty flight over to LA, we got our stories straight. Then we spent Saturday night with our friends, having an excellent time, my tears forgotten. Lisa was there too, and I found that lying to her was the hardest thing I had to do that evening, but I couldn't tell her the real reason we were a day late.

Our first fight changed our relationship. We were no longer

just lovers; from that day on, we became partners. Each of us brought the other as our plus one to industry parties and events. Both of us carried headshots of the other in our portfolios, ready to slide on top of casting directors' heaps when no one was looking. Both of us put in good words with the directors and producers every chance we got.

Then, we had our evenings out, just for the two of us, and they were each a night to remember. Adrian outdid himself setting those up, thinking of new places we could go, even on a small budget. Sometimes, it would be sandwiches by the Hollywood sign after a hearty hike up Mount Lee. Other times, peanuts served from a supermarket jar, to go with beer chilled in a cooler bag, laid out on a blanket in Ascot Hills Park or El Matador State Beach, watching the sun set over the Pacific. He never ran out of ideas.

Then we'd go home, to the small Lexington Avenue apartment when Lisa was out, or to his studio rental in Universal City. I remember making passionate love with him, then spending hours talking, lying in each other's arms until we dozed off, spent and satisfied. My love for him deepened as our lives became more entwined, holding on to each other on our way up professionally, finding our place in the world holding hands. Our relationship evolved into a collaborative bond, fascinating and highly rewarding.

And a bit frightening.

I used to be afraid of losing him, back then. Remembering that stirs me, knowing I've lost him since. How did that happen? I still can't remember, or perhaps I'm afraid to open the drawer that hides such heartache. I'm drawn to it, though, eager to find out, even if I brace myself before urging my brain to cooperate and reveal its secrets.

Sifting through fragments of scattered memory, I try to find what I'm looking for. Instead, I hear that agent's raspy voice saying, "Take my advice, kid, sign this dotted line and the sky's the limit for Adrian Sera. Hell, women will line all around this block for a night with Adrian Sera." Then Adrian shouting angrily, "I don't want to hear it, Lyle. I won't do it."

Why wouldn't he sign the paperwork? He already had the role. The question buzzes through my mind unanswered, until the memory of Adrian's voice shifts into my own, screaming.

Help! Someone, help me . . . Let me go!

I see myself running, turning my head, and faltering, landing hard against the wall, then pushing myself away. I reach the door and try to open it, but can't. I fumble with the lock, and turn to look behind me again, just in time to see the arm raised above my head, ready to come down, while a look of pure hatred stares me in the eyes, terrifying, paralyzing.

I'm sick and tired of these invasive memories, or whatever the hell they're called. Nothing but pieces of mental garbage.

I'm about to doze off, when the word comes to me. It's *intrusive,* not invasive. I can remember this piece of entirely worthless information. I wish I remembered the important things, like who put me here, in this damn bed.

Was it Adrian? My paranoia gnaws at me. But it doesn't feel possible. Not in the depth of my heart. He was incapable of such violence.

Will I ever know? Perhaps the police will, one day, give me a call and tell me who it was. Tell me I'm safe.

The sound of raised voices arguing outside my door has me wincing. I try to catch what they're saying. Perhaps I'm about to find out, and I'm not ready for it.

Jasmine sounds defeated, while a man's bellowing voice draws closer to my door.

"—can't let you in, sir," Jasmine says. "You have to understand. My patient is resting. She's been sedated."

"I will initiate legal proceedings against your patient and you personally for impeding this process. What is your name? What's your role here?"

I breathe. It's not the killer, coming to wrap up the loose ends. But it's probably someone just as bad by the sound of it: Steve's attorney. Perry Sheldon was the name Dr. Sokolowski found in my messages. I still remember that.

"Jasmine," I call weakly. "It's okay. Let him in."

TWENTY-FIVE

Cold air clings to the man like a shroud, bringing the freshness of mountain winter inside my room, tainted by the scent of expensive aftershave and weathered leather. I can visualize him in my mind's eye: expensive suit, designer wool overcoat, and a leather briefcase matching the color of his Italian shoes. A few snowflakes, still clinging to the shoulders of his coat, melting quickly. I can't picture any colors; most people like him wear dark grays, so I'm willing to go with that, since it's all in my imagination anyway.

As for Perry Sheldon's face, I can't imagine anything.

"I'll take it from here," he says and waits, standing a few feet from my bed.

"Whatever," I hear Jasmine replying sarcastically. "But I'm right outside this door, so don't go doing anything to upset my patient."

When the door closes, the attorney starts pacing around the room, probably looking for something, although I can't be sure. This uncertainty scares me. All the cues I'm missing make me feel powerless.

After a few endless moments, I hear the chair being rolled

across the floor. "This will have to do," he mutters. Briefcase latches snap open. Something touches my leg through the covers, and I wince, wishing I could pull away, the thumping in my chest suffocating. Then I realize he must've set his briefcase down on the bed by my side.

"Mrs. Wellington, I was sent—"

"Duncan," I correct him coldly. "That's my name, Emma Duncan. Are you sure you have the right cripple to harass?"

"Oh, I apologize." He overly dramatizes the words, as if that's going to make me feel better. "Your husband—"

"Ex," I correct him again, wondering for a moment how he can function as an attorney if he routinely gets his facts wrong. Then I realize it's a tactic. To throw me off my game. "But you already know that, don't you?"

"Again, I have to apologize." The drama is now completely absent from his cold inflections. "Your ex-husband is quite concerned with your well-being, especially after the accident, and has asked me to speak with you."

I bite my lip, trying to stay quiet, but anger gets the best of me. "It wasn't an accident, and he knows that. He probably knows that quite well," I insinuate, but he doesn't take the bait. *Of course he doesn't.*

"Ms. Duncan, once again, I'm sorry for the confusion. I can tell this is a highly sensitive matter for you and I can appreciate why." He pauses for a moment, but I remain quiet, seething. "Your ex-husband believes, and I agree, that a conservatorship might be beneficial for you during your recovery. It's purely about ensuring your needs are met and your affairs are in order."

Conservatorship? I'm shocked. That's what he wanted the whole time. To take everything from me. *Oh, no. I can't let this happen.*

"Affairs in order? Isn't that something dying people are encouraged to do?" I reply, instead of telling him what I really think about his idea, or Steve's, or whoever the hell it was that came up with it.

"It's just a figure of speech, in our profession—"

"I'm still alive, Mr. Sheldon, and planning to stay that way. You're wasting your time." My voice is level and calm, but I feel like I'm suffocating. The heart monitor's beeping hastens, giving my unwanted guest insight into my state of mind.

"And Mr. Wellington wants nothing less for you than to recover without an undue burden from trivial matters such as paying the bills. A conservatorship would allow him—"

"—to take back the house he lost in the divorce. Yes, I know exactly what this is about."

Did Mikela put him up to this?

I still can't believe Steve would hurt me. Only he already did. For her.

Sheldon breaths deeply through his nose, probably infuriated by my resistance. "I understand why you might assume that. Conservatorship is a legal tool designed to assist those who are unable to manage their affairs. It's not about taking anything from you. The courts supervise this entire process, ensuring that your interests are protected."

I decide to hide my bitterness for a moment, desperate to know more, to have an inkling into Steve's real intentions, while an annoying thought buzzes through my mind.

Did you put me here, Steve? Was that you?

Faking a sigh, I stay silent for a long moment, as if considering the alternative. "How would this work, really?"

Some papers are rustled somewhere close to my left calf. "Mr. Wellington will assume responsibility for your care, with everything that entails, from medical decisions and expenses to managing your assets."

"Where would I live? Would he put me in one of those assisted living homes?"

He clears his throat, as if my question is making him

uncomfortable. As if he wishes I'd never asked that. "No. Absolutely not. Mr. Wellington has expressed his intention to take care of you himself, with specialized help, of course. He feels this is the best way to assist with a speedy recovery."

"Okay, but where? Where exactly would he do all that?"

A beat of tense silence. "In your own home, ma'am," he replies. "Mr. Wellington and his fiancée would move—"

"So, it *is* the house they're after, isn't it?" No answer from him. "Yeah, that makes sense. He wants my house, that's all he wants. For his mistress, pardon me, fiancée. I've always wondered how he'd go about it. Now I know."

He was willing to kill for it. He still is.

Perry Sheldon clears his voice again. I hear him shifting in his chair. I've made him uncomfortable.

Good.

"I can understand how you might think that's the case, but in fact, this is all about giving you the opportunity to restore your health without any worry. This process is court-supervised, and—"

"And what? I'm supposed to just trust this process? Trust *him,* after everything that's happened?"

"I'm not asking for blind trust, Ms. Duncan."

"I believe that's exactly what you're asking for, when you're asking for a whole lot of undeserved trust from a blind person."

"I—um, I apologize for the choice of words. It was unintentional, I can assure you."

I let him sweat it in silence. Sheldon is prepared to fight this, and I'm up to par, now that I know who tried to kill me.

"What I'm suggesting is a structure that could empower you to focus on recovery without the burden of managing—"

"That's the third way you've said exactly the same thing. I don't want to hear it anymore. Steve wants to move into my house with his new love interest. I get that. I didn't see it coming, but then again, I didn't see that little bitch coming either. Gee, I must be blind or something."

Perry Sheldon, attorney to Hollywood's somewhat famous, almost chokes with a frustrated sigh. His breath carries the faint smell of quality cigars toned down by breath mints. "The person appointed as your conservator could even be an independent third party, if you have concerns about—"

"Like who?"

For a moment, all I can hear is that little fly banging its head against the window.

"Well, Miss Mikela Murtagh has expressed—"

Rage is suffocating me. "Are you kidding me right now? Of course, she has 'expressed'! She can go express herself straight to hell."

"Ms. Duncan, there's no need for such language. These people want nothing but what's best for you, when you're clearly out of options. I would give their offer some consideration, especially when the alternative is to lose said property anyway, when you won't be able to make the mortgage payments on time."

The beeping of the machine surges as I struggle to settle down enough to see this through. "Let me make it very clear, Mr. Sheldon. Unless there's a court order, my ex and his fiancée are not welcome in my house. They would be trespassing, and will be dealt with as such. Do we understand each other?"

"I can see you're upset, Ms. Duncan, and I'm really sorry to do this to you, but believe me when I say it's for the best."

"Let me tell you something, Mr. Sheldon." I pause a moment, for dramatic effect. "I'm willing to die on this hill, because I have nothing else left to fight for. This is the only answer you'll get. Please convey to my darling Steve, with emphasis, my determination to do everything in my power to win this battle against you, him, her, or the entire world if I have to."

He stands and leans over the bed; I can hear his overcoat against my sheets. I can smell his aftershave. His breath touches my forearm when he latches his briefcase and picks it up. "I'm hoping you might reconsider this, once the shock of the idea has worn off."

The beeping is about to turn into one of those droning alarms I've grown so sick of. "And I'm hoping you'll get the hell out of here already, Mr. Sheldon. If you please."

He walks away with slow, determined steps that pound into the floor, but doesn't make it to the door before someone enters the room.

I wait, every muscle tense. Is it Steve?

"You need to leave." It's Dr. Sokolowski. I breathe again. "Right now."

"Who are you?" Sheldon asks, his voice high and aggrieved.

"I'm Dr. Sokolowski, the attending physician in charge of Ms. Duncan's care."

"Interesting. Who's paying for all this?"

Exactly the same question Steve asked.

Why do they care?

I'm terrified at the thought of the medical bills I'm incurring; they're mine to pay. But what's up with them?

"Insurance." The one-word answer is delivered in an icy-cold voice, fading into the distance as the doctor walks the lawyer out.

"Insurance? From where?"

"From none of your business."

An argument ensues, but it's out of earshot, and I can't make out much of what's being said. The voices clash for a while, then a door is slammed shut so forcefully a window rattles somewhere in my room.

But I barely notice it. That slammed door sounds familiar, bringing a chill to my spine as a memory flickers in my mind.

It doesn't make any sense.

For a few minutes, I keep waiting for Dr. Sokolowski to return, but he doesn't.

I'm alone again. The beeping of that annoying machine is slowing down a little, and I can breathe better. But the events of the day have left me drained, dizzy, and nauseous. Too weak to fight it, I turn my attention inward, replaying the sound of that door in my mind, over and over, hoping I'll figure out why it sounds so familiar.

I can't place it. Mostly because the sound of Steve's voice intrudes in my thoughts. "I'll destroy you, Emma! To think I was ever in love with you . . . it makes me sick." Then, later, after the divorce was finalized, the deathly glare he gave me along with the house keys, right there, in front of the judge.

There isn't a shred of doubt left in my mind.

My ex-husband tried to kill me. After what happened today, I'm sure he'll try again.

I must tell somebody about it. I need to call that detective.

TWENTY-SIX

I must have dozed off with that thought, waiting for someone
to come by so I could ask them to make that call. In my restless
dream, I was running through the long hospital corridors, all dark
and empty, just my steps echoing in the eerie silence. Then the
PA came to life. "Code blue, room 1204," it announced, and I
froze, looking around, trying to read the numbers on the many
closed doors.

All the rooms were labeled 1204.

Including mine.

I looked into one of the rooms and saw myself lying on the
bed, a swath of white gauze wrapped around my head. The
heart monitor was droning steadily, its screen blinking red
numbers—mostly zeroes—and a steady green line where the
rhythm of my heart should've been. Two people, a man and a
woman, both wearing scrubs, moved quickly and almost word-
lessly around the bed. Injecting something into my vein. Pulling off the covers. Lowering the head of my bed until it was flat.
Rolling the defibrillator cart and readying the paddles, a silent
hum of electricity as they charged. Then a jolt, and I saw stars,

a rush of stars coursing through my blood, my brain, my entire being.

Startled awake, I exhale slowly, trying to get a sense of my surroundings. I can't hear anyone else in the room; the only breathing is mine. But in the depths of my mind, the sound of that slammed door still plays over and over like a broken record.

Why would anyone slam a door inside a hospital? Didn't Perry Sheldon realize he was disturbing people's rest?

My fingers start their workout while my mind still wanders, stuck on the stupid door. As my hands travel up and down the fleecy cover, a little faster today, I ask myself a different question. One I should've asked myself already. One that freezes the blood in my veins.

What door?

I haven't seen that many swinging doors in hospitals, and none that anyone can slam. Most of them are sliding, some automatic, with motion sensors making them open whenever anyone approaches and close when they're gone. But it's been a while since I've been inside a hospital, before this happened to me. Years, really. Who knows how things are these days at Baldwin Memorial Hospital in Lake Tahoe? That must be where they took me. It's the closest trauma center to my house.

In the distance, a phone rings and no one takes the call. My mind drifts, remembering the unsettling dream. I can still feel the effects of all the meds they've been pumping into me, lurking in my brain after I wake, holding me hostage in a state of permanent confusion. Every time I wake up I feel like this: infuriatingly slow, my brain engulfed in fog, my memories mangled together in a jumbled narrative I cannot call reality.

It's hell.

And still, the memory of that dream persists. My foggy mind picks on that PA announcement and plays it like a song I partly recall the lyrics to. How many times have I heard the code blue announcement? How many people have died in these rooms, their resuscitation efforts failed? I don't have an answer to that. It feels like I've heard it a few times, but what do I really remember?

Has it always been room 1204? No, that's just a stupid dream.

But the announcement I play in my head doesn't work with other room numbers. Doesn't ring familiar. I try it for the heck of it, whispering to myself. "Code blue, room 1203." I'm sure I've never heard that before. "Code blue, room 1211." Still not a fit. The tune in my head goes with 1204, and 1204 only.

I challenge myself to remember, to understand, riling myself up into a senseless frenzy. It doesn't make any difference what I think I remember when it's not at all reliable. When I can't make any sense of my own thoughts. Just as I bring my hands together over my chest, fingers entwined for a brief moment of respite, the PA system goes off.

"Dr. Parrish to the nurses' station," the automated voice calls.

Breath catches in my lungs. The only sound I hear for a while is the thumping of my heart.

Was Dr. Parrish ever called elsewhere but the nurses' station? I just can't remember, and I wish my stubborn brain would let go of this already.

But it doesn't, because it's hardwired to finish things. That's why people get earworms, those catchy pieces of music that stick in their heads. There's a simple solution. Just listen to the entire song. It's stuck in your mind because the brain can't finish the song, doesn't know how it really ends.

My earworm is a song made of PA announcements. Code blue is in 1204, it seems, and Dr. Parrish is summoned to the nurses' station. But what comes right after the code blue? Dr. Parrish? Or someone else?

I play the sequence tentatively in my mind, and it doesn't fit.

But Dr. Jones fits. He or she is needed in the ICU, from what I can recall.

Then an ambulance pulls in.

After a while, a couple of nurses chat about some dude named George, and debate where they should go for lunch. Their voices are young and carefree, they giggle as they talk, and lower their voices when this George comes up. How many times have I heard them chat? I don't know. I just don't.

But only after the issue of lunch is addressed does Dr. Parrish get called to the nurses' station.

As I keep diving into the rabbit hole, I feel dizzier, sick, about to throw up and faint at the same time. In what world does any of this make any sense? What if I've never heard these things the way I think I did? What if I'm not remembering correctly? Perhaps Dr. Parrish was only called once the entire time I've been here. Just like I dreamed about the code blue, I could've dreamed about all the other stuff.

My hands are trembling, frozen by the chill that won't leave my body. What can I do to find out? To be sure? If I start asking people, they'll think me insane. Worse, they'll up my meds again, and I'll never emerge from the abyss.

But how can I be sure?

I'm going insane on a whole new level.

Unless I can remember what came after Dr. Parrish in this twisted, deeply disturbing earworm of mine.

Out of the storm of shattered thoughts, a memory emerges, a fond and cherished one. My favorite professor at UCLA, himself a method actor who used to be famous before a car crash ended his acting career, taught his students to think of the lines in the script like a melody, a song we had to sing, with sadness or joy, with gusto or *andante,* making the part easier to remember and act.

The PA calls were a song too, one stuck in my brain on the frayed edge between reality and dream, between shattered, blurry memories and real nightmares. And in that song, after playing it again in my mind, I'm sure that the next PA announcement should be Dr. Whitting, called to the emergency room.

Unless I'm completely crazy, and I've imagined the entire thing.

I start waiting for that announcement to come. Or not come.

I don't know what's scarier.

But if I'm not crazy, and the next announcement confirms my theory, what does that really mean? In which reality would that make sense?

"I don't know," I whisper to myself. "Whatever it is, please don't let it be Dr. Whitting. And not to the bloody emergency room."

I'm almost asleep, drowsy like I usually am, an easy prey to my demons. A new nightmare is starting to take shape when the PA system chimes and the robotic voice makes its announcement.

"Dr. Whitting to the emergency room."

Panic overtakes me in an overwhelming wave of irrationality. *Am I losing my mind? Am I imagining this? How can it be real?*

The beeping of the machine seems distant and fading. The only sound I can hear is the rush of my own blood, drowning out everything else.

A faint cry leaves my lips, then gains strength and turns into a desperate question.

"Where am I?"

TWENTY-SEVEN

I hate to see my Emma agitated. It makes me feel powerless, and powerless I am not. Staring at her lovely face, I can't help gritting my teeth. I'm aching to give that Perry Sheldon the "accident" he so badly deserves. The road he's about to take is a winding road across Mount Rose, stunningly beautiful this time of year, also treacherous and slippery in places. He rented a Mercedes-Benz at the airport, black and upgraded, because nothing else would've been a fit with his self-assured, entitled persona.

I don't believe that Benz would do that well on icy roads. No rear-wheel-drive vehicles ever do. It would be a slice to send that asshole over the railing, tumbling into a steep ravine and making one hell of a bonfire. It would take some doing, figuring out how to mess with that car without leaving any traces, but the point is moot, so to speak in lawyer lingo. He's gone.

He's probably going to return. And still, I won't touch a hair on his balding head.

I'm a rational man, or so I like to believe. It carries too much risk to start cleaning up all the trash that surrounds Emma's life. People might notice. Law enforcement people.

I know the cops are searching for me. They've been looking for a while, and I knew that was going to happen. Emma called them. Every time I let her see me, she became increasingly afraid of me. Sometimes, after such an encounter, she called them again. Begged them to keep her safe.

From me.

That's hilarious.

One time, a few months ago, she came straight at me, angry as hell, looking for a direct confrontation, my recklessly brave girl. I wasn't ready for it, for our moment of truth. I didn't have the right words to say to her. So, I ran, barely had time to disappear behind someone's RV and wait for her to give up looking for me.

That night, she didn't call the police again. She just gave up, her voice brittle, her anger turned inward into bitter tears.

Nevertheless, I don't want cops near my Emma. If people connected with her start experiencing a shortened life expectancy, they'd start swarming, and they'd probably find me then.

I'm right here. Always. Close to her, wherever she is.

That's why I decided, regretfully, to let that bastard drive off in his rental Benz undisturbed. I'm sure he made it to the airport in one piece. Later, though, when enough time has passed to obliterate his connection to Emma, I might pay him a visit. He so dearly deserves it.

I know all about him.

He's no ambulance-chaser, Mr. Sheldon. He's got offices on Sunset Boulevard, and represents some well-known names, but mostly B-graders, not A-listers. I'm sure he wants to make it to the A-list club, but he's not there yet. Which makes him dangerous, because he's so close to the prize he can taste it. He's willing to do anything for it. His nose flares when he's interviewed in the local media about some case or another. He always speaks of the settlements he got for his clients in tabloid-worthy divorces, and *his mouth always curls up a certain way when he pronounces, "millions," with the enchanted enjoyment of one tasting a good dessert. I'm sure his percentage isn't too shabby either. He lives in Thousand Oaks, somewhere up on the hills, in a sprawling house on an oversized lot, kept private from the public's eye behind thick boxwood hedges.*

I like to look at what people are choosing to drive. It tells me lots about who they are, what matters to them. This particular attorney drives a Land Rover. Not a Lexus, as I would've expected, based on his profession's statistics; not a Porsche either, reserved for people who want to make an immediate and lasting impression. A Land Rover. Perry Sheldon is headstrong and completely self-absorbed. He probably sped twenty over the limit the entire trip to the airport, just because he could. He's focused on appearances more than anything. A stickler for convention, and loyal only to the highest bidder.

That said, I'm a bit wary of him. He could be dangerous. His kind often are. He knows Emma is vulnerable right now, out of reasonable options to manage her life, and he's brutally pushing Wellington's agenda. Emma probably doesn't know that this was Perry Sheldon being nice. He could easily turn and file for conservatorship against Emma's will, and probably make it happen.

Things will have to change quickly around here.

But Perry Sheldon isn't the root cause of some evil either, because he was only hired to do another man's bidding.

Steve Wellington is that root cause. I'll take care of him first.

TWENTY-EIGHT

No one answers.

It becomes clear to me, after a while, that no one can hear my cries. No one will rush over and help me fight my demons, not unless I code again. Not unless that machine by my bedside breaks out in all sorts of dissonant tones.

So, I wait. And all I can do is think, while my panic is still strong, numbing my limbs. I'm struggling to stay alert, awake, ready to fight for my life. Despite the terrified thumping in my chest, drowsiness creeps up on me, sticky like molasses, a death trap.

I can barely keep fighting it as the memory of my anguish starts fading away.

What *did* just happen? I knew what PA announcement came next? Well, I've been here for a while, right? Or perhaps I knew it just how sometimes I know what song will play next on the radio. Once I listen to something for long enough, I could assume I know what's coming next. But I'd be wrong.

I have to be. The thought brings peace to my weary mind. I must be wrong, because nothing else makes sense. And Steve . . .

I should tell the police about Steve. He wants my house. With those thoughts, I slip into a deep slumber that resembles unconsciousness.

When I wake, I hear someone by the bed. In that split second, panic rises like bile in my throat. I will myself deathly still, while I listen intently. But it's not a sound that brings me the answer; it's a smell. A hint of basil and leather and spice, so faint it's barely there.

Dr. Sokolowski.

"Good evening," he says, as soon as I make the tiniest move. His clothes rustle and give a whiff of fresh laundry and disinfectant. "How are you feeling?"

For a moment, I can't find my words. "Where am I?"

"You're at home, of course."

The casual words resonate strangely in my mind, as if they belong to an alternate reality. I can't be at home. I'm in the hospital. "What do you mean?" Fear quickly overwhelms me, and that annoying machine gives me away.

I sense Dr. Sokolowski's gloved hand squeezing mine. "The hospital released you into the care of your husband."

"What? No!" Those few words light a fire inside my brain. "We're not married anymore! He's not my husband. I told you I didn't want to see him again!" I pause, afraid of what he might say. "I did tell you, right? I didn't dream it?"

"No, you told me, that's correct. Let's see what happened." He stands—and with a nightmarish feel to it, there's the sound of a chair rolling away from the bed. When he walks to the foot of the bed and takes the chart, the plastic clipboard rattles against the bed frame.

I know this noise. Nothing in my house sounds like that. I can't be at home.

Papers rustle as the doctor reviews the chart, looking for something. I have so many questions, each more terrifying than the next.

"He was listed as your next of kin. A Mr. Steven Wellington."

"He's the man I told you to keep away."

"I am so sorry, Emma." He sounds genuinely embarrassed. "I know you told me, but the hospital didn't check my notes. It's right here, in the chart."

"How did it happen?" I ask, more as a desperate wail than an actual question I'm expecting an answer to.

"The hospital's procedure is to locate the next of kin and ask them to accept responsibility. Mr. Wellington accepted, and they discharged you into his care."

"So, I'm at home? In my house?"

"Yes. Pine Street, in Lake Tahoe. In the master bedroom."

My mouth gapes open. "How can this be? Everything is the same as the hospital. The bed. This ... machine that beeps, the chair on wheels—" A sob rips through my chest. This can't be true. It's a nightmare, and I'll wake up soon.

"Mr. Wellington arranged with the hospital to rent some equipment, to continue with the standard of care we provided for you at Baldwin Memorial. The chair is part of the equipment that was leased; it comes with the crash cart." He touches my hand gently. "I see you're concerned about this. You don't remember the move?"

"No. I don't remember anything! I just—when did you move me?"

He leans forward and rolls up my left sleeve, then checks my patch. "I wasn't there, personally, or I would've said something, knowing you expressed concern about your ex-husband. They moved you yesterday morning." He changes the patch with quick, expert gestures. The fresh patch gives me a chill. "You might've been asleep through all that."

Yesterday! The slammed door ... it was my front door. That's why the sound was so familiar. Steve had slammed that door hard enough to put a crack in the wall.

And that's why Perry Sheldon visited. I'd already been discharged into Steve's care, and the asshole hadn't bothered to mention that.

What am I going to do?

"So, it's the same bed as before?" I'm starting to understand what happened. With that understanding, my panic recedes somewhat, although it leaves behind tidepools of fearful thoughts. But things don't seem surreal anymore, except the part about Steve being in this house again, looking to strip me of my rights. With *her.* After he tried to kill me.

"It's not exactly the same bed. They took one out of storage, I guess. It's only slightly different. You can't tell, but the side rails are more rounded and have integrated controls. The heart monitor, the crash cart and the chair are exactly the same."

Silence fills the room for a while, barring the beeping. Dr. Sokolowski is jotting down something in my chart; he presses on the pen forcefully; I can hear it scratching the paper. Then the chart rattles against the bed frame, back in its usual place.

"How about the nurses?" I swallow with difficulty. My throat is dry. "And how about you?"

"Well, Baldwin Memorial is only ten minutes away." There's a draft of air as he lifts the blanket off my feet and checks my reflexes. "The hospital administrator has agreed to provide temporary assistance, while Mr. Wellington sorts out the details of your care. I will see you twice a day, mornings and evenings, right after my hospital rounds. The nurses will rotate through shifts, to handle your meals and administer your medication." He moves to one elbow and gives it two quick taps. It still feels numb. "And if there's an emergency, I will be paged immediately."

I do my best to stay calm. I can't imagine going through this without Dr. Sokolowski. If he's gone . . . I don't know what I'm going to do.

"Emma . . . it will be all right."

"Is it still going to be Jasmine? And Isabella?" My voice trembles pitifully. "Or did I lose them too?"

The hand squeeze returns. This time I relish the contact, the warmth of his touch. I cling to it mentally as if his hand is a life saver thrown my way.

"Sometimes, the mind plays tricks on people with a traumatic brain injury, filling the gaps with what would feel plausible." He pauses for a moment. "It hasn't been Isabella in a long time. Your medication, Versed specifically, can make you a bit foggy in the mornings."

"I noticed." The reply comes weakly, while I'm still struggling to process.

"Things will improve faster, now that we're weaning you off the Decadron. Your brain swelling has subsided almost entirely. You're doing great."

"I thought it was always Jasmine. And Isabella. I can't believe it's been so long since she's been here."

I can't count on anything that comes out of this fractured mind. I can't trust myself.

"Some such issues are to be expected," he says, as if reading my mind. "Don't think too much about it. It will pass."

My fingers squeeze his lightly. "I'm terrified. I can't count on anything I notice, and the people I thought I recognized were, in fact, complete strangers." I pause for a moment and bite my chapped lips, hesitating. "I'm not safe here. It was Steve. He tried to kill me."

"Emma, you're not alone," he says, standing and letting go. My time with him is coming to an end. "Are you sure you remember correctly? We can call that detective if you're ready to make a formal statement."

It's what I've wanted to do since I realized it was Steve, and yet now that the possibility is here, I shy away. How can I be sure of anything? When I still can't see his face clearly in my memories?

"Don't leave me here," I whisper. "Not with him. I can't trust myself to remember clearly, but what if it was Steve? He'll try again, I know he will."

A tense breath of air leaves the doctor's lungs. "This is a serious concern. There's also the issue of the next of kin being out of date, and your specific instructions regarding your ex. Let me take this back to the hospital and discuss it all with administration right now. We might have some options."

"Until then?"

"I don't believe you're in immediate danger. He'd be a fool to try something right after you were brought here. But I'll work on this as quickly as I can, I promise."

He takes a few steps toward the door, when I ask, "What about the PA calls? How can that happen if I'm at home?"

He returns to my bedside. "What PA calls?"

My heart skips a beat.

"I've been hearing things like, 'Dr. Jones to ICU', or 'Dr. Whitting to the emergency room'. I'm quite sure I heard those today, earlier, before I dozed off, as if I were still in the hospital. How can that be?"

A long moment of silence, the kind I've learned to fear. "Emma, you wouldn't hear the emergency PA system from your hospital room. It's rarely used outside of the ER. Now we have mobile phones, and there's no need to disturb the patients when someone needs to report somewhere." He pauses, while my thoughts are racing desperately. "I'll ask for a psychiatry consult. Sometimes, TBI patients develop hallucinations that could be early indicators of post-traumatic psychosis."

"No..." I feel as if I'm sinking deep into an endless chasm that's about to swallow me whole.

"Don't worry about it, all right?" He pats my forearm, then quickly retreats. "Whatever it is, we'll help you."

His words fade in the distance, while my thoughts keep racing.

Psychosis? Hallucinations?

It explains why I never heard those PA calls when other people were in my room. Because they weren't real.

I *am* losing my mind.

TWENTY-NINE

I dreamed of Adrian.

As I slowly awaken, drowsiness refusing to be satisfied with the sleep I have had, I can't help lingering in the memory of that dream.

I don't want to let it go; it felt so real.

At first, it was a good dream, of our days working together, being together, a smooth and blissful sailing through a fairy-tale romance. Then the dream shifted to a horrifying scene where Adrian was calling my name, and I couldn't answer. His voice was riddled with fear, as if he was trying to warn me about something, while I was opening my mouth, his name on my lips, but no sound was coming out. I was lying flat on my back, staring at a large, bright ceiling lamp with a circle of bulbs, seven I believe. I could see that light, and it was terrifying—not how I'd imagined seeing light again would be. But it was a dream, and I couldn't do anything under those powerful lights but shiver, my skin prickling with goose bumps as if the wind were touching it.

That sensory, scary part of the dream I hate. But the earlier part, where I could feel Adrian's love warming my heart, I want to relive. It carried the promise of unveiling a new chapter of my forgotten past, if I followed the thread wherever it took me.

As I start remembering, the sense of loss deepens, slicing through my heart with unspeakable pain. We used to be so happy. What happened to us? I still don't remember how we came to part ways, but I'm starting to recall more and more about who we used to be. Perhaps, at the end of this journey through blurry memories, I'll find the answer I'm looking for.

At that weekend birthday party at the Bernards, Adrian's career got a shot in the arm from a television producer who seemed to enjoy chatting with him, while I wandered and mingled, a smile on my face, a glass of champagne in my hand. People were polite, yet uninterested, most of them laser-focused on their own agendas. Despite my best efforts, I still carried the stigma of having divorced Steve Wellington.

Adrian signed a new deal with that producer the week after the party, and started working the week after that. He tried to push my name for that show, but it didn't take. The female roles were already assigned, and contracts already drawn up. I went back to auditioning and staying home when I wasn't working, and taking the weekend shifts at the Black Bear in Tahoe, just because I wanted to go home every now and then—not that it made a whole lot of sense to keep going there, when my entire life was in Los Angeles.

Still, I resisted the idea of getting a house in LA. When Lisa was on location, we stayed at the Lexington apartment. But Adrian steered clear of her for some reason. The weekends she used to spend in Tahoe with me became rare occurrences, because Adrian needed his rest and wanted us to be alone; to do whatever we wanted in that house, to make love in every corner of it, to lie naked in front of the fire. None of that could happen with Lisa visiting. Though I regretted my lost girlfriend time, I caved to his insistence. It felt good to overwrite the history of that house.

Lisa made it easy for me and stopped coming. She must've sensed my hesitation whenever she mentioned she had the weekend off and it was ski season in Tahoe again, or that it was the perfect weather to hike the lake shore.

About a couple of months after the Bernard party, we were invited to another mixer at the home of a relatively obscure film producer. This time, Steve and Miki were there. My step faltered when I locked eyes with Steve as I entered the fancy backyard. The place was delightful, lit with warm white bulbs on ropes that zigzagged between palm trees, yet all I could see was my ex. Adrian held my arm, and I could feel him stiffening at my side.

As for Mikela, she was attached to Steve like ivy—clinging and parasitical. She wore a sequin halter neck in sheer silver mesh, leaving very little to the imagination. Her thigh emerged through a high slit, and she made sure it did, keeping her left leg a little flexed and to the side. It worked. Not many men, except for my Adrian, had eyes for anyone else but her.

I wanted to leave as soon as possible, although Adrian and I had debated extensively how we would handle the eventual interaction with my ex. We knew it would happen; we all worked in the same industry. Filmmaking is a small world, more like an incestuous bedroom community, full of gossip and sin and political maneuvering.

Restless, I tugged at Adrian's arm and looked pleadingly into his eyes.

"The hell if we will," he whispered back, his voice firm despite his charming smile. "We have no reason to back out when Steve Wellington makes an appearance. Not if you want to work again in this town."

He was right. We stayed, but the evening seemed to drag on forever, while people gravitated around Steve and Miki the way they used to do around me and him when we were married.

Occasionally, Miki gave Adrian a provocative look, but he only glared at her and shifted his gaze. And both men did their best to keep at least twenty feet of distance between them, at all times.

For a while, things were peaceful, manageable, and I started to relax just a little bit. We ate delicious hors-d'oeuvres, and drank enough champagne to feel a light buzz. With Adrian by my side, mingling was an easier task. His handsome looks and charismatic personality drew attention and interest. After a couple of hours of working the crowd, we decided to have some fun for ourselves.

It didn't last long.

Adrian and I were dancing to the host's amazing collection of rock ballads, lost in each other, when Miki's voice came into earshot.

"... don't think she'll amount to too much as an actress," she was saying. "Her entire value expired when she left Steve's bed." An unforgiving roar of laughter ensued, but I couldn't see who was there as my back was turned to her.

I recall wishing the earth would split open and swallow me right there and then.

Adrian stopped dancing and turned to stone, his muscles tense, his eyes glinting with rage. He walked over to Steve, while I tugged at his arm unsuccessfully, trying to hold him back. "Do you agree with that statement, Steve?" he asked politely.

I held my breath, knowing Adrian's apparent calm was thinner and more fragile than a snowflake falling on a summer day.

Steve looked at me, seeming a little embarrassed. He seemed inebriated, a rather rare occurrence in the composed and disciplined man I knew him to be. His face was red and his eyes a touch glassy. Seeming a bit dizzy, he turned to Adrian. He patted him on the arm and smiled. "Nobody meant any harm. All right, sport?"

Adrian didn't budge; he just glared at Steve's hand on his arm until Steve pulled away, taking a faltering step back. "Do you agree with her, Steve? Yes or no should suffice."

The crowd around us had stopped talking and were gathered in a thick circle. The music playing in the background had been turned down a notch. I tugged at Adrian's arm again, holding on to it with both hands, but he didn't even look at me. His eyes were drilling into Steve's, both men locked in a wordless and motionless battle of wills. Miki was staring at Steve, her glossed lips pressed tightly together and her four-inch-heel tapping nervously against the granite pavers, as if expecting him to do something or say something to please her. To take her side.

"No," Steve eventually said, his baritone voice level and menacing. "I don't agree."

Adrian nodded, and for a moment, I thought the crisis was over. I was wrong.

"Well, then, I suggest you muzzle your bitch."

A split moment of shocked silence, then the gathering gasped in unison, Miki's voice higher than everyone else's.

Steve's fist came toward Adrian's jaw, but he pulled to the side nimbly and Steve missed. A second punch, aiming for his jaw again, went the same way.

"You son of a bitch," Steve muttered. His face was splotchy and red, his eyes fixed on Adrian with a deathly scowl.

"Adrian, please," I whispered, knowing it wouldn't take much longer before he struck back and decked Steve with one blow. "It's not worth it."

He scoffed with a cynical, lopsided smile as he sidestepped a third punch. A couple of guests came to hold a hollering Steve back. He was disfigured, his face scrunched in rage, his hair in disarray. I'd never seen him like that.

Adrian put his hands up in a pacifying gesture. "No need for blood here today, but an apology would be nice."

"Yeah? Not gonna fucking happen, asshole," Miki shouted, pouncing on Adrian and trying to claw at his face. Someone held her back too, while we walked away slowly, leaving the upsetting ruckus behind with as much dignity as I could muster.

Adrian apologized to our host, who seemed quite uncomfortable at first and didn't know what to say, but ended up shaking his hand. They even half-hugged, the way men do, and patted each other's backs, while I waited, feeling dozens of merciless eyeballs on me.

I knew this little piece of sordid gossip would be on everyone's lips by tomorrow. But I didn't think any less of Adrian for it. He had defended me, and, although I didn't feel I needed to be defended by any man, I felt loved and cherished. Protected.

Perhaps Adrian knew about Steve from that day on. Maybe he'd seen who he could be, way before I had a chance. The violence in him, when rage fueled his inner fire and brought his blood to the boiling point. That was new to me.

Do I think it was Steve who attacked me? Yes, wholeheartedly. I *know* he put me in this bed and destroyed my life with one swift, rage-filled blow. It feels right, even if the face in my memory of the attack is still hidden.

My sense of safety is gone, knowing that I'm at home now, and that in this home, Steve can come and go as he pleases. I can't do anything to defend myself. There are no medical personnel around, there's no security, no screening of visitors at the entrance. I'm just as vulnerable as I was the night I was attacked; even more so, because now I can't run. If Steve wants to kill me, he can, and I won't see him coming.

I wish Adrian were here, by my side, ready to strike him down with one punch, the way he was that night. He used to be my knight in shining armor, and I, his damsel, but not in distress. That fairy tale fell apart somehow, the reason still lost in the persistent fog of my broken memory.

Well, I'm in distress now, but my knight isn't here.

I do recall the way Adrian was calling my name in that dream, the sense of urgency in his voice, the despair. As if I were about to fall off a cliff, and he was too far away to bring me back to safety.

He's too far away now. Gone from my life. Lisa told me we broke up months ago.

And no one will believe me about Steve. Not after Dr. Sokolowski wrote a psychosis diagnosis on my chart.

THIRTY

Despite all the meds making me drowsy, I can't sleep. I'm too afraid to let myself fall asleep deeply. I just doze off, only to immediately startle awake. Then I listen hard, and if the silence is perfect except for those annoying heart monitor beeps, I doze off again.

For a minute or two.

Now the silence isn't perfect. Voices, at first unrecognizable, are drawing closer until I can catch what they're saying. And who's saying it.

The pleasant, slightly raspy voice belongs to Jasmine. The baritone is Steve. And the screeching, fake-friendly one is Mikela.

"Don't worry, sir," Jasmine is saying. "I will let you know as soon as that happens."

"You're amazing, Miss Jasmine," Steve purrs. I bet he's looking her in the eye right now, making her blush, the manipulative bastard. "I'm immensely grateful to you for all your hard work taking care of our poor Emma. What would I do without you?"

Jasmine laughs quietly, flattered. "Let's hope we don't have to find out, right?"

There's the sound of the door to my room opening and Jasmine's, "There you go."

She lets them in.

It was her all along.

I can see it now. She's the only nurse who was with me every day. I'm sure Steve made it worth her while to do any amount of overtime just to keep an eye on me and make things easy for him. She knows I don't have anyone to take care of me, because I told her as much. I'm sure she ran to him and filled him in, to earn her prize. I wonder how much she sold me for.

"I'll leave you to it, Mr. Wellington, but I'm right outside if you need me," the traitor says, before closing the door.

I wince, listening to them approaching, knowing what they want.

Damn them both to hell. If there's any shred of hope I can still win this battle, I will, I tell myself, then I wait. I don't say a word; I just wait for darling Steve to show his hand.

When he does, his voice is seething. "Emma. I know you're not sleeping, so why don't we cut the act?"

Son of a bitch. "I'd open my eyes for you, to show you I'm awake, but I'm afraid that won't be possible. I do apologize." My sarcasm is thick, merciless.

Miki scoffs in the background, farther from the bed, toward the window somewhere. "Unbelievable," she mutters.

Steve approaches with a firm gait and stops uncomfortably close to my bed. I can feel his breath on my face, distant, but close enough to sense. The head of my bed is elevated, and I'm propped on some pillows, but I still feel small, powerless, with a man looming over me like that.

He breathes sharply. I can tell he's angry. "Perry Sheldon's visit was your opportunity to do this with some civility, Emma. The only opportunity you'll get. You're ungrateful and selfish, and you're refusing to take the one helping hand that anyone's extending your way right now." He paces in place, almost stomping his feet against the floor. "I happen to know you don't have any other options left, not unless you want to go live with your sick mother, back in Lubbock."

Damn him for mentioning her. If he tells her anything, if he calls and harasses her, I'll kill him.

I steady myself, thinking of the stupid machine next to me that gives away my emotional state to the enemy, on a platter.

"Steve, this is not your house anymore. Accept it, and stop trespassing."

"Emma, this is ridiculous! I'm not trespassing. I'm offering you a way out of the mess you're in. You can't help yourself. Can't feed yourself, can't do anything without help. Your recovery could last—"

"Steve, this won't be your house ever again, for as long as I live. Do you understand? I'd rather set it on fire with me in it."

"Well, then, it's great that you can't even light a match, isn't it?" Mikela intervenes, walking quickly across the room in loud-clacking stilettos.

"Miki," Steve says quietly. "That's enough."

"Whatever," she throws, walking away slowly. She's probably inspecting her fingernails, and possibly chewing gum.

"Emma, please be reasonable." Steve takes my hand. I struggle to pull away and he eventually breaks contact. "I still have strong feelings for you. No one's taking your house, I promise. But what else could we do? Move you with all this stuff over to LA? You have your people here—nurses, doctors, everyone who's been caring for you since this happened."

For a split second, I believe him. I forget what he did, and only remember how much he used to mean to me. How much I used to trust him. Then anger rises inside me like a wave.

"Nothing *happened,* Steve. *You* put me here, in this godforsaken bed. You—"

He takes a step back, so suddenly it shifts the air around him. "Emma, are you crazy?"

"You already tried to kill me once, you son of a bitch. I'm just wondering when you'll try it again. But even so, the house won't be yours. I've spoken to people about this." As I say the words, I realize I must do that. Make some sort of will.

Mikela curses under her breath. "She's batshit crazy, Steve. Let's go. I have a two o'clock facial at the Zalanta."

Steve ignores her. "Who did you speak to, Emma? You know this isn't right. I'd never hurt you. We were married for years, and I never raised a finger to you. How could you possibly believe that?"

"I *know* it was you, Steve." My voice is losing steam; I'm exhausted and drowsy and can't keep going at it for as long as he can. I'm not strong enough. "I remember it clearly." Lying comes easily to me, the only weapon I have left.

He slaps something and I wince. Must've been his own forehead, in his signature gesture of frustration, one I remember well. "I thought we could reason with you, but you do have a traumatic brain injury, so it's only logical you're confused."

I can't think of anything to say. As always, he twists things around with the same brilliance he has as a film director, when he knows how to shift the camera to show a completely different picture.

"Honestly, the more unhinged you appear in front of the judge, the easier it will be to obtain the conservatorship."

I gasp silently. He is relentless, I'll give him that.

I thought I was getting somewhere, but he's too determined and resourceful. Some of the things I loved the most about him are the ones hurting me now.

"Face it," he says, starting to pace again next to the bed, slowly, methodically, probably thinking and planning his next steps. "There's nothing you can do to avoid this. You'll thank me later, when you get back on your feet and you still have a place to live and a career you'll be able to pick up where you left it." He pauses for a moment, while my thoughts are racing, desperate to find a way out of the trap he's laid open in front of me.

"I'll be fine, Steve. Please, don't worry about me. Your obligations to me ceased the day you signed the divorce papers. You should've stayed away."

"Emma, there's no one else to take care of you. Do you understand that? You'll run out of money, then what? Live off residuals?" He scoffs, and I bet he makes a dismissive hand gesture, like he always used to do to underline his contempt. "How much did you make last year? Ten grand, if even?" His pacing stops next to the bed; he's close enough for me to pick up the scent of his aftershave, mixed in with leftover traces of Miki's sickly-sweet floral perfume.

"I'll be fine. And I'd like you to leave now. You tried to kill me, Steve. Pardon me for not wanting your company."

"Jeez, Emma! You'll end up on the street, and I'll buy the house from underneath you! In foreclosure, for cheap. You won't see a dime from it."

All I hear for a while is my own blood rushing to my head, until Miki's clacking heels draw close to the foot of my bed. Plastic clatters on plastic, then some papers rustle.

The bitch is reading my chart.

She breaks out in a bout of harsh laughter. "Stop wasting your time, babe. Says here hallucinations and post-traumatic psychosis. I told you she belongs in the loony bin. No one's gonna believe shit."

"I know what I remember," I say, as strongly as I can. "Get the hell out of my house."

The door opens, and Dr. Sokolowski's voice carries over Miki's continuing laughter. "Mr. Wellington, a word, please."

Steve walks out and closes the door behind him. No matter

how hard I try, I can't hear anything that's being said outside; only tense, loaded whispering.

"You have no idea how easy it was to replace you." Miki's minty breath lands on my face, then her acrylic nails trace my cheek, lightly, but I'm screaming inside. I don't want her touching me. I can't do anything about it.

"Poor Steve was craving some decent sex for a change, ya know? He wasn't getting any of that from you, was he?"

The tip of a long fingernail tugs at the corner of my mouth and I lie there, taking it, unable to move. The best I can do is turn my head away a little. Not enough to escape her.

Her breath is now touching my ear, prickling the skin on my neck, raising my hackles. "But I *want* this house, you see? Don't fool yourself . . . I'll do anything for it." Her words, barely a whisper, send ice chills through my veins. "You've already lost . . . only you don't know it yet. You'll die in this bed."

Her fingernail traces a line across my throat, as if she were slashing it open. A moan escapes my lips and I hate myself for it.

I gather myself, fighting the wave of panic emptying my mind. "The game's not over yet," I reply, coldly. "Was it Steve who tried to kill me that night? Or was it you? I see you have plenty of motive." She pulls away as if my skin burned her fingers. "Psychotic or not, cops love to hear about means, motive, and opportunity." I hold my breath for a moment, trying to figure out where she is. She's drawing breath angrily some two or three feet away. "I'd work on securing a good alibi if I were you."

She gasps, right as the door opens, and Steve's voice carries through.

"This isn't over yet, you hear me?" he bellows. "I'll get to the bottom of this. What kind of doctor are you? What's your specialty?"

"The kind who won't hesitate to call the cops if I suspect

abuse. Lay a finger on Emma Duncan again, and there will be hell to pay."

Steve walks into the room angrily, and I shake for a moment, thinking he's coming for me. But he seems to walk to Mikela and leave with her hastily, probably holding her arm in a tight grip, dragging her out of there, because she doesn't seem too happy about it.

Their footsteps fade in the distance, then the massive front door slams forcefully. I wonder if the crack Steve put in the upper corner of the wall has widened.

I listen for a moment, hoping Dr. Sokolowski is still there with me, but he's gone too. I don't know where, and I don't know when he's coming back.

Tears start soaking the dressing wrapped around my head. I miss Adrian. He knew how to take care of me, to make me feel safe. I wish he were here.

Adrian, my love, where are you?

THIRTY-ONE

The smell of fried chicken seeps into the air, stirring my stomach. For a moment or two, I think this smell might be a memory, triggered by reliving the times Adrian and I used to retreat home for the long winter weekends. I used to make fried chicken then, using my mom's recipe for the herb-loaded, crispy breading, and serve it with golden, buttery mashed potatoes.

Dishes clatter in the distance as the smell becomes stronger. I hear the beeping of the microwave, then plates being set on the granite countertop. A few moments later, Jasmine walks in, groaning lightly.

Well, of course, doing so much overtime must be a killer.

"Are you hungry, Emma?" Jasmine asks cheerfully. "I have a surprise for you, to celebrate being in your own home again."

I don't share her mood; I'm wary of her, now that I know who she's sold me to. I consider asking her directly if she's working for Steve, if he's bought her off, and what his money actually paid for. But what good would that do? She'd deny it, swear it wasn't true, then be pissed at me for figuring it out. While I'm at her mercy.

The kind of money Steve could afford to throw at her makes

her dangerous. I'm afraid to eat the chicken I was craving, the mouthwatering smell becoming stronger as Jasmine brings the tray to the bed.

"Have you always been my nurse? Since the day I was attacked?" I ask, fighting to resist the craving for normal food. I've had enough hospital food to last me a lifetime.

"Yes, hon, uh-huh." She groans again when she sits on the side of the bed. I pull my hand away from her, slowly, tentatively, but I manage to do it. "Well, look at that," she says. "You're getting much better. I think you could eat this chicken all by yourself."

"Not yet."

"Ah, in a week or so, you'll get there. Let me check your patch real quick, okay?" She rolls up my sleeve and exposes the upper arm. "Sometimes it gets loose."

I follow her motions, my senses focused on her moves. Her fingers run the edges of the patch, but I don't feel that she does anything but test the corners to see if it's sticking to the skin, tugging gently. Then she lowers my sleeve with a satisfied sigh. "It was a little loose, but it's okay now."

"Thanks. How about Isabella? Was she my nurse?"

"I don't know her. But I don't work twenty-four-seven, you know. Just a few hours at a time. I'm sure there were other nurses. If she was a temp, through one of the agencies, they come and they go as shifts become available."

"Was there anyone else taking care of me, when you were out?"

"I'm sure there were others, hon. I usually work evening shifts, but you had three meals each day, right? Medication needs to be checked, vitals monitored and documented on your chart, positioning, hygiene, all that is a nurse's job." A metallic utensil chinks against the plate. It's not plastic anymore, like it used to be. It's real cutlery and porcelain. "Let's hold the fork together, all right? I cut the meat in small pieces. It will be easy."

I turn my head away slightly, wondering if I can trust her enough to eat from her hand. I've been doing it for a while, and nothing ever happened to me. "Why wasn't I allowed normal food until today?"

"Doctor's orders. I'm sure he felt it was too risky. We had to make sure there weren't any issues with deglutition—your ability to swallow. Medication could make you choke, or the TBI. We were just being cautious, that's all. Ready?"

I reluctantly let Jasmine hold my fingers on the fork. The contact with her hand, even if through the nitrile glove, burns my skin. I don't want her touching me, or being in the same room as me. Was she telling Steve everything? What I eat, my medications, what I discussed with Dr. Sokolowski? Or just the fact that no one will fight on my side in this grim battle for survival?

The chicken is absolutely delicious. It tastes perfectly fine, and it doesn't kill me on the first bite. I didn't really expect it to, but the thought crossed my mind. The recipe is different from Mom's, with fewer herbs and a restaurant-like taste, but the meat is juicy, and I relish sinking my teeth into it. I realize how hungry I am, and welcome a few more pieces.

I'm almost ready when the doorbell rings. Jasmine stands and takes the tray with her, not before patting my mouth with a moist tissue and offering a straw for a drink of water.

For a moment, I'm alone again, wondering who's at the door, dreading that it might be Steve again, or that attorney. I feel a bit stronger, though, after my first real meal since other people started feeding me. When a jay cries outside my window, a smile flutters on my lips. There are blue Steller's jays in my backyard. I remember that. How I wish I could see them, bolting in short bursts of azure flight from one aspen to the other, filling my heart with joy.

"Hey, lazy girl, whatcha doing there?" Lisa's voice fills the room with cheer, and I smile, breathing at ease.

"Hey, Lil." I remember how we last parted, when my baseless accusations drove her away crying, and it fills me with shame. "I'm really sorry for what I said—"

"Get over yourself. If I wasted brain space to remember every little stupid thing you say, there wouldn't be much room left for those lines, right?" She places a quick smooch on my cheek. She smells of fresh mountain air, of winter, and the world of the living and the free.

"You're a real friend, as always."

"Not as real as you, Em."

I can tell from Lisa's voice she's dying to share something with me. I pretend I don't notice, an old game we used to play. "I don't know what you're talking about."

"Denise signed me up." I can hear her happy dancing next to my bed, giggling and swirling like a dervish with her hands up in the air. It's easy for me to imagine that display because I've seen it many times, at least once for each successful audition.

"Ooh, congrats!" A pang of sorrow clouds the happiness I feel for my friend's achievement. I remember being completely irrational about her, afraid of her, thinking she was involved somehow in my attack. Now I know that's not true; the real villains were just here. But there's still a trace of sadness I feel at the thought of the chances that were taken from me, and Lisa's presence reminds me of that, acutely. She reaped the benefits, even if that doesn't make her the villain. I'm still grieving the loss of my life as it used to be.

She stops spinning and lands on the bed, making it bounce. "Oh, shit, I didn't hurt you, did I?"

"No, relax."

"Whew." She pants a little, catching her breath. "I didn't tell you the best part yet." She pauses for a moment, but I don't say anything. "Denise already got me a new contract. Mid-budget romantic drama, as lead."

"Oh, wow," I whisper. "You're gonna be awesome."

A brief, loaded silence. "We'll have to see about that. There's a wrinkle."

"What happened?" I hope it's not about how she doesn't like the costumes, or that her co-star is ugly, or that his stubble will scratch her delicate skin when they kiss. I wish I had those problems again.

"Steve's gonna direct it. We start filming early next year."

Her words fall heavily on me, seeding more doubt in my heart. Did he buy her with his role? What exactly did he buy?

"It'll be weird, working with him," she says, taking my hand. It's the gesture everyone makes, regardless of their relationship with me. This time, I respond. I'm able to squeeze her fingers just a little. It doesn't feel as if it's happening to someone else anymore; it almost feels normal. "Hey, you're getting better!"

"Slowly." A deep sigh leaves my chest. "What else is new?" I can't think of anything else to ask her, without risking another accusation I can't prove.

"Oh, it's all fabulous. I can't tell you enough what a blessing it is to be rid of old Lyle. I couldn't stand him anymore. He's a dirty-minded, libidinous old man who must be popping Viagra like breath mints. He's always screwing some young, pretty chick who thinks he's her ticket to Hollywood's wall of fame. But he's just a faker. I'm so glad my contract is done. You should've seen his face when I told him I wasn't renewing. He was floored! And he's not making a dime off my current job, the one that should've been yours. He didn't get me that audition. So"—she blows a raspberry—"buh-bye, Lyle."

I usually love to listen to her banter, but my mind wandered away the moment she mentioned Lyle Crespin. He was Adrian's agent. Lyle was there the day we met, shouting at him, insisting he sign something. The memory is still blurry, only pieces of it there for me to find, in one of the darkest drawers of my mind.

I remember Adrian eventually signed the paper Lyle pushed his way, but there was something else. Something that gnaws at the raw edges of my mind, a partially obscured intrusive memory just like the one from the day I was hurt.

I must remember. If for no other reason than to be rid of this and focus on the more important things, like how to survive.

Who cares why Adrian didn't want to sign his agent's paperwork? It's just a stupid brainworm memory . . . stuck songs are earworms, so I guess stuck memories can be brainworms.

"Em? You still with me?" Lisa asked. "Maybe I should go, if you're tired."

"No, don't go just yet. I need a favor." Even if doubts flood my mind about her working with Steve, I need her help.

"Shoot."

"Do you see my phone anywhere?"

"Yeah, it's right here, on the night table."

"My doctor helped me figure some things out from calls and text messages—at least, he tried. I forgot to ask him to look at the pics."

"Sure, what do you need?"

I swallow with difficulty, my throat feeling parched. I'm about to trust her with my life, and I'd better not be making a mistake. "Is there anyone else here?" I ask in a whisper.

"No, it's just us."

"And the door is closed?"

"Yes. You're freaking me out, Em. What's going on?"

I keep my voice low when I speak. "I was bludgeoned here, at the house. I must've let my attacker in myself, because the door was locked when I tried to run. Now I know why. It was Steve."

"What?" She springs off the bed. "What are you talking about?"

"Steve came to kill me that night. Seems he missed, left me for dead with my head split open in a pool of blood."

"No . . . I can't believe it, Em."

"Don't tell anyone yet. Promise me."

"I promise," she replies weakly, her voice filled with doubt for my sanity. "What are you going to do?"

"The police are investigating. But they might not be fast enough. He might come after me before they catch him." I swallow hard, my throat suddenly dry. "In case something happens, Lil, now you know. And you'll be able to tell them."

A whistle of amazement tells me what she thinks of everything I've just said. She probably doesn't believe me. I half-expect her to fend everything off with a joke, in her usual style.

"Girl, this will make my new movie project a new level of interesting. Super awkward, if he still directs it, knowing what I know now. Or maybe he'll be in jail. What happens to a movie when the director's arrested? I hope we get a new one."

Yes, maybe he'll be locked up by then. The thought makes me smile a tiny bit.

"About the phone . . . I wanted to see if I called someone before that night, inviting them to the house. If there were any messages, my doctor didn't find anything. And I forgot to ask him to look at the photos. I had a stalker, remember? We talked about this."

"Uh-huh, I know about your stalker. I saw him too. I guess you're not a really famous Hollywood personality until you get one, huh?"

I can't help a smile. "Yeah, right. Well, I'm thinking I might've snapped a picture of him with my phone. I remember standing by the living room window, hiding behind the curtains, looking at him. It was dusk, and he was leaning against a tree trunk, and I had my phone in my hand."

"Say no more." Her fingers tap quickly. "Yes, there's a photo of him, taken about three weeks ago, but it's really grainy. I'm enlarging it and can't make out his face. But maybe the police can."

"That's it? Just that one pic?"

"Yup. Sorry." I hear the sound of the phone's screen locking feature. Then it lands on the table with a light noise.

"Let's try something else. I think I could pinpoint where my amnesia starts using the photos. I want to know how much time I'm still missing. Tell me what pictures you see, and I'll stop you when I remember taking them. Start from the most recent ones, and go back."

"Just like time travel. Huh . . . Interesting idea." Her fingers tap on the screen some more. "Selfies of you and Bryan, about seven of them. Do you remember taking any selfies with him?"

"I can barely remember anything about Bryan," I reply, with a deep sigh. "What's next?"

"You and I on the ski slopes in October. I stayed here, with you that weekend. We roasted marshmallows over the firepit and drank tequila. Remember that?"

"Nope."

"The stalker I mentioned, and then, before that, the two of us and Bryan together for your birthday dinner. You turned thirty, in case you don't recall. Lots of candles to blow."

September 19. I press my lips together. *Was I happy?* I don't find the courage to ask the question out loud. "Next, please."

How come I remember taking the stalker's photo three weeks ago, but don't recall my birthday, more than two months ago?

"Adrian and his car on your driveway. He has roses in his hand."

I hope you still like roses, my love. The memory resounds clearly in my mind, but that moment didn't happen on my driveway. "Next."

"Lots of pics of you and Adrian in Vegas, about forty or fifty of them."

Tears prick my eyes. "Nope." All the life I'm missing . . . it's heartbreaking.

"Some random stuff on movie sets, a shopping list in your own handwriting, a billboard off the highway with an ad for teeth whitening services. You don't need that, by the way. Then, you and Adrian in Cancun. Sound familiar?"

I remember going with Steve to Cancun. The rising moon over the ocean, the pink sky in Mom's picture of Steve and me. "No. Isn't anything in there of you and me except the ski slopes? We didn't go out?"

"While you were dating Adrian, you became scarce for us mere mortals. You just went for auditions, shoots, and out with him, and that was it. I thought I'd lost you. That relationship swallowed you whole, girlfriend. I had concerns, but you were so deliriously happy, I was happy for you, patiently waiting for the honeymoon to be over so we could hang out again."

"I—I'm so sorry," I whisper, remembering how much I used to miss her. Our production schedules didn't match too often either, but there were weekends when we could've gone out together, and I said no. Just so I could be alone with Adrian. I was addicted.

"With Adrian in Texas. You took him to meet your mom?"

I struggle to make sense of my scattered memories. "No, I don't think so. Mom still thinks I'm married to Steve."

"You know that's been over for a while, right?"

I let that pass unanswered. I still can't tell Mom. "Must've been on location. We did a TV show together, I think."

"Yes, you did! *Echoes of Tomorrow*. You won an award for it. Let me see . . . Yes, it was shot on location in Texas. I think that's when you and Adrian became a thing. Remember that?"

"I think so. When was that?"

She doesn't answer right away. I'd like to think she's just checking the date on the pics, but I suspect she's actually afraid to tell me.

Her fingers find my hand. "Almost a year ago."

I can't believe I'm missing so much time. "I see. It's okay, don't worry," I say quickly. "I've started to remember, so it won't take long, I guess. It will come back. I'm just sorry we drove you away, Adrian and I. We shouldn't have stopped going out just because I was—"

"You didn't have a choice. I understood that later." Lisa lets go of my hand and opens a bottle of something. The cap pops and hisses as if the drink is carbonated. "That stalker was everywhere, remember? The police didn't do much, not even when he came onto your land. You were both afraid to leave the house, and I don't blame you." She gulps down some of the drink. A faint scent of Coke comes my way, but I don't pay any attention.

That's why we secluded ourselves every chance we had? Because of the damn stalker?

"Want some?" she asks.

"Yes, please, but I need a straw. There should be one around here somewhere."

"Yeah, got it." She brings the straw to my lips, and I draw gulp after gulp of refreshing Coke and don't stop until the straw sucks air. "That's all I have, but I can bring you more."

"No . . . it's okay. My nurse would throw a fit if she knew I'd had caffeine and sugar."

Silence fills the room for a while as my mind wanders and comes back empty-handed. No new tidbits of memory to feast on, my questions still unanswered.

"Why did Adrian leave me?" I ask, the tremble in my voice giving me away. I'm afraid to find out.

"Em, you never gave me all the deets. You guys just broke up and that was it. I'm sure you'll remember." She stands by the bed, seemingly ready to leave. "For a while, I thought you'd just stopped living, after Adrian, but when I came back from location, you told me it was because of the stalker. He came to your house one night, and you were terrified of him."

Screw the stalker.

Did Adrian cheat on me? Did we have a fight? That's what I have to remember.

"I gotta go, but I'll be back tomorrow, I promise." She places a quick kiss on my cheek, then lowers her face. "Seriously now, how sure are you that Steve tried to kill you? Maybe it was this stalker, you know? He was there in your yard, staring at your house, when you took that photo. That's really creepy."

I know Steve tried to kill me, and I know why he did it.

THIRTY-TWO

Last night, after everyone went home and the night nurse dozed off, I snuck into Emma's room and kept her company for a while. I brushed her hair, placed the lightest of kisses on her cold lips, careful not to wake her, and told her how much she means to me. She didn't move, didn't realize I was there.

When I was about to leave through my usual back-door route, I nearly ran into Jasmine. She was leaving, about forty-five minutes before the end of her shift, thinking no one would know.

Officially, no one does.

I have about thirty minutes until the day nurse shows up. I use it to grab a quick shower and something to eat from the fridge, then visit with Emma once more, my steps completely silent on the hardwood, dampened by the thick wool socks I borrowed from her drawers.

I hold my breath, but she stirs when I walk in. I stand perfectly still, a couple of feet from her bed, and look at her pale lips, twitching in a dream. A nightmare, most likely. Not surprising after what I've seen and heard so far . . . The gall of that conniving bitch, Mikela, to harass Emma like that! For a moment, I close my eyes and imagine how it would feel if I held her tied up and *blindfolded, while I'm slowly carving into her skin. What would she say then?*

But that's not my style. I do my chores quickly. I don't play with them.

When a car pulls onto the driveway, I make my way quickly out of there, closing the door gently behind me, and disappear just as the nurse unlocks the front door.

By myself again, I can't help but obsess over what I saw yesterday. The visit from Lisa was most disturbing. The way she talked about me. The way both of them did, as if I ruined Emma's life.

The stalker. They keep calling me that, perhaps because it's true—from their perspective anyway. I don't see myself as a stalker, but a man in love. A protector. Someone who should be trusted, not feared.

I know she fears me, and it's upsetting me deeply. She'll come around, once she realizes what I did for her. Once all these people go away and leave her alone.

Until then, I wait. Not for much longer, because there isn't too much time left. At some point, I'll have to face the consequences of what I've done.

I'm not talking about going to jail. LA cops have better things to do than waste resources on a stalker who, as far as they know, never hurt anyone. The Tahoe cops, with ski season upon them, are buried in driving fatalities, assaults, batteries, the occasional drunken rape. Even murder, up there on the slopes. It happened last year—I promise it wasn't me. I prefer deep ravines layered with thick snow, where bodies don't get found for a while. Or ever.

No . . . I'm talking about Emma.

Will she ever forgive me?

THIRTY-THREE

It's the first time I don't feel drowsy in a very long time. Since Lisa left, I feel energized, and my mind seems to be working a little better. Not a whole lot, though, because it takes me a while to figure out why.

It must've been the Coke I drank.

It makes me wonder what sugar and caffeine would do for my recovery. I'll ask the doctor the next time I see him. I've never heard of doctors prescribing stimulants on top of sedatives and—perhaps soon, if the neuropsychiatrist finds me delusional—antipsychotics, but it's worth asking the question.

My mind wanders again, this time deciding to fixate on that damn stalker. Lisa's comment about fame made me laugh, but the truth is, I would've very much appreciated to have the house paid in full before acquiring myself a stalker. I feel very broke for a famous person, someone worthy of being tailed.

If Mom knew about it, she'd be horrified, then immediately blame it on me and that stupid *Summer Love* scene, where I bare my chest for half a heartbeat. Perhaps that's why American movies show less and less nudity, because people are not mature enough to deal with it like responsible adults. Unlike other cultures, Americans have an obsession with sex; probably because talking about it is taboo, and no one educates the young about it the right way. Without guilt or shame or stigma. So some of these people never forget what they see on the screen. They think it's real, not fictional, and feel motivated to take action. They choose to ignore that it's nothing more than a job for us. And, every once in a while, the wrong individual, with the wrong combination of psychological characteristics, sees the wrong movie, and bam. I have a stalker.

I try to visualize him, to remember a little more about him. Now I know for sure this man has been at the center of my life for the past year or so, perhaps longer. Who would do this? Instead of obsessing over his face as I have done a few times unsuccessfully, I'm trying to think of the mind behind the fixation.

He is fixated, all right. Lake Tahoe in November is a very cold place. To stand in someone's backyard for hours in the hope of catching a glimpse of them as they walk past their living room window takes a lot of stamina. The trunk of that aspen might've shielded him from the bitter wind rolling off the mountains, but it was still below freezing out there. And he only wore a hoodie. Have I ever seen him wear a parka? I don't recall.

Perhaps he's suffering from delusions, like I vaguely remember someone explaining to me—perhaps it was the cops. Someone who might've fallen in love with me without ever meeting me, someone who can't imagine I don't love him just as much as he loves me. He probably can't take the rejection, and how could he? If his expectations are based on the delusions haunting him, daydreams of romantic liaisons with the object of his desire, he'll never go away. It's called erotomania, if I'm not mistaken. Or, perhaps he's a narcissist I once met and didn't feel like dating; someone like that never forgives being turned away. There were a few invites to dinner I declined in the past couple of years.

They say that if you walk through the grass long enough, you will eventually step on a snake.

Seems that I did.

The memory of that one time, at the shopping mall, comes back to haunt me. He came really close that day, and still, I only saw a man in a gray hoodie with shades on. I remember staring right at him, from across the concourse. It was busy that day, with lots of holiday shoppers. He came close enough for me to tell a police officer about it. Or was that a dream I had? Because there's no merry-go-round at the shopping center, and I seem to remember there was one.

Speaking of delusions, what the hell am I going to do if I can't tell what's real? What if I am psychotic?

That thought makes me shiver inside, but I know it's not true. Yes, for some reason, my memories are confusing and unreliable, but that will get better. I'm not hallucinating, I know that. There's an explanation for everything and I will find it.

I wonder what the stalker thought when he saw me with another man. Was he jealous? I'm trying to remember a time when that happened, but I can't. Instead, I remember one time when he followed me the entire time I ran my errands at a small plaza by the lake. I drove straight home and crashed into Adrian's arms, breathless and scared. He held me tight and rocked me back and forth until my tears dried up. Then he called the cops.

It wasn't the first time we spoke to the police about the stalker, but this time Adrian insisted I file a formal complaint. "To force the lazy assholes off their butts and out there, investigating," he'd said. They weren't lazy nor assholes; they just didn't have a lot to go on. I gave a description of someone who could've been anyone, really. Medium build, no idea about hair because of the hoodie, eyes covered with wide shades, three-day stubble barely visible above a black scarf, perhaps white but could've been Hispanic. He was human; that much was the only thing I was positively sure about. Nothing else. I can't blame the cops for looking at each other in disbelief as they took our statements. They advised us to be careful, encouraged me to keep my distance, but look closely at his face if I saw him again in a public place. How was I supposed to do that? "Perhaps take a picture, if you can," they said. "That would be helpful."

After they had left, I wanted to go out on the back patio and sit by the fire, watching the moonlight glimmering on the distant lake. But I didn't get too far before a thought filled my heart with dread. What if he was out there, watching us? I turned around and went inside, but the floor-to-ceiling living room windows that I had loved so much now scared me. The light reflected in the dark windows, and I couldn't see anything outside.

But the stalker could see us just fine if he was out there.

Adrian's arms wrapped around my shoulders as he listened to me talk about my fears. Then he placed a quick kiss on my lips and propped his hands on his hips. "Is that it?"

"What? You don't think it's enough? We've lost our privacy, Adrian. We don't have that anymore."

"Piece of cake with a cherry on top, babe," he said cheerfully, folding me into his arms again. I loved his little phrases, the things he said and did to cheer me up when I needed it the most.

No matter how much I insisted, he didn't say anything else that night.

The next day, when I returned from the grocery shopping I had reluctantly agreed to do on my own, the house was swarming with people. They were installing curtain rods on all the windows, and had covered the sofa with fabric swatches for me to choose from. By the time the moon was rising, heavy draperies in reddish-brown with streaks of light tan, the colors of hardwood timber and pine, covered every inch of glass on our windows.

Our home was ours again.

Our patio was a different story.

"What?" Adrian had reacted, reviewing a quote for a fence, a security system with motion sensors, video surveillance, and flood lights. "You have to be kidding me! I'm not going to fork out six figures for a fence."

The contractor left soon after trying to negotiate the price and failing. He explained the lot was large and mostly rock that had to be excavated, that posts needed to be set in concrete. And Adrian didn't want to fence just a part of the backyard. He wanted it all. And that was expensive.

"Let's get a dog," he suggested, after the contractor left. "One of those mean German shepherds that would die defending you. What do you say? He'd rip that stalker to shreds the moment he sets foot in the yard again."

I was back in his arms, feeling safe. "Um, I don't know. We're gone days in a row, sometimes weeks when we're on location. We'd have to get him a permanent sitter, too. A stranger, living here . . ."

"That's true. Well, let's at least get a top-of-the-line security system for the house. Then, some motion sensors with floodlights should do the trick to keep him away. They'll go off for every racoon, but who cares?"

He had solutions for everything. I smile with sadness, remembering how it felt to be loved by him, to have him near.

Then my mind shifts, returning to the stalker. What if Steve put someone up to it? To drive me crazy, make me abandon the house? But that doesn't fit. As much as I'm willing to blame all evil things on my ex, that creep was stalking me in LA too. And was on my tail one time I know for sure Steve was filming in Aruba. But he still could've hired someone to follow me around.

The door opens and rubber soles squeak on the floor. As always, I hold my breath, until I recognize Jasmine's footfalls and tired, muffled groans.

"Did I wake you?" she asks, setting something down.

"No, I'm up, so to speak."

"You should be resting."

And not paying attention to what you're doing, I think coldly, remembering how chummy she was with the man who tried to kill me. *You wish.*

"I just woke up," I reply instead.

"Are you moving better? It was nice seeing you work those hands over dinner."

I try to lift my right hand and I manage with a lot less effort than I'm used to. My chest fills with hope. That Coke did wonders.

"This is great," she says. "Try the other one." My left hand is less cooperative. I struggle hard, panting from the effort, but it barely lifts a couple of inches off the covers. "Interesting," she mutters, returning to her clattering objects and rustling wrappers.

"You know what would help? If I could have some Coca-Cola," I say, hoping I can catch some good will. Maybe Steve didn't pay her to withhold soda from me.

"Uh-uh, sorry, hon. You're on Versed," she replies, feigned regret in her voice. "The doctor will kick my ass straight to the curb if I do that."

"What if I ask him?"

"Sure, if he says yes, I'll bring you anything you want." She comes over to the bed. "Keep working those fingers. Actually, since you're doing so well, you could probably use the controls for your bed. These buttons, right here." Gently, she takes my right hand and guides it to the railing. I can feel some buttons underneath the tips of my fingers. "Can you press this?"

I try my best, and the head of my bed lifts a little. I squeal with joy. "How do I bring it down?"

"Here," she says, guiding my fingers a little farther down.

I press and the head of the bed moves down. "Thanks, Jas, I appreciate it." As soon as she's gone, I'll be messing with those buttons until I teach myself how to do it quickly.

"There's more. This one makes an alarm go off, if you need it. This other one should control your TV, but it's not connected yet. I don't know how to do it."

"I have a TV?"

"Yes, you do."

Oh, it will feel so good to hear something else other than beeping and my own breathing.

"Tell me about Dr. Sokolowski," I ask, shifting gears toward what interests me the most, getting my hands on some caffeine. I feel like one of those hopeless, shaking addicts looking for a fix. "What kind of man is he?"

"He's a very good doctor," Jasmine says, helping me turn on my side, and fluffing my pillows. "Seems he's taken a special interest in your case, and that's great. The last thing you want is for them doctors to forget you exist, until it's time to bill you." She chuckles lightly, working near my side. There's a faint scent of sweat underneath the smell of disinfectants and pharmaceuticals. She's probably been working all day.

"That happens, huh?"

"Don't worry, hon. You're in good hands. He's coming to see you twice a day, which is the best you can hope for."

I feel the IV tubing moving. She's probably replacing it. I'm about to ask her what's in it when a thought occurs to me. "That's it? Only twice a day?"

"Yes, that's the norm. These doctors, they're super busy. Insurance calls the shots, how many patients they have to see in an hour and all that. I'm surprised he finds the time, but Baldwin Memorial isn't far; I guess that helps." She adjusts my sheets and straightens the covers. "You sleep a lot, you know. Maybe that's why you don't realize he's only here twice a day."

I wish I didn't sleep that much. And having the brain fog lifted, even if for a little while, is wonderful.

"What does he look like?"

Jasmine chuckles in a low, hushed voice. "He's dreamy, if you want to know. If I didn't like my men chocolate mocha, I'd make a pass at that. Tall, dark hair, bit of a beard, and he's not too old. Thirty-five, forty, maybe?"

That doesn't tell me what I wanted to know, but reminds me I wanted to ask something else. "How about Dr. Winslow?"

"I don't know him. What's his specialty?"

"He's the neurologist."

Jasmine walks toward the foot of my bed, then I hear papers rustling as she looks at my chart. "I see him on your chart, but I don't recall meeting him. It's a big hospital, hon. I've never worked neurology. Only trauma and emergency, that's it. And I took these extra hours to take care of you because I need the cash. Why else, right?" She laughs, her voice strained, tired.

Perhaps she's ready to confess about the other cash she took.

"How old are you, Jas?"

"I'm forty-nine, going on seventy." She laughs again, rolling up my left sleeve. "Just checking here, and we're done." A slight smell of vinegar tickles my nose, but I don't pay attention.

"How do you know my ex, Steve Wellington?"

Her fingers don't falter while she's checking the edges of the patch. My question didn't bother her. She's not going to tell me anything. I don't know why I believed otherwise.

"I don't. I met him when he came to see you, that's all. But I do get excited when I meet famous people, you know?" I feel a slight tugging at my skin. "Just checking to see if it sticks right." She rolls my sleeve down. "You're good to go."

I'm not buying it. First off, Steve's not that famous. He's no Spielberg or Scott, even if he'd keel over and die if he heard me say that.

Jasmine gathers her things and walks toward the door, then stops. "Should I leave the TV on for you?"

I almost say yes, when I realize it's a really bad idea.

I can't afford not to hear him coming.

THIRTY-FOUR

Jasmine didn't seem bothered by my question about knowing Steve, but what does that really mean? Was she telling the truth? Or was she perfectly relaxed, knowing I'm crippled and blind and can't do anything about anything anyway?

Not knowing for certain is driving me insane.

She's gone for the night, or so it seems. The house is perfectly still. She left before I could ask all my questions. I wanted to know what Versed does and why I need to take it, which drug leaves me so groggy in the morning, and what's in that IV she keeps changing. I could ask the doctor, but I don't want him to think I'm challenging him. He's the only ally I have, and I can't afford to piss him off.

Perhaps Steve has Jasmine following a different game plan than I imagined, to keep me in limbo until he can snatch the house. Until that conservatorship is finalized. And who better to help Steve achieve all that than the woman handling my medications? Recently, she's a little too preoccupied with the patch on my arm. Dr. Sokolowski told me that's the pain medication. Is Jasmine screwing with that? When she last checked it, a few minutes ago, I caught a whiff of a strange smell, pungent, like vinegar or bleach. I don't remember that distinctive odor before, although those patches have been on my arm since I first woke up.

Is she adding something to that patch? I can imagine her getting a couple of drops from who knows what vial or bottle, in an eyedropper, unseen. While she's "inspecting it," she could tug at the corner and flip it up, add the drops to the pad, then pat it down, to make sure "it sticks right." Her words, not mine.

But why? And why would Steve risk his career and his freedom to get the house? Why would that warrant all this effort on his part? Yes, he has a motive to try to kill me, but I don't see how it's easier to kill someone than buy another house. In Lake Tahoe, if that's what matters to him.

I hate to say it, but Lisa's motive seems stronger than Steve's. Slipping into my place for the lead role in *The Charade* is a career-maker. Getting on Denise's list will ensure she'll climb to fame and fortune way faster than I could, because she's talented and driven and she didn't divorce Steve Wellington. And she was chummy with dear old Jasmine; my nurse had her phone number, after all. How come? I nearly bought Jasmine's story about her excitement in the presence of famous people, but having Lisa's number was a different story. I wonder how she'd lie her way through explaining that one.

But she's not here, so I can't ask her.

My mind drifts back to the stalker, and how he changed our lives. Lisa's stories triggered new snippets of memory.

I remember Adrian and me sitting on the sand on Santa Monica Beach, not able to enjoy it, afraid to lie down, looking over our shoulders all the time. I made a joke at some point, trying to lighten the atmosphere, and said it would be something if he showed up there in his hoodie. It was a hot summer day with a crystal-clear blue sky and glimmering waves crashing gently at the shore. Adrian barely looked at me, not responding to my attempt at humor with the tiniest smile. He kept on frowning.

After that day, although the stalker didn't show up there, in Santa Monica, change seeped into our lives, slowly, unstoppable. We stopped going out. Only performed the bare minimum of networking, with less pressure since both Adrian and I had jobs lined up. Quickly, life turned boring and stifling and scary. Freedom was right there, outside our door, but we were held captive by the steel bars of our own fears.

"Stalkers can turn violent," Adrian said one night, after we debated going out and eventually gave it up. "Some become rapists, others break and enter and kill everyone in the house. You never know."

I had no reply; he wasn't saying anything new. The cops had told us to be careful for the exact same reasons.

There was no more hiking the lake shore at sunset. No more skiing under the powerful lights at Kirkwood or Sierra. No more eating out al fresco in LA, my personal favorite. We were officially hunkered down, in hiding. Defeated without the opportunity of a real, honest fight.

Every phone call jolted me, and I had grown increasingly afraid of the dark. Most of all, I felt guilty, as if his fixation on me was somehow my fault. Adrian was sweet as always, never said anything about it, and I didn't expect him to. If some freak decided to turn into a stalker based on something he's seen in a movie, that's not the actor's fault. It was well understood by everyone.

The police still had no ID, but they were starting to get some information back to us. They'd investigated the footprints he'd left in the backyard and told us he wore size eleven boots, military grade. Based on some grainy video obtained from a mall ATM the day I saw him there, they concluded he was over six feet, weighing about 200 pounds. They couldn't do a composite based on the video; he wore shades and a scarf that covered his mouth.

They still had nothing.

Almost a year flew by like that, in a flurry of flights between Reno-Tahoe and LA, and periods of intense work on movie sets, alternating with time off that passed incredibly slowly. I was afraid of weekends, which were spent looking at TV shows we didn't care to watch, and making a hobby of cooking dinner and eating too much.

Then something changed.

As the fog of oblivion starts to lift, a chill travels down my spine.

If what I recall is true, I might never leave this bed.

THIRTY-FIVE

I don't know the precise moment when it happened, but I recall Adrian and me working together on the set of another movie. Both of us were cast in supporting roles. My name was the sixth billed; that bit of information has stuck clearly in my mind, even if the movie title is a blur, still inaccessible to me. My screen time was only twelve minutes overall; some days my call sheet was just general production notes and upcoming highlights.

Adrian had significantly more screen time; he was the lead's sidekick, third billed. That left me with lots of spare time on my hands to use as I pleased.

I got in touch with Denise and had a couple of lunches with her; it felt good to spend time in her company, while learning a few more things from her. While Adrian was stuck on set, filming, I went on a couple more auditions, including one for a ten-million-dollar budget action thriller, as lead.

And I got the part.

I was thrilled, exhilarated, thinking the gods of career fortune were smiling down on me again. I didn't say anything to Adrian about it, while I tried my best to get his name added to the cast. I would've loved to have him as my co-star.

It didn't happen, though. The producer wouldn't budge; his mind was made up in favor of a rather butch ex-bodybuilder I didn't particularly like.

Nevertheless, when the contract was signed, I went back to our hotel room with an oversized bottle of champagne tied with a red bow. Adrian was wrapping up his filming that day; I was hoping for a memorable celebration, then a flight home to Tahoe the next morning.

Adrian was gloomy when I got there, enraged almost, sitting on the side of the bed with his head in his hands. He gave my champagne an uninterested side glance and looked at me with vacant eyes as he congratulated me on the role. I quickly abandoned the bottle on the desk and pulled up a chair in front of him. I reached for his hands, and stayed there, waiting, for a long moment, until he took my hands in his.

"What's wrong?" I asked, holding my breath. We were happy... No one's ever ready to lose that once they finally have it.

"I heard... Congratulations, I guess, but I'm afraid for you," he eventually said. "With that stalker out there. While we're filming together, I can still keep an eye on you, make sure he doesn't get to you. But if we're on different locations, I can't protect you anymore."

I pulled my hands away and shoved them in my pockets, steadying my breathing. I was enraged by his concern for my safety. Yes, the stalker was out there, but Adrian had made things perhaps a little worse because of this exaggerated need to protect me. Planning a dinner out had turned into a tactical exercise of sorts, where he said things like, "We're too exposed there," or "I don't like the greenery next to that patio. He could sneak up right next to you."

It suffocated me. It made me mad.

Men are so threatened by a woman's success, and Adrian seemed to be following that rule. He was acting as the strong protector, when I'd started to wonder if anyone—if I—really needed that much protection. We'd stifled our lives and squandered countless opportunities just to feel safe from some crazy creep, who had nothing better to do than waste his time on me.

"Adrian, we'll be all right. There's always security on sets, and the days are so incredibly long, I won't have time to do much anyway. I'll be working all the time."

"How about the hotel where you stay? Will you have security there? And the restaurants? And anywhere else you might decide to go? Where are they filming it, anyway?"

"I believe it's here, in LA, with some location shoots in the Grand Tetons. It's an action—"

He scoffed and stood, starting to pace the room. "In the bloody *woods*. If that isn't just perfect for him, I don't know what is."

"He won't know where I'm going, Adrian. It's not like I'm some hot-shot rock star that everyone's tracking, going to shows on a set schedule."

"But fans can find out, and you know it. They have their ways." He stopped squarely in front of me. "No, you need to drop out of this contract. Tell Denise to invoke some force majeure or something."

"Absolutely not."

"I couldn't stand it if something happened to you. Please, Em, do this for me. Play it safe. They'll catch him eventually."

"No, Adrian. Hell, no." Our eyes locked fiercely for a moment, mine enraged, his cold and unyielding. After a moment, I softened, and so did he. "This could be my big break, baby. Lots of residuals too. This kind of flick has enduring appeal. It can sell for decades."

"We don't need the money. I have—"

"That's it. That's *exactly* it. *You* have. Not me." I stabbed his chest with my finger as I shouted. "Well, newsflash. I want to have something too. A career. My name out there. Another golden trophy on that mantel would be nice."

He didn't say another word. Just stared at me for a moment, then walked out of the hotel room.

"Adrian?" I called, as the door latched closed. He didn't return.

After the bout of rebellion, I started feeling guilty. Ungrateful. Ashamed for being so selfish. That man loved me so much, constantly worried about me, and what did I do? I screeched and clawed at him like a scalded cat.

He came back later that night. Without a word, he went straight to the bottle of champagne and uncorked it. Much of it spilled with the pop; it had gotten warm. He filled two glasses, then brought them to me, out on the terrace, where I was staring at the Hollywood sign, hazy but visible in the distance.

"Congratulations, baby." We clinked and I took a sip. It was warm, but good. Good to have him back by my side, smiling, kissing me with unbridled desire.

The next morning, after catching only a few hours of sleep, I wasn't feeling so well. I got through the day with the help of some extra coffee, and thought nothing of it. But the following day, I was worse. It felt as if I were immensely tired, my muscles too weak to keep me on my feet.

We were back in Tahoe as planned, and I rested for a couple of days, hoping it would get better without needing to see a doctor.

My sleep became restless, sprinkled with bouts of migraine so intense they'd wake me up from the superficial snoozing I was able to manage. When I woke up in the mornings, I felt depressed, saddened without any explanation—after all, everything was going well. Adrian was there, by my side, catering to my every need, occasionally insisting we call a doctor. The stalker had been invisible for a while, and I even summoned my courage and spent some evenings on the back patio, by the fire.

It scares me to remember all that now, because I realize that the lack of muscle tone the doctor talks about, the lack of physical strength I've been struggling with, could have something to do with what they found when I eventually let myself be talked into seeing a doctor.

I had fibromyalgia, I was told, after completing endless rounds of testing. And there's no cure for it.

The moment I heard that doctor voice the life sentence she gave me, everything started making sense. The struggle I'd been having memorizing my lines. The restless sleep. The stress creeping up on me all the time.

There was no cure, just fistfuls of pills that came with side effects and made things worse. It was my new reality, impossible to evade.

As I remember those days, panic seeps through my blood. The attack might've made the fibromyalgia worse. And Dr. Sokolowski doesn't know I have it. I never went to Baldwin Memorial Hospital with it; there's no record of my illness in their systems.

I have to tell him . . . for what little good it might do.

My hand reaches the bed railing. I push the button to elevate the backrest, but it doesn't help me feel less upset.

Jasmine comes into the room and walks to the bedside quickly. "What happened, hon? Are you in pain?"

"No . . . just can't sleep." She takes my hand, but it doesn't do anything for me. There's no hope left. It's pointless. All the fight to make my hands move, everything I tried to do to revive my broken memory. The fibromyalgia won't allow me to walk again.

"Would you like me to give you a little something to help you sleep?"

"Yeah," I whisper, surrendering myself to the oblivion I tried so hard to fight. I listen to the sounds Jasmine makes, anticipating the sweet relief of oblivion. A vial is popped open. A syringe is unwrapped, and the plastic needle protector is discarded on a tray. The needle sucks the fluid from the amp.

I'm ready for it. I don't care if I don't hear Steve coming to finish what he started. Let it be, already.

I push the other button to lower the backrest into a comfortable position for sleep.

Then, without thinking much about it, I do something else.

I scratch my nose.

I don't realize it at first, the gesture so ingrained in my body's memory it seems natural. Only it hasn't been, not for me, not since I landed in a hospital bed with my head split open.

"No," I cry. "I'm sorry, I changed my mind. Please don't give me the drugs." I quickly put my hand back down in its usual spot, unwilling to let Jasmine see my progress if she hasn't already.

"Okay," she says with a sigh, followed by the sound of the contents of the tray being dropped into the trash can. The lid grinds to a close. "Page me if you need me," she says, walking slowly toward the door. "The button's next to the bed controls."

"Thanks, Jas. Good night."

The moment she closes the door, even if it takes every bit of strength I have, I scratch my nose again.

And smile.

THIRTY-SIX

I dream of that blinding light again, a circle of bulbs above my head, much like an operating room lamp. It is so unbearably bright I close my eyes, and my world becomes dark again. I see Adrian's face in my dream, close to mine, calling my name in a panic, despair coloring his voice. I don't listen, don't follow him, but I feel his pain. The panic in his voice turns to anger, rage almost, but I turn away. Close my eyes, because the lights are too bright. I pull away from his touch, then instantly feel the pain of missing him.

I wake up, engulfed in darkness still.

As the remnants of last night's drugs scatter, I remember how Adrian and I broke up. The memory catches the breath in my lungs. I explore it fearfully, as one would read a heartbreaking novel, afraid to turn another page.

After the devastating fibromyalgia diagnosis, I had only a few weeks left before starting work on the action thriller. Adrian and I moved to LA in a rental house, to be closer to "better health-care," he'd said, but also to be together while he worked on a new television series he'd signed up for. If I was in LA with him, he could come home every night. During the better days, I could accompany him on set, so he'd stop worrying about that stalker for a while.

I'd seen that son of a bitch only twice in the past couple of months: one time when I looked out the window of a Tahoe restaurant where I'd snuck in by myself to have dinner while Adrian was in LA; another time, also in Tahoe, while I was walking to my car after getting my hair done.

I was still scared of him, terrified of his persistence, of the way he stood in the distance, arms always crossed, staring at me from behind those mirrored shades. I had nightmares about the things he would do if he managed to kidnap me or be alone with me somehow. I tried to take his picture, but he always turned away and ran when I grabbed my phone. The bastard knew what I was trying to do. After the last encounter, I didn't even call the cops anymore. It was pointless. That stalker had become a staple of my existence.

Damn him to hell for that.

Almost every night, Adrian hinted or downright insisted I claim medical reasons and cancel my upcoming movie contract. He didn't understand me at all. That opportunity was the one thing keeping me from losing my mind. What did I have without it? A loving, overprotective, and health-obsessed boyfriend, and the prospect of spending the rest of my life ill, popping pills, struggling with pain and side effects.

Meanwhile, Adrian had assumed the responsibility of managing my care. I didn't expect him to, but he was quite insistent on it. Every minute he could spare, he rushed home. Had my pills on a schedule pasted on the fridge door. Took me to aerobics twice a week, and took a tai chi class with me. Insisted I take up meditation, which I did for a while and saw very little effect. I'm not sure I was doing it right, though.

Counting the days until I had to board the flight to Jack

son, Wyoming, I felt stifled by what my relationship with Adrian had become. It was always about the stupid illness. Never about romance, future plans, or just plain fun. When he was out working, I used the time to work on my lines, to rehearse, even if I felt ill and drained, and sometimes so weak and shaky I could barely stand. That part could've been my fault somewhat, because I flushed the meds whenever he wasn't looking.

Illness is tough on a marriage; on a new relationship like ours, in its first year, it simply doesn't belong. It did things to us, changed whatever was left undamaged by the stalker until we became old before our time. I wasn't spending a fun Saturday night with my hot boyfriend, going to town in heels and a curve-hugging little black dress. No, I was choosing the right nutrition out of a very restrictive, anti-inflammatory diet plan, which he would make while I watched TV by myself in the living room, fatigued and hopeless.

I was grateful for everything he did, and loved him very much. I just desperately wished he could remember I had wants and needs and some ideal of life I still believed I could make happen. Despite the stalker. And the illness.

I just wanted to feel alive one more time before I'd have to call it quits and resign myself to suffering and living a half-life.

A few days before my flight out of LAX, I stopped taking the meds altogether. Adrian was filming on a Monday through Friday schedule, making things easier for me. Every night he came home tired to the bone, and had to set his alarm for five each morning.

An entire week went on like that, and I didn't find the right time or the courage to break the news to him; I was flying to Wyoming on Saturday.

Friday night he came home with flowers and a small bottle of champagne. Thinking back, I believe he was celebrating the assumption I had canceled my contract. He knew filming was scheduled to start the following Monday, at the Grand Teton National Park.

He had no idea my bags were packed and stashed in the trunk of my car. No clue that I had already checked in to my flight. I remember the guilt weighing me down that night, hard to bear when looking at his beautiful smile and his mesmerizing hazel eyes. He was happy. I couldn't ruin it a moment too soon.

Come Saturday morning, it would be ruined anyway.

But I had to do this for myself. One more project. My swan song.

He was sleeping soundly when I snuck out of bed and dressed quietly. I broke the news in a text message I sent from on board my flight, right before takeoff.

> I hope you can forgive me. I didn't have the heart to tell you last night. I'll be in Wyoming until we're done with location, then back in LA, in a couple of weeks or so. Please, be happy for me. It's probably going to be my last film.

My phone rang before I could turn it off, Adrian's loving smile displayed on the screen. I took the call.

"I'm really sorry—"

"How could you do this to me?" he was shouting, stuttering, choking on his rage. "How can I focus on my work when I don't know what's going on with you? Do you ever think of anyone but yourself? Jeez, Emma, you're driving me insane."

"Adrian, it's not that I—"

"I don't want to hear it! What am I supposed to do? Put filming on hold here so I can run to Wyoming and take care of you?"

I didn't need him to take care of me. He never understood that, and that kindled my own frustration. "I don't expect you to. I'll be fine. It's just a couple of weeks." A moment of tense silence on the call, while I heard his breathing, rapid, almost panting. "I just wanted one more shot at doing something. You know damn well that I can't memorize my lines with this illness. I'm not going to last like this. I'm finished."

"No, you're not," he replied, exhaling forcefully. Then he hung up without another word, just as the flight attendant was starting to give me the stink eye for still being on the phone.

I don't believe he ever forgave me for what I did with that text message, with my own cowardice not to look him in the eye as I broke the news. I still believe I deserved every bit of his anger. It was an unbelievably shitty thing to do to a man who loved me so selflessly.

I cried almost the entire flight to Jackson, making countless plans on how to get Adrian to forgive me.

Once I was on location, with all the adrenaline, the excitement keeping me on my toes, I started feeling better than I'd felt in a long time. Despite long days spent filming, when I read my lines in the evening, from a lounge chair with one hell of a mountain view, I memorized them with ease. I felt in my element, not a trace of fatigue or pain to slow me down. Exhilarated, I gave everything I had in me in front of the cameras. And I shined.

When I went back to LA, my stomach was in a knot at the thought of seeing Adrian after almost three weeks of text messages and tense, frigid phone calls late at night.

He met me at the airport, red roses in his hand and a faint smile on his lips. His eyes didn't light up when he saw me; he was still mad. As I returned home, everything I'd left behind came crashing back down on me. The sense of suffocation. Fearing that damn stalker. Adrian's overbearing helpfulness.

The following morning, my joints hurt so badly I winced when I got out of bed. He rushed to help me. Holding a cup of tea to my lips seemed difficult, my strength depleted after the flight home.

I thanked him for the tea, then set the cup down.

"I need to go back to Tahoe until we start filming on location," I said calmly, knowing I was about to ignite a powder keg. "I can't—"

"How will you manage?" he asked, his voice high-pitched with concern. He ran his fingers through his tousled hair and looked around desperately as if searching for a way out. "We have a couple of weeks more in this season, then we break until September. Can't you wait for me?"

It was a reasonable request, but I didn't have it in me to live like that for another day. I needed time away, time to think about us, about our future. "I'm sorry, Adrian, I need to do this."

"You're incredibly selfish, Emma. It's always been about what you need. What you want. Where you want to go. When everything turned to shit because of that guy out there"—he pointed at the window—"that wasn't my fault."

"Why bring him into this? It has nothing—"

"Why? We never had a bloody chance at a normal relationship, because of you. Your needs. Your career. Your baggage. Your ex. All your countless problems. That's what my life's been since I fell in love with you." He stopped talking and propped his hands on his hips, glaring at me. "Playing whack-a-mole with your endless predicaments."

I was speechless, gaping at him in disbelief.

He took one step closer and locked his eyes onto mine. "You know what? I've had it. I'm out of here. Give the landlord notice on your way out. He can throw my shit in the trash for all I care." He grabbed his jacket and keys on the way to the door. "Have a nice life."

The slamming of the door echoed in my mind for a while. I stood there, shaking, heartbroken, devastated at the thought of having lost him. Terrified his words might've painted a picture I had somehow failed to see. Had I been that selfish?

There were no tears that night, only a gaping opening inside my body, like a black hole that had swallowed my heart. Later that night, when I peeked outside the window, hoping to see Adrian's car pulling into the driveway, all I saw was that damned stalker, hiding in the shadow of the house across the street.

"This ends now," I muttered, angry as hell. I grabbed my jacket and rushed outside, then ran across the street, where I'd seen him only moments ago.

He was gone.

"Where are you?" I shouted, my voice carrying over the peaceful neighborhood and raising up the barking of several dogs. "Where the hell are you?"

Nothing but silence. I walked up and down the street, looking for him everywhere. Then I turned back, striding quickly up my own driveway. From my doorway, I looked at the street one more time. A couple of houses had turned on their lights. It was almost two in the morning.

"I'm right here, you son of a bitch," I said loudly.

"Shut the hell up," a voice called from two houses down, where a guy in his pajamas was gesturing furiously, flipping me off. "We need to work tomorrow."

I spent that night awake, unable to sleep. Expecting Adrian to come back. Or the stalker to take me up on my invitation and show his face. To settle this, whatever *this* was.

Nothing happened.

It feels like this scene took place a long time ago, only I feel sure it hasn't been that long. I miss Adrian dearly, and wish I could take everything back, to make amends somehow. I blame myself for the damage I've done to a kind and loving heart. Yes, I've been selfish.

It's too late to fix anything. He's gone.

He's probably moved on. Denise mentioned something about a supermodel girlfriend. He had every right to seek happiness elsewhere.

All I have now is regret. And fear I won't survive the next attack.

THIRTY-SEVEN

I wake up feeling just a little bit stronger than yesterday, although my sleep was haunted by nightmares that still make my skin crawl. They felt so real, and I relive them with a shudder. Then my mind shifts away from the world of dreams to that of memories, with the fragment about the day I met Adrian. It infuriates me, the recurrence of this partial memory, how it stubbornly pops in my mind. It keeps bothering me, as well as the one about the attack, where I am screaming and running, and still can't see the face behind that hateful, burning glare.

I need to remember how these particular memories end, so that the brainworm can dissipate and leave me be. I have nothing better to do, while waiting for the nurse to start my day with breakfast and blood tests and medications and the ultimate form of humiliation known in hospital lingo as "personal hygiene," so I let myself become immersed in the moment I still can't recall completely.

I see myself walking onto location for *Summer Love,* with Denise by my side. I was stressed out about that film, about baring skin in front of the crew, other actors, everyone. I entered the house with my head held up high, projecting a self-confidence I was hoping to start feeling soon.

As we were walking in, the first thing that caught my attention was that agent's raspy voice saying, "Take my advice, kid, sign this dotted line and the sky's the limit for Adrian Sera. Hell, women will line all around this block for a night with Adrian Sera."

Then I noticed Adrian, tall, handsome, with a strong jaw and mesmerizing eyes that lit up when he saw me. His dark hair, a little tousled. His voice, shouting, "I don't want to hear it, Lyle. I won't do it."

"Son, do you ever want to get laid again? Then sign the damn paper. It's your only chance."

Lyle kept pounding, stabbing at Adrian's chest with his stubby finger, but Adrian turned away from his agent, dismissing him with a hand gesture. "I said no. It's not who I am."

Lyle grabbed Adrian's sleeve and held him back. "Listen, no one can—"

Lyle's words faded into the background, because I was distracted by someone. The director, summoning us in the other room. Denise, leading the way and beckoning me to follow.

I stop trying to relive that memory. It's clear I will never know what that document was unless Adrian someday tells me. But why would he, now that he's gone from my life? And why does it matter? My brainworm is nothing but a pointless annoyance. There's no hidden meaning to it, nothing of any importance that my subconscious mind might be trying to say, as Dr. Sokolowski suggested.

However, I remembered more about that day this time around. That, in itself, as pointless as it may be, is encouraging, worthy of a tiny smile, as my fingers find the bed controls almost effortlessly and lift the head of the bed.

Distant voices make me hold my breath again. My smile

withers when I recognize Steve's voice. *Oh, no. I can't face him.* I don't care what the doctor said, I'm not safe with Steve in the same room.

"This is a legal document," Steve is saying, his baritone sounding closer, louder, with each step he takes. Menacing. "Miss, you don't want to be the one who keeps my wife from seeing these papers. Trust me, you don't."

I wouldn't expect that she does. She must be terrified of him. The nurse's voice sounds familiar and intimidated. It's not Jasmine; I don't know who it is, but I've heard her before.

Steve has his way of getting things done. "Get with the program, or get out of my way," I heard him say so many times I lost count. He doesn't say it this time, not with words anyway, but I'm sure he projects it just fine.

The door opens and he walks in, his heavy steps accompanied by the clacking of stilettos.

Mikela.

"Hello, Emma, how are you feeling?" Steve asks. He brought in a whiff of winter freshness and a faint scent of wood smoke. Somewhere nearby someone's sitting by a wood firepit, or perhaps grilling over that fire, although I'm not picking up the smell of barbecue. No amount of snow can keep the locals away from the grill. I miss that.

Instead of barbecue, I pick up Mikela's sweet floral perfume, the one that never fails to turn my stomach and rile me, all in one single breath.

"I'm fine, Steve, as fine as I can be. What do you need?"

He exhales without trying to hide his annoyance with my attitude. "I brought the documents we discussed. They're ready for your signature." He unlatches a briefcase, and papers rustle near the bed. In the distance, chewing gum pops. I smell mint.

"All right, leave them on the table. I'll read them as soon as I can." The sarcasm in my voice is heavy.

"Well, you don't have to." I gasp quietly. I can't believe the nerve on him. "We can get a notary public in here to read the papers to you and sign them in your place, with two witnesses. Or direct your hand to the right spot, if you can manage it yourself."

Oh, he's thought of everything. "And who would those witnesses be?"

"Anyone, really. We'll figure something out." He pulls the chair closer to the bed and takes a seat. "Have you reconsidered? It's a win-win, you have to admit. I promise, we'll take good care of you."

For a second, I imagine Mikela performing the duties of the morning nurse. The thought rattles me to my core. I couldn't survive it.

I fill my lungs with air, steadying myself. I can't lose control, can't start shouting the way I feel the urge to, can't seem even more unhinged than these people paint me to be.

"I've had plenty of time to think, yes," I say, then pause for effect, letting him build up some hope. "And I realize now that, when you lost this house, you lost way more than the actual piece of real estate, didn't you?"

"What are you talking about?" His voice is a low, threatening whisper.

"You lost your Nevada address, and with it, about ten percent of your income, which the State of California gets in taxes now because you live there. I didn't realize it at first, but I'm sure you did." I wait for him to respond, but he's breathing heavily, enraged, while I'm starting to feel fear again. "It took me a while, but I think I finally figured out where your obsession with this house is coming from."

"You've lost it, Emma." He slams the stacks of paper against the bed. I feel it through the blanket, on top of my legs, and I flinch. The papers aren't heavy, just rustling continuously as sheets start slipping off the bed and landing on the floor.

I brace myself. "Is that what you came to ask that day? To keep using this address as your tax residence?"

"What?" He springs off the chair and pushes it aside, then starts pacing the room angrily. "You're out of your mind!"

"Is that why I'm here, blind and bedridden and at your damn mercy, because I said no?"

Mikela breaks out into laughter. She's a few feet away, probably by the window. "Told you, babe, she's psycho." She says the word in a singsong voice. "Just do what you got to do, and let's get the hell out of here."

It takes all my willpower to ignore her. "I wondered why you didn't just buy another house in Nevada, if taxes are your issue. Why getting this one is so alluring to you, even if it meant becoming a criminal."

"Yeah, you're right," Steve says, farther in the distance, probably speaking with his fiancée. "We're wasting our time here."

"Then I realized you can't afford to buy anything anymore, can you?" I drive the point mercilessly, like a dagger. "She bled you dry, didn't she?" It's my turn to laugh, and I make it the best performance of my career. "I've seen girls like her. *Leeches* like her. It's always something. One more dress, another diamond bracelet, let's take a trip to somewhere exotic, I need a new car. Until you're broke, and no matter how hard you work, you can't climb out of the hole she put you in with a sway of her hips."

The stilettos are approaching quickly, the feet in them stomping the floor angrily. She's about to hit me, slap me probably, and I brace for it. I could push the button and call for help, but I choose not to.

"Miki, no," Steve says. There's a struggle happening a few feet to my left. He's probably trying to hold her back. "There's a security system in this house. Cameras in every room." Those words end the struggle like a bucket of ice water poured over a fire. Mikela walks away, while Steve approaches the bed.

"You need help," he concludes. "Until now, I didn't fully understand the extent of your brain injury. It is now my duty to bring your case to court. I'm sorry, Emma, but you've left me no choice."

"Get out of my house, you son of a bitch." For a tense moment of silence, I'm thinking hard and fast for a solution, for something that could keep him away. "I'll sell it," I eventually say. "I'll list it for 10 percent below market and sell it to anyone but you. Then we'll see what you'll do with your conservatorship."

He inhales sharply, with an unnatural, rattling noise. Perhaps he's not feeling well, because he lets himself drop on the side of my bed.

"I might let you spend money on lawyers first," I whisper, knowing he's close enough to hear me, "but the day I'm called in court is the day I sell this house. I swear. Get the hell out, Steve."

The door opens and footsteps rush inside, soles on hardwood, one with a slight squeak.

"Mr. Wellington," Dr. Sokolowski says firmly. "Follow me, please."

Steve stands with some difficulty, breathing heavily, but then his breathing accelerates. "I checked you out, Doctor whatever your name is. You're not even board-certified."

"Not all doctors are," he replies calmly. "Now, let's go. You're disturbing my patient. Again. I believe she made that clear."

I listen as hard as I can, each tiny rustle of clothing or shift in the air painting a picture. I believe Dr. Sokolowski grabs Steve's arm and leads him out of the room. Then the door closes, and their voices fade.

I breathe, relieved, then freeze when stilettos approach the bed slowly, quietly. The bed tilts under Mikela's weight, and that repulsive perfume invades my nostrils.

For a long moment, nothing happens. Then she takes a strand

of my hair and plays with it—I imagine her twirling it around her fingers. In the distance, the doorbell chimes. I'm hoping that whoever's at the door hurries the hell up.

"Don't touch me," I whisper, shaking inside, not with fear but with all-consuming rage.

"Or what?" she asks, also a whisper, mocking me. "What will you do about it?" I can feel her smoothing the strand out, running her fingernails through it, then twirling it again. Then she laughs, like someone without a care in the world. "Ah, sister, you and I will have so much fun together. If you behave, I'll let you watch." A gentle tug at my hair. "Oops, sorry, you can't. I'll let you listen instead. I can teach you a thing or two. You see, us leeches really know our shit. I bet you never made him scream and beg for mercy, did you?"

I can't think of anything to say to that, but I force a smile on my lips. It doesn't go unnoticed. The tug turns stronger, pulling at my scalp, tilting my head. I resist the best I can, still smiling, wondering why Dr. Sokolowski has been gone for so long.

"Tell me, is your name what happens when people who can't spell have children?" I laugh quietly as she gasps.

The door swings open, and Mikela bounces off the bed. I finally breathe. It's Dr. Sokolowski.

"Miss Murtagh, Mr. Wellington had to leave." I hear keys jangling in his hand. "His assistant just picked him up. Something urgent with the production set and casting for—um, sorry, I forgot what he said. He asked you to take his Beemer back home." Keys ring as they probably change hands.

"How could he leave me here?" Mikela's voice climbs to a high pitch of frustration. "He's never done that before. Who picked him up?"

"Please, feel free to discuss that with him," the doctor replies, unfazed. "And I ask that you never return here until such time as you have a valid court order. Am I understood, Miss Murtagh?"

"Take your hand off me, asshole," she snaps, but the stilettos are clacking toward the exit. A few moments later, the front door is slammed once more. Seems that my door takes the brunt of all the drama in my life.

I listen, trying to hear if Dr. Sokolowski has come back.

"I'm here, Emma," he says gently, when he returns. Something rustles by the bed, and the IV tubing moves slightly against my arm. "And you're safe. You can go to sleep now."

No...I'm not safe. Not when he's not here with me. Not when I'm alone in the dark, locked inside a betraying body.

But within moments, my awareness disintegrates, and with it, so does my fear.

I fall asleep.

THIRTY-EIGHT

"I'd love some coffee, please, or some Coke. Whatever's easier," I add, hoping it's the right moment to broach the subject with Dr. Sokolowski.

It's the next morning, I believe. I'm still a little fuzzy about the passing of time, still feel disoriented. But I remember having dinner sometime after Steve left and I slept a little. Jasmine helped me guide the fork to stab pieces of delicious roasted potatoes with herbs, and I took them to my mouth with very little assistance. Jasmine covers the night shift, according to her, so that must've happened last night. I wonder if she's still working with Steve, and what exactly she's doing.

"Emma, I'd love to, but I'm afraid it would conflict with your medication." He's tearing open some packaging. There's a faint smell of disinfectant. "Have you been eating well?"

"Yes, I have." I wonder if I should mention Jasmine's skill with fried chicken. Perhaps that's also conflicting with some medication. "By the way, what are you giving me? What meds?"

"Quite a few. You're still on Decadron for your brain swelling."

"I thought—"

"That's gone down, yes, but not 100 percent. We doctors like to err on the side of caution. Then Versed to help you sleep better and relax. It also helps prevent seizures, which can occur in TBI patients. Fentanyl in a patch for the pain, and you're on IV fluids."

"Which one's responsible for keeping me caffeine-free?"

He laughs, a bit muffled from the mask. "That would be Versed."

"Let's just take that one off the list. I'm doing so much better." I reach the control panel on my bed and lift my backrest. "See? I can do this now."

"Congratulations, yes, that's really good. Your muscle tone is improving. Can you move your legs?"

"A little. I've been wiggling my toes with some success, but lifting my knee off the bed is a different story." I hesitate, wondering if I should mention the fibromyalgia, but I don't. Something indefinite holds me back, more like a gut feeling than a rational thought. Probably thinking I won't be able to flush my meds if I open my mouth about it. I'm sure Dr. Sokolowski would rush to treat it.

"How's your memory?"

"Eh...slightly better. Still trying to fill the holes, and it doesn't always work. But I'm remembering more."

"Do you remember the attack?"

"Y—not entirely." I correct myself mid-word. "I know what happened, I just don't remember all the elements of *how* it happened. I know my ex tried to kill me."

"You told me about an intrusive memory, about being chased and looking over your shoulder to see him coming. Was that Steve you saw?"

I don't reply for a moment, trying, yet again, to lift the fog off that particular stretch of damaged memory. "I can't see his face yet. I know it's him, though; there's no doubt in my mind."

As we chat, he starts checking my reflexes. Flicks my middle fingernail. Taps each elbow twice. Runs a pointy object on the soles of my feet. Has me squeezing his fingers, which I do much better than I recall doing in the past.

"Do you know where you are?"

"At home," I reply quickly, amazing myself at how easy that feels—to find the right information inside the maze of my awareness. "Released from hospital into the care of my ex," I add bitterly, with just a hint of reproach in my voice. If I could, I'd roll my eyes at him, although he wasn't even there. "Any progress with fixing that?"

"Let's just take a moment and celebrate the return of your anterograde memory. You're forming new memories well, retrieving them quickly and without hesitation. Bravo, Emma." His fingers trace under my jaw, then my neck, feeling the lymph nodes. The faint, elegant scent of basil and suede fills my nostrils. I've come to like it just as much as I like his company.

He turns my head gently, left and right. "Any pain?"

"N—no. There's some in the back of my head, dull, like an enduring migraine, but not too bad."

"Dizziness? Nausea? Disorientation?" My chart clatters in his hand as it hits the bed, his pen scratching against paper.

"None of that. Lots of brain fog, though. Mornings are the worst. That's why I believe you should prescribe me some coffee." I smile, but he doesn't say anything. "And I can't form new memories that well, even if you want to celebrate. Sometimes I wonder if what I remember actually happened, or if I'm dreaming. Or making it up to fill the holes, like you said."

"This is great progress, Emma, but we have a long road ahead, with all sorts of rehab." He seems preoccupied with something else, barely paying attention.

"How about my eyes? I tried to peek under my dressing and couldn't. They feel heavy and mushy."

He tugs at the edge of my dressing, lifting it a little. I don't see anything, and still can't open my eyes. "Dr. Winslow said you shouldn't stress your eyes at all."

"But they feel weird, and I'm afraid it's not normal."

"They're treated with a lubricant to protect the cornea, because you can't blink under the gauze. That's why they feel mushy. It's perfectly normal, don't worry about it. Try to remember instead, and tell me how you feel about what you discover."

"What do you mean?"

"As we discussed before, some people with post-traumatic amnesia don't remember more because they're afraid of *what* they could remember. Of reliving the trauma of the attack. We could set you up with a psychologist to help you." He lifts the bed rail and locks it in place.

"Thank you, I'll think about it." I can't tell him I'm not sure how I'm going to pay the medical bills I've stacked up so far. All I can do is avoid adding more. "I don't think I'm afraid. It's something else, like key pieces of information are hidden. I guess it will come to me, because it is starting to, but it's just very slow."

"Your blood values are improving across the board, with inflammation markers dropping. Very good." Some papers rustle again. "Oh, about you being released into your ex's care. That's taken care of, but there's a catch."

"How is it taken care of? Was Steve told about it? He didn't mention anything about that, and I was surprised, but—"

"Yes, I informed him right before he left yesterday. You're technically in limbo now, from a paperwork perspective, but you could easily fix that if you hired your own caregiver. If, of course, a neuropsychiatrist can certify you're able to make sound decisions."

"Oh, I see." Fear grabs my gut and twists it mercilessly. I remember what he said when I asked about those PA announcements. Psychosis. Hallucinations.

I'm so screwed.

"How can we make that happen?"

"I'll arrange a consult. But for now, you're fine, because you have nurses with you around the clock."

"Thank you." I keep myself from worrying what will happen if I don't pass the psych evaluation, if I'm found mentally deficient, or whatever nice, complicated phrase they use to say I'm crazy. "Can I ask a favor?"

"Sure."

"I got a text message earlier this morning. I heard the beep. Could you please read it for me?"

He takes the phone and enters the passcode I give him. "See? Forming new memories beautifully. Okay, it's from Denise. She wants to know if she can visit you tomorrow. What do I reply?"

"Um, yes, sure, she can visit anytime." Why did Denise text me? She knows I can't see. That's a bit strange. Still, I smile at the thought of her coming to visit. She's my rock, my cornerstone.

A familiar whoosh as the message is sent. "What do you say I pick up some ice-cream after my hospital shift? To celebrate your progress. Would you like that?"

My smile widens. "I'd love that."

After he leaves, I find myself feeling hopeful, but hope is dangerous. Hope can make frail humans have false expectations and be crushed when they don't come to fruition.

Then, after the self-admonishing about hope and its dangers, I think about that Coke again. It made me feel good, stronger, more coordinated. But I continued to improve for almost two days, way after the caffeine left my system. I'm puzzled by that realization. I don't know what caused the improvement and that bothers me, because whatever I did that worked, I want to do more of it.

After a while, tiredness catches up with me and I'm about to doze off, when Jasmine's words come to mind, the way she spoke about pain, how it's useful, how it reminds us we're alive. She's seemed obsessed with my fentanyl patch lately, tugging at it, checking it, although it's always Dr. Sokolowski who places it on my arm every few days, and it stays there. It never slips.

What exactly would happen if I lifted the corner just a bit? I suspected Jasmine of tampering with it, of adding something with a vinegary scent to it, but I'm not sure. What if fentanyl smells of vinegar and bleach? I have no idea what it's supposed to smell like.

It's easy to suspect people when you're completely in the dark, or when you're paranoid. I know for sure Jasmine did something to that patch, something she didn't mention to me, and that's very suspicious, especially considering how chummy she is with my ex. Or with Lisa, whose number she had. Lisa, who had a bigger motive to kill me even than Steve.

Fentanyl is a powerful sedative, an opioid painkiller and anesthetic, if I recall correctly what I heard about countless overdose deaths on the news correctly. Perhaps the caffeine in that Coke reduced its efficacy for a while.

I'm going to reduce it more, and perhaps my memory will thank me.

That is, if I can find the strength and coordination in my fingers to lift my damn sleeve enough to reach it.

THIRTY-NINE

Warmth spreads across one side of my face. The sun, as it rises over the mountains, must be shining through the window. In the distance, the lake must be sparkling with golden specks on shades of topaz and sapphire and aquamarine. My fingers brush against my left cheek, tracing the sun's warmth, feeling its heat mirrored on the back of my hand. I bask in the sunshine, slowly turning my aching head toward the left, welcoming its faint touch on my skin.

Then I resume my efforts to lift the edge of my sleeve above the patch. I'm obsessed with it, motivated to do what I've set my mind to do, and frustrated with the intense struggle needed to complete such a basic task as rolling up a sleeve, or at least slide it up a little.

I don't have enough dexterity and strength to grab the hem and lift. If I want to touch the tip of my index finger with my thumb I can, but there's not enough strength in my muscles to do more than just touch it. "Severely low muscle tone," Dr. Sokolowski called it, and did a good job explaining what that means. I understand why it happens; I just need it to stop happening already.

Lowering my arm, I breathe heavily, defeated. Then I find the control panel and lower the backrest until it's almost horizontal. Perhaps I can save the strength spent lifting my fingers and use it to push the fabric up just an inch or two now I'm horizontal.

My mind wanders as I struggle with the fabric. I keep thinking of those PA announcements that made Dr. Sokolowski voice concerns about psychosis and hallucinations. What if he was right? What if I was imagining things, trying to fill the holes, to paint the picture of my hospitalization in imaginary sounds and events, so that everything wouldn't be so scary and quiet? Perhaps that's not as bad as psychosis, right? Dr. Sokolowski said that would be normal.

Was there anyone with me when one of those PA calls happened? I think hard for a moment, and I can't recall a single occurrence. I would've commented on it with whomever was there. I would've asked who that doctor was, because I'm naturally a curious person, hungry for any tidbit of knowledge I can find.

But then again, how could anyone have been with me when a PA call happened, if they weren't real? And I know they weren't. Code blue only happened in room 1204. No one needed Dr. Whitting anywhere else but the emergency room. I ponder on that for a moment. They weren't real; I'm absolutely sure about that.

No, whether I like it or not, it seems I was making them up. Hallucinating, or just filling the holes with sounds that matched a hospital, my memory a garbled mess at the time. Seems I can't trust myself worth a damn. The neuropsychiatrist better not pick on that to slam a mental deficit label on me and tie my life up with a nice bow as they lay it at Steve's feet.

Not gonna let it happen, I promise myself. *Whatever it takes.*

I grab the fabric of my sleeve and lift it a little, but it slips right back. Repeating the same action with hope of a different outcome, also known as the textbook definition of insanity, takes a few long minutes. Until I decide to slip the lifted sleeve under my arm, to hold it in place.

It stays put. Finally, some progress. I run my trembling, weak fingers along the edges of the patch, then try to lift the corner a little. My fingers slip on the glossy surface and cannot grasp it. I'm about to curse out loud when the door opens. Light, rubber-soled footsteps approach quickly.

It's not Jasmine.

I don't know who it is.

"Hello?" I call weakly, lifting the backrest of my bed, as if that helps with anything. Lying on my back makes me feel more exposed, but I'm completely vulnerable anyway.

"Hello, Emma," a familiar voice replies, drawing near. Something rustles near my head, and I flinch. "It's me, Isabella, checking your vitals. Would you like a sip of water?"

I breathe. "You're back."

"Yes, I was off for a week." She sets something down on the table beside my bed. "You remember me, that's excellent." She sounds genuinely happy for me. "Straw coming," she announces, then the plastic touches my lips. I down a few sips thirstily. It feels so good.

"Thank you."

"How are you feeling?"

Stuck is my first thought, but I don't voice it. "You were my nurse in the early days, right?"

"I was, yes. One of them, anyway."

"Was I, um, making sense at all?" I want to know if I was hallucinating, but how is she supposed to know what monsters my damaged mind was battling?

"To be honest, I don't remember much." She laughs quietly, apologetically. "A week off has that effect on me, especially after taking three screaming kids skiing on five of those days. I'm spent now."

So, I probably wasn't making too much sense, and she's embarrassed to tell me. Or she wants to spare my feelings. Medical personnel put way too much stock into hope and positive mindsets. Being clueless is more dangerous than anything.

Moving quickly, she changes the bed sheets. One by one, the pillows are removed from the bed. Fresh linens fill the air with the scent of laundry detergent, a brand I might have used myself. It's possible they're my own sheets, laundered in my own laundry room.

"Do you know a Dr. Whitting?" I ask, firing a shot in the dark. How could she possibly know the figment of my over-drugged imagination?

Her hands don't skip a beat dressing the pillows. "Yes, he's a trauma surgeon."

Her reply chills the blood in my veins. "How about Dr. Parrish?"

She laughs quietly, seeming a little confused. "He's the resident OB-GYN."

I'm shaking, the chill entering my bones. "And Dr. Jones?"

"He's the ICU resident," she replies casually, putting the pillows back on the bed.

In my mind, the sound of the PA echoes faintly. "Dr. Jones to ICU." That's what I heard. How is it possible? How could Isabella know what my hallucinations were about? Or is she lying about these doctors, and saying Jones is in ICU was just a lucky shot? Not likely.

And why would she lie?

"Why do you ask?" She fluffs a pillow and slips it under my head, gently supporting my back. "You know all these doctors?"

"I remember hearing PA calls, like code blue and Dr. Jones to ICU."

She chuckles, punching another pillow. "Ah, that makes sense. It's much better at home, isn't it? It's peaceful."

"Yes, but—"

I stop, frozen in mid-phrase, unsure what to say, what to believe about all this. I'm a traumatic brain injury patient. My memory is not fully recovered. I don't know when to trust myself, and whether I'm imagining things.

I might be imagining the conversation I'm having with Isabella right now. What if she's not real either? How would I know?

"Okay, we're done for now," Isabella announces with a short, satisfied sigh. She starts moving around the room, collecting things, opening the trash can, throwing something in.

The can closes with that familiar metal-on-metal grind. It's not a rental trash can; it's the same one it's been since I can remember.

Before I can say anything, Isabella asks me, "Do you need anything else?"

"N—no." Her question has thrown me... there was something I wanted to say. Frustrated, I ask the first thing that comes to mind, "Do you work in the hospital?" I don't know how to uncover the truth about what's going on, which questions to ask. I'm poking randomly in the dark, hoping I'll hit something.

"Yes, at Baldwin Memorial."

"What's your specialty?"

"Trauma. I work in the emergency room." She collects a few items that clatter when she dumps them on a tray. A metallic clatter, like cutlery landing on stainless steel or something like that. "Why? Do you need anything?"

"And you work in people's homes too?"

"Usually no, but I responded to an ad for a side gig, and you're it. I took a couple of shifts, then I went on vacation, and now I'm back." She stops for a while, then adds, "Emma, if you're not comfortable with me, please say so. I'm trying my best, but—"

"No, it's not that, I promise. You're great. It's just these PA calls, I can't get them out of my mind. I thought hospitals don't use the PA system anymore, or something. Did you hear it recently?"

"Ah." She sounds relieved. "They stopped using the PA on the patients' floors, but they're still using it in the ER and the operating rooms, where people can't check their phones that easily. But the system is there. If we have a multi-cas emergency—"

"What's that?"

"A multiple-casualty emergency, like a highway pile-up or a building fire."

"I see."

"Then the hospital turns it on again, because people can't take their attention off their patients to check messages all the time. So, it depends." She walks over to the bed and stops. "What else can I do for you?"

"Could you please ask Dr. Sokolowski to stop by?" I have a ton of questions for him.

"He's not here. I believe he's on day shift in the ER today. I don't think he'll be back here until tomorrow, or he might swing by later, after his shift."

I feel sad at the thought, anxious, but push it away. My face feels warm on the left side. I remember the sunshine is piercing my room through the window and I shudder. The curtains must be completely open. "Could you please pull the curtains shut at dusk? There's someone out there, a man who's been stalking me."

A brief moment of hesitation before she replies. "Sure. Jasmine will be here by then, but I'll leave a note." The clipboard clatters. "I see you have some tests scheduled for tomorrow. Blood tests in the morning, then a psych eval at ten."

Sometime after that, Isabella goes, and I barely acknowledge her wishes for a good afternoon. My mind echoes with the sound of my own shrieking voice, reverberating over fragments of memory like shards of shattered mirror. I see myself, broken, in a million different images of the same terror.

Help! Someone, help me . . . Let me go!

I see myself running, turning my head to look behind me, and faltering, landing hard against the wall, then pushing myself away. I reach the door and try to open it, but can't. I fumble with the lock, pull the door open, and turn to look behind me again, just in time to see the arm raised above my head, ready to come down, while a look of pure rage stares me in the eye. Then I see the asphalt of my own driveway rushing to slam against my face, before my entire world goes dark.

I push away the intrusive memory after searching it again, desperate to see Steve's face in it, needing to hear the words that preceded the blow.

I can't.

Another question, just as terrifying, keeps me locked in a restless whirlpool. How did I manage to hallucinate PA calls with real doctors? Or did I? If the calls were real, why were they repetitive? Or did I hear everything only once, but those sounds echoed in my mind whenever I needed sounds to reassure myself that I was still alive, not alone, in a hospital where I was safe?

If that's the case, how did I know ahead of time that Dr. Whitting would be needed in the ER?

Then again, why would I trust anything that comes from such a screwed-up mind?

As my shaky fingers try to grab hold of the edge of my fentanyl patch, I wonder why I can't recall anything else distinctive about the hospital, other than those PA calls. No specific smells. No cleaning crews. No passersby chatting, other than those two girls discussing their lunch choices. No footfalls outside my door, or ambulances pulling in. The sheets feel the same. The water tastes the same.

That damn trash can and its grinding lid. The same.

As my fingers finally manage to lift the corner of the patch and start peeling it off, I recall the fresh air that came off my visitors when they entered the room, as if they'd just stepped inside from the cold. Unless my hospital room was right next to the entrance, it doesn't make sense.

Stubborn and determined, I peel off the patch completely and hide it under the covers, then lower my sleeve to hide what I've done. No one can figure it out, especially not Jasmine, or she'll slap a new one it its place.

A fly buzzes at the window, butting its head against the glass, looking to break free. It happened before, when I was in the hospital. What did Jasmine call it? Positive pressure something, keeping critters out of hospitals. Hearing it chills me, as a terrifying new thought emerges from the abyss inside my mind.

What if I'm being held hostage?

What if I was never in the hospital?

FORTY

The heart monitor by my bed is beeping furiously. I feel I can't breathe, my own powerlessness suffocating. I wish I could spring out of this bed and look around and figure out where the hell I am and what's happening to me. Am I completely losing my mind? Have I become paranoid, or psychotic, or some other medical explanation for what's going on with my fractured mind?

More than anything, I wish I could get some answers, ones I can trust to be true. But the only person I can absolutely trust is myself. Although, I have to admit, the threat of hallucinations casts a shadow over that.

I know what I remember, and it's not some hallucination. I was attacked. I remember screaming for help, running, the killer's arm raised above my head to strike. I remember falling to the ground. My memories are real. I can still feel the rush of adrenaline, of fear, as it came in that desperate moment. The searing of my panting breath burning my chest.

My pain is real too. My body doesn't lie to me. The throbbing in my head is now starting to increase, probably since I removed the painkiller patch, thinking it would help me clear my mind faster. Curious and afraid at the same time, I place my hand at the back of my head where the throbbing seems to emanate from. I feel the gauze covering that area and tap it lightly, until I find an area that hurts badly. It's an oblique stretch of about four or five inches, raised and bumpy. Probably a laceration that has been stitched up, like Dr. Sokolowski said.

That wound is real, as real as it gets. It can barely take the weight of my own head lying on the pillow. The throbbing is severe at times, but I endure.

So, that part is real; I've established that beyond any doubt.

Then, after I fell to the ground with my head split open, what happened? Logic indicates I ended up in the hospital. Everything points in that direction. The doctors, nurses, medications, blood tests, medical equipment, even the PA calls. The fact that I survived that injury, and that I'm getting better. All that points to a hospital taking me in and nursing me back to life, even if not yet to full health.

The only thing that doesn't fit is those PA calls, the fact that they were repetitive. Nothing else. That conclusion sends a chill through my blood. What's more likely, that I hallucinated the PA calls anomaly? Or that someone orchestrated a very elaborate hoax without any obvious reason?

I could've dreamed the entire PA thing; I have to admit it. But my gut won't settle for that conclusion. Who can I call for help? And how? Who can I trust with my life? And do I really need to call anyone, or will I make things worse, by causing additional concern for my sanity?

Whatever monsters took over my mind were created by a traumatized brain flooded with drugs. Now I'm slowly starting to make sense again. I can move a little better, too; seems my guess was right. That painkiller patch was making me weak. As the effects disappear, the throbbing in my head becomes almost unbearable, but my strength improves. It's a trade-off I'm glad to live with.

In the distance, someone flushes a toilet—probably Isabella. The tank refills with a multi-tonal whistling sound I recall hearing before. Of course, I *have* heard it before. If people are camped in my house to care for me, they're using the facilities. And it's my toilet. I must've flushed it hundreds of times. My brain struggled to recognize the familiar sounds of my own house through the haze of drugs. That's all there is to it; must be, even if the timeline seems off somehow, as if I heard it while I was still in the hospital. But since the fog started to lift with that Coca-Cola, things are beginning to come back to me, and it's all clear now.

Dr. Sokolowski was right. My mind must've fabricated explanations for the missing pieces of information. It plugged the holes the best it could.

But my own paranoia is infuriating. I've never suffered from anxiety, but I'm guessing this is what it must feel like. An excruciating sense of dread, sucking the life out of me, turning me into a dysfunctional wreck. Pure hell.

A chime coming from my phone reminds me just how powerless I really am. Such a simple pleasure, reading one's text messages without having to ask people for help. Without having someone else privy to every bit of personal communication.

I wonder if it's Denise again. I still can't think why she texted me in the first place, when she knows I can't see. I'll ask when she gets here. The decision eases my anxiety for just a moment, but it's long enough to think of something I could try.

I lower the backrest of my bed again until I'm almost flat, then take both my hands to my face and find the edge of the gauze covering my eyes. I struggle grasping it, just like I did with the sleeve and the patch earlier, but I feel it's going a bit better. I can lift the gauze a little, and I try to peek from under it. But my eyes refuse to open, my eyelids heavy, held shut with gauze.

But nothing hurts except for my head, and I press on.

I don't see much at first, just a bit of hazy light, a narrow band through eyelids almost entirely closed. I desperately try to blink, but my eyelids don't move much. The head dressing is tight, pressing hard on them, but if I look down, I can see a thin sliver of what's out there.

It's bright. Unbearably so. And it's exhilarating to see again.

Defying the pounding migraine, I force my head back until I can catch a glimpse of where that light is coming from. It's a circle of seven powerful bulbs right above my head. Tears burn my eyes and I close them completely, the effort to stare into that light unbearable. After a while, when I stop seeing smudges of green against my shut eyelids, I peek from under the dressing again, looking around me, slowly moving my head left to right.

I'm in my own master bedroom, at home. I recognize the drapes, the furniture, everything, except for the hospital gear Dr. Sokolowski mentioned. There's a crash cart with drawers by the dresser, next to the window. A mobile heart monitor, perched on a wheeled stand with five casters, displays my vitals in red and green, just as I imagined. A lab stool on wheels is near the bed and, next to the wall, a small table with a metallic tray on it. My king size bed has been replaced with a white hospital contraption with railings on both sides and a complicated control panel on the right.

Everything else I recognize; it's my bedroom furniture.

Except the ceiling lamp, the seven bright bulbs shining like the sun above my head. That's not mine. There used to be a three-blade fan up there, with a soft, central light with a remote-controlled dimmer.

I've seen this lamp in my dreams. And as disturbing as that thought is, I take a moment to acknowledge what it means.

I can see.

The sense of relief washing over me is suffocating and exhilarating at the same time. It's intensely liberating.

Perhaps I always could see. I might've opened my eyes

when they changed my dressing, and I don't remember any of it. Because of the drugs.

My eyes peek from underneath the gauze again, as if I can't believe it's true. I relish seeing the world around me, every little detail. Even that metallic trash can I kept hearing—now I see it too. The logo on it *is* black, not red. I smile, wondering how I knew that. I blink repeatedly, even if I still can't open my eyes fully, trying to focus on that logo. Tears wash off a bit of the lubricant, and my vision clears some more.

It's not biohazard circles. It's the three leaves of a LuxeBin logo. It's the automatic trash can from my own kitchen.

It always has been.

My subconscious mind was trying to tell me that, with my obsession with the black logo, only I didn't listen.

And with that thought, fear returns like a wave, crashing over me until I'm breathless. I have to talk to someone about it. I should call someone, right now. Frantic, I recall the detective who I was told visited me and the business card she left, the one with the round logo. It has her mobile number on the back—that's what Dr. Sokolowski said.

It's a huge, breathless, and painful effort to force my hand to reach that far. I have to turn my entire body, and my legs are not working yet. I feel along the surface of my nightstand for the small piece of stock paper, and eventually find it. Brushing the large, round, raised ink logo with the tips of my fingers, I take it and bring it in range of the sliver of vision I have.

The logo doesn't say *Lake Tahoe Police Department.* I read it again in disbelief.

Heal Home Medical Rentals.

I close my eyes and feel the logo with the tips of my fingers, trying to make sure it's the same one I touched before. That I'm not delusional or simply mistaken.

It's the same one.

Dr. Sokolowski lied to me.

FORTY-ONE

I spend a good stretch of time wondering if I should remove my head dressing and be done with it already. Knowing that I can see has been liberating and scary at the same time. But why did the doctor want me to think I'm blind? I should confront him, only I know I'm too weak to do that. He could've already seen me peek under the gauze already, if he knows to watch the security videos.

I need help.

Until I can figure out what's happening, I'm better off keeping the gauze in place and pretending that nothing's changed. The decision is not an easy one; I'm way past ready to be rid of this bed and all these people. But the doctor's betrayal is heartbreaking. Why did Dr. Sokolowski lie to me? Is Steve paying him to get me to accept the conservatorship? Is that it? All for this house?

When I pushed his buttons, Steve's voice was tinged with despair. I noticed how terrified he was at the prospect of me selling the property to anyone else but him. He was an entirely different man when we were together, before Mikela came into the picture. He was rational, cold-blooded, even, about his decisions. Yes, we had our dry patches, when the right projects didn't land on his desk, and we endured through his decision to wait for the right one, while I worked to pay the routine bills. I was fine about it, even if he wasn't. Something about this house business doesn't add up. Unless I have to believe what Mikela said, that she wants this particular house, she wants to see me kicked out, because this is where they had sex for the first time. In my bed.

Well, I'll have to remember to set that bed on fire, if it's still here somewhere. I'll take it out on the back patio and douse it with gasoline, then light a match and watch it burn.

Because I can *light a match, bitch.* A couple more days, and I'll be able to flick a lighter, too.

Satisfied, I start making fists in the air, then spreading my fingers as widely as I can. After a while, I move on to my legs, trying to bend my knees and force my thigh muscles to work harder. Infuriatingly slowly, it happens. I can flex my knee and push my leg up just a little.

"Good evening, Emma." When Jasmine walks in, I straighten my legs and set my hands alongside my body, hoping she didn't notice what I was doing.

"Hi, Jas." I'm panting a little from the effort I put into my workout. "How's everything?"

"I'm okay. Just a little tired, is all." She sighs as she approaches and sets something on the bed. I hold my breath, knowing she's looking at me. She might notice the missing patch. "Your heart rate is a bit high," she says after a while. "How are you feeling? Any pain today?"

"N—not really, no. I'm fine." My head is throbbing, and I need to learn how to lie better. *Oh, and by the way, I can see.* The thought brings a tiny smile to my lips.

Jasmine doesn't reply. She busies herself in the room, walking back and forth with a slight limp and an occasional groan. She tweaks my IV, while I cringe, knowing she's standing right there, next to my patchless left arm. I'm hoping the sleeve is covering the crime I committed, and she won't be the wiser.

"You're a little dehydrated," she says. "I've increased the saline, and I'll bring you some water. Aren't you thirsty?"

"Yes, I am," I reply enthusiastically, knowing that fluids will help wash the fentanyl out of my system. When she brings the straw to my lips, I forget myself and grab it with shaky fingers, then empty the entire glass.

"Very good," she commends me with excitement in her voice. "Soon you won't need me anymore." She pauses for a moment. "That's my wish for all my patients. To stop needing me."

I laugh quietly. Then I remember who she works for, and the laughter dies on my lips. I can't trust her worth a damn. I wish she'd get out of here already, and leave me alone.

Dinner is delicious—mashed potatoes with cheesy omelet—and I make quick work of finishing everything. I'll need all my strength soon. She still guides my hand to my mouth, but my grip is much stronger, and she notices. I could probably feed myself just fine, if it weren't for this damn gauze.

"Any chance we could skip the Versed tonight?" A pause. Her breath lands on my elbow. "That's what it's called, right? My sedative?"

"I don't know about that," she replies quietly. "It's not just a sedative. It prevents seizures in TBI patients. I'd have to ask the—"

"No," I rush to stop her. "Never mind, I'll ask him myself. Just don't give it to me before I get a chance to ask him. Please."

Another moment of silence. "Sure." She gathers a few things, throws away the trash, and grabs what she'd set on the bed by my side. "If you're in pain more than you can bear, buzz me and I'll take care of it. Do you remember how to do that?"

My fingers find the control panel without much effort. "Yes, it's here, right? This button?"

"Exactly, good. I sleep in the guest bedroom, across the hall, so I can hear you if you call me, or if the machine throws an alarm, all right?"

"Yes, thank you. Good night, Jas. I'll be fine, really."

The door closes after her. I listen intently for a moment, and I'm the only one drawing breath in my room. Then I reflect for a moment, reliving our strange interaction. She's never said that before, not the bit about pain being unbearable, or that she'll sleep nearby, within earshot.

Am I supposed to be scared more than I already am? Did she notice I took off the patch? I may never know. All I can hope for is that she's tired enough to fall asleep and forget all about the Versed.

A door opens in the distance. A microwave beeps. A phone rings after a while, and Jasmine takes the call, her voice muted and indecipherable through the walls. She talks for about ten minutes or so. Then, eventually, all noises stop, after the toilet flushes and that whistling two-tone tells me the tank is now full.

Once the house becomes eerily silent, I grab my phone and set it on my chest, then lift the edge of the gauze and catch a narrow stretch of its screen, enough to retrieve Denise's number. I connect the call, then pull the cover over my mouth to hide the sound.

"Hello, Emma," she says, probably seeing my name on her phone's display. "How are you feeling?"

I don't have time for any of that. "Please help me," I blurt, my voice a rushed, panicked whisper. Jasmine or Dr. Sokolowski could walk in any moment. "You need to call the police. I believe I'm being held hostage here. I think it's Steve. He wants to take my house."

"What are you talking about? I can't believe this. Are you sure, darling?"

"You don't know what he did. He had a lawyer come in here. He wants me to enter a conservatorship agreement, so he can

move in here with Mikela. He wants to take all my rights away."
I start sobbing, and bite my lip to make it stop. "And I can't fight
him. I can't fight them all."

"Oh, honey . . . This doesn't sound like the Steven Wellington I know."

"Yeah, no kidding. And you don't know the half of it." I stop
short of telling her Steve tried to kill me. I'm not sure why; perhaps because I still can't see his face in that memory.

A beat of heavy silence makes me wonder if Denise believes
anything I said. It's hard to; in her place I'd probably be just
as shocked. *Come on, come on,* I urge her, knowing my time is
limited.

"Are you sure you're not overthinking things? You're taking
lots of medications, and you had a brain injury, Emma. Is it possible you're imagining some of these, um, events?"

A long, shattered breath leaves my lungs. I'm not surprised
she thinks I've gone insane. Sometimes, I think so too. "Denise,
if there's one thing and one thing only I could ask of you, that
would be to trust me. Help me, please. I need you to believe me
right now."

"I'll, um, I'll make a few calls—"

"It's the most important thing you could do for me. Please."

"All right. Give me a few minutes. Can I call you back?"

"Yes." I end the call scared she won't trust me after all. But I
trust her. If she said she'll call me back, she will. I lower the volume setting on my ringer and wait, my ears perked up, listening
for the tiniest noise outside my door.

When the phone rings, it gives me a start. I struggle a little to
accept the call, my finger clumsy and uncoordinated, but eventually I manage. "Denise? Did you call them?"

"I spoke with your doctor." Hearing her words, my entire
world collapses. "He explained why this is happening, and that
it's perfectly normal in cases like yours, where the brain has
been traumatized. He said no two brains are alike, and it's hard

to predict what will happen as the brain rewires itself after the trauma. But he gave me the number of your neurologist, a Dr. Winslow. I left a voicemail for him. He'll probably get it in the morning."

Tears are flooding my eyes. "You don't believe me," I whisper. "You were my last hope. And now he knows—"

"I'm not done," she says quickly. "As always, you interrupted me. I'm coming over, first thing tomorrow. I'll watch over you myself, all right? I understand how all this is terrifying, but don't do anything, don't say anything. Just get some rest, and tomorrow you can leave it with me. I'll sort everything out."

"Thank you," I whisper between tears. The call ends, and silence returns, heavy and menacing, just as I realize I never asked why she texted me when she knew I couldn't see. I decide to text her instead of calling her back. It makes less noise that Jasmine or Dr. Sokolowski might hear.

With weak, trembling fingers, I switch over to messages.

The first thing I notice makes me gasp. The earlier text wasn't from Denise. It was from Steve's assistant, Tim, with the news that Steve's gone missing.

With a chill, I recall that Tim is deathly afraid to fly.

He would've never picked Steve up at the house for some studio emergency. Something else happened. And Dr. Sokolowski lied about it.

And now Steve's missing. Per Tim's message, no one's seen him since he visited yesterday.

What's going on?

Panic shears through me. Frantic, I stare at my screen, thinking about what to do. How to save myself.

Panting heavily, I scroll through my contacts, looking for a name I can trust. Then I tap on one, staring at the handsome face displayed on my screen. Memories come crashing into my mind, sweet memories of the good times we had. Of the love we shared.

The avatar smiles at me, the smile touching the man's mesmerizing hazel eyes.

Unanswered, the call goes to voicemail. Hearing Adrian's voice on the recording stirs me up inside—too many clashing emotions to make sense of. A sense of loss and longing, remnants of the old love, and also fear, probably at the thought of speaking with him again. He'd be well within his rights to tell me to go to hell.

I'm already there.

I wait for the beep, then speak, my poorly chosen words a breathless whisper. "Hey, Adrian, it's me, Emma. I know it's been a while, and you've moved on. You don't owe me anything, but if you could, please come by my house. I need you . . . something happened. Please."

Then I wait.

FORTY-TWO

Time crawls slowly when you're waiting.

For me, it's much worse than that. I'm afraid of the moment that door will open, of who will step through it and what their intentions are. I'm not nearly strong enough yet to defend myself.

The screen of my phone shows me the passing of time. It grounds me. Those numbers on a digital display are my lifeline to the world, to reality. I know it's almost ten in the evening, and the deep silence means Jasmine is probably fast asleep. She's probably going to be here until morning sometime, but I haven't heard a sound coming from the guest room in a long while. It's across the hall and to the left, and has its own bathroom. The one with the whistling toilet tank.

Flushing that toilet will probably be the first thing she'll do when she wakes up. And I'll hear it and be ready for her.

But where's Dr. Sokolowski? Wasn't he supposed to swing by tonight, with the ice-cream he offered to pick up? To celebrate my anterograde memory returning, he said. I shake my head in disbelief, gently, because it hurts.

I don't know what to believe anymore.

I give it about thirty more minutes to be sure he's not going to come by tonight, using the time to work on my legs. Because there's something I absolutely need to do, tonight. I can't wait for Denise . . . can't live in this terrifying uncertainty. I have to know.

While I count the painstaking leg exercises I manage to do under the covers, I recall meeting Adrian for the first time, on location. I was lead in that chick flick; he was my co-star. We actually kissed for the first time filming that movie, under the director's professionally focused stare. I recall feeling guilty over how much I'd enjoyed kissing a stranger.

I think again of his strange conversation with Lyle, his pushy agent. And something else reveals itself to me.

Through the fog of time, I hear a voice. It's Lyle, Adrian's agent, the one who loves to channel Joe Pesci. The memory swirls in my mind, invasive and obnoxious and still incomplete.

"Take my advice, kid, sign this dotted line and sky's the limit for Adrian Sera," he was saying, his voice hoarse, as if he smoked two packs a day and drank himself under the table each night. "Hell, women will line all around this block for a night with Adrian Sera."

Adrian had shouted, "I don't want to hear it, Lyle. I won't do it." Seeming fiercely determined for a man who was about to do the exact opposite a few seconds later.

"Son, do you ever want to get laid again? Then sign the damn paper. It's your only chance."

Adrian had turned away at that, dismissing him with a gesture. "I said no. It's not who I am." Then he started walking toward me.

And Lyle had grabbed Adrian's sleeve and held him back. "Listen, no one can—"

Lyle's words faded in the background. That's where the memory ends, the story unfinished, my questions unanswered. I know he signed the contract moments later, but what was said in the meantime is lost to me.

Why the hell does it matter now?

I wish this memory would leave me the hell alone. Nothing but a brainworm, an artifact, that's what it is. If Adrian comes, I'll ask him what that strange conversation with Lyle was all about. Then it will stop haunting me. It feels important, in my gut, that I solve this mystery somehow.

It's almost eleven when I decide I've waited long enough. I elevate the backrest until I'm upright, then proceed to unwrap the gauze from my head. I move slowly, my arms shaky and weak, keeping them working above my head a difficult task. When I'm almost done, I move even slower, the gauze sticking to my stiches, making me wince. It takes patience to untangle it from my hair without pulling at my scalp. When the last of it is loose, I lower my arms and let them rest for a minute.

Next, I try to open my eyes properly, infinitely slowly, afraid of what could happen. My eyelids resist. I feel my face with my fingers and find pieces of tape holding them shut. It's a struggle to peel off the tape, but I manage eventually. Then I finally open my eyes, familiarizing them with seeing again, with the light in the room.

The lamp above my head is dimmed, not as excruciatingly bright as I remember it from earlier. I recognize the dimmer remote, on the nightstand by my side, and I turn the light lower still, to give myself time to adjust.

Then, holding my breath, I unlock and lower the left side rail of the bed. I look at the control panel on my right, until I locate a pair of buttons with arrows on them and a graphic depicting a bed going up and down. I press the down arrow and the bed descends with me, quietly, until it stops with a faint beep. Then I remove my IV, leaving the needle hanging loose from the tubing.

The heart monitor wires are next. Before peeling them off

my skin, I turn my head and look at the machine closely. I can't afford to have it blaring an alarm because a lead disconnects. In the lower right corner, I catch a glimpse of an on/off button. A moment later, the beeping finally stops, and I'm engulfed in perfect, absolute silence.

I turn on my left side, then push myself into a sitting position. My feet touch the floor. I push against it, trying to see if my legs will support my weight. It's doubtful, but I don't have much choice. Holding on to the lowered rail, I ease myself off the bed.

My knees are shaking badly, but I'm standing. After a long moment of self-doubt, I let go of the rail and take a couple of steps, afraid my legs are going to give out on me, and I'll fall. But I don't. Fists clenched, I make it to the cart with drawers, over by the window.

One by one, I open the drawers quietly, rummaging through the contents. One is filled with wound dressing essentials: gauze, pads, tape, scissors, sterile suture kits. The one above it is stocked with medications in pill and vial form, even a couple of IV bags. Another drawer is stocked with labeled, plastic-wrapped equipment: endotracheal tubes, laryngoscopes, and suction catheter kits, even a cricothyrotomy kit. Nothing I can use.

I strike gold with the last drawer, where I find prefilled syringes with all sorts of drugs, color-coded and organized neatly. I take one labeled VERSED, and hold it in my hand. I know what Versed can do. It knocks me out within minutes.

A moment's listening tells me Jasmine's sound asleep. From my bedroom doorway, I can hear her light snoring. Moving as lightly as I can, and running my hand along the wall for balance, I make my way along the corridor until I reach the living room. From there, I sneak into the study and open the closet.

Inside the tiny space, a desk holds a small monitor, a keyboard, and a wired wheel mouse. The control unit for the home security system is installed on a shelf fixed to the wall. A small, three-legged stool is tucked under the desk. I pull it out, not letting go of the syringe in my hand, and I sit, not minding the dust.

Dr. Sokolowski told me that the police took the older security system videos, the ones from the night of the attack. I don't know if that's true. Even if it is, it happened before Steve's last visit. I wake the system and wait for the monitor to display the menu and the array of camera views, then choose the one that covers the door to my room. I fast rewind, staring at the time codes changing rapidly, nothing happening on the screen for a while, with the exception of a nurse who must be Jasmine coming and going, and Isabella before her. Then I reach the place where Dr. Sokolowski had left my room. A few minutes earlier, he'd gone out with Mikela. Another few minutes earlier, with Steve.

I want to know what happened to him. I'm willing to bet my life Tim didn't fly to Lake Tahoe to pick him up.

I memorize the time code and shift the camera to the one outside the front door. Nothing happens then. A few minutes later, I see Mikela exiting the house, then climbing behind the wheel of Steve's blue Beemer and driving off.

Frustrated, I go back to the indoor cameras and choose the living room, then access the time code I memorized. I see Dr. Sokolowski talking with Steve, both men appearing riled up, gesturing widely, posturing, staring each other down. Then Dr. Sokolowski seems to invite Steve to leave through the back patio door. There's something eerily familiar about the doctor's gait, although the image is blurry and distant and from a bad angle. As if I've seen him before.

Perhaps I have, at the same time I saw that lamp, and I don't remember.

Holding my breath, I switch camera views to the one overlooking the backyard. As if watching a silent horror film, I see both men continuing their argument. Steve takes a threatening step toward Dr. Sokolowski, who takes a small step back. Then, lightning-fast, Dr. Sokolowski punches Steve in the throat.

I gasp, then cover my mouth.

On the low-resolution screen, Steve chokes and falls to the ground, both his hands at his throat, as Dr. Sokolowski watches him without making a single move to help. After a while, Dr. Sokolowski walks over and puts his foot over Steve's throat, pressing down until Steve stops writhing and falls still. A minute or so later, after looking around carefully, Dr. Sokolowski checks Steve's carotid for a pulse, then drags his body into the woods behind the house. He comes out of there with a set of car keys in his hand, and goes back inside.

I watch, still covering my mouth, trying to control my racing heart. I know what I have to do now. I have evidence. I can call the police myself, right now, and that will be the end of it.

Grabbing the edge of the desk for support, I ease myself up. I turn off the monitor and turn to leave, then I freeze.

From the doorway, Jasmine is staring at me.

FORTY-THREE

"I knew it," Jasmine mutters angrily, more to herself. She stares at me from head to toe with eyes rounded in shock. "Oh, dear Lord. Come on, let's go."

She's taller than I had envisioned. A bit slimmer, but still heavyset. She wears dark blue scrubs and a stethoscope around her neck. Her hair is in long, graying braids neatly pulled back into a bun. Her mouth is slightly open in dismay, horror even.

I'm finished.

I'm not strong enough to fight her or make a run for it past her. Terrified, backed into that small closet, I realize there's no way out, unless I figure one out. "I can explain. Please, don't hurt me."

"Hurt you? I'm the least of your problems, Emma. I started peeling off that patch because I suspected something was off about it. It smelled funny."

"Fentanyl doesn't smell like vinegar?" The words come out of my mouth in a faint whisper, the effort of speaking taking almost everything I had left.

"Fentanyl doesn't smell of anything," she says, holding

my arm for support. I leave the closet hesitantly, still afraid to trust her.

"Why didn't you say something?"

"Against a doctor?" She looks at me, her eyebrows raised, yet apologetic and ashamed. "I need this job. My husband had a stroke last year, and I can't afford to have any complaints. I just peeled the patch back a little, hoping I'd notice a difference in you. And then I'd know, and have some proof, and be able to tell someone." Her eyes glisten with tears. "I should've called someone sooner. I'm so sorry—"

"You told me he was a good doctor. You never said—"

She lowers her head for a moment, ashamed. "What would you have done in my place? Tell a bedridden patient you never met her doctor? I should've—"

"We need to run," I urge her, tugging weakly at her hand. "We can't be here when he comes back." I think of what could happen and shudder as I clasp the Versed syringe tighter in my hand.

"Can you walk?" she asks, letting go of my arm. "I need to go check on that guy out there, the one on the monitor." She shifts her chin at the security camera screen behind me. "He could still be alive."

"You remember Steve, don't you?" My voice turns cold, tainted with suspicion. "You have his number. Did he pay you and the doctor off? To make me sign those papers?" I hear myself and realize I don't make much sense.

Jasmine stares at me, visibly confused, her brow furrowed. "I heard you talking to him, that's all. He seemed to be one of the few people who cared about what happened to you. He gave me his number and asked me to call if you had any problems. I swear, that's all."

"But didn't you say—" I stop, realizing how foggy my memory is, about everything that's happened to me since I was attacked.

"Never mind . . . let's get the hell out of here." She's still staring at me, unsure what to do. "Yes, I can walk. Go!"

She speeds out the back door, and a gust of cold air rushes inside, chilling me to the bone. I'm barefoot on the cold floors, wearing a flimsy hospital gown that flutters around my body as I walk. My teeth are chattering, my limbs are starting to feel numb; I'm too weak to last a moment outside, dressed like this.

Moving like a zombie, I make my way inside the master bedroom closet and rummage through the drawers. I take thick wool socks, a pair of sweatpants, and a sweater, and throw them on as quickly as I can. The Versed syringe, removed from its wrapping, lands in my pants pocket, but I'm unwilling to let go of it for too long. I keep my hand tightly wrapped around the thin cylinder as I stumble out of the room.

As I'm making my way to the front door, I nearly fall a couple of times. I keep looking over my shoulder, listening to every noise, afraid Dr. Sokolowski might be back. The lights of the house stay off, thankfully; strangely, I feel safer in the dark now, feeling my way around this familiar place, listening for telling sounds.

Just then, the key turns in the front door lock, and I freeze in place, merely a few feet away from it. I keep my hand on the wall for balance, too weak to run back and hide.

The door creaks lightly as it opens. "Emma?" A man's strong voice calls out from the doorway.

It sounds eerily familiar, because it is.

"Adrian," I say, the relief swelling my chest as I run into his arms. "Help me, please," I blurt, looking at his concerned face as my story rolls off my tongue in a jumble of words. "I was attacked, and I—I landed in the hospital, but then I don't know what happened. It must've been Steve, who wants the house, but the doctor was lying to me. I think they're drugging me. Please, we have to run. He killed Steve. He'll kill me too."

"It's okay, Emma, I'm here. I came as soon as I could." His

arms wrap around my shoulders, and I breathe, then start sobbing quietly. "It's all right, baby. You weren't answering the door, and I still had my key. I was scared for you. It's going to be all right."

My legs tremble with the effort, but I have Adrian to lean against. He senses my weakness and supports me. My face rests against his chest as I remember how it used to feel in the warmth of his embrace, back when we were together. Safe. Loved. Protected.

I shove the syringe in my pocket and wrap my arms around his neck, still sniffling. And in that moment, a flashback engulfs me, vivid images streaming through my mind like a runaway film reel.

After he left me that night in LA, I carried on with my work during the days, and sobbed myself to sleep at night. Stayed put in that furnished rental for about two weeks, giving him time to forgive me, to come home.

He didn't.

I moved into the Lexington Avenue apartment that Lisa still had. She was filming on location somewhere, and I was all alone, content to be by myself as I grieved the loss of my and Adrian's love. Slowly, I started feeling better. The pain dissipated in a few days, and I felt energized, able to memorize my lines, to perform at my best. Just as I'd felt in Wyoming, where I blamed my improvement on the fresh mountain air and the excitement of working on something new.

My follow-up doctor's appointment found me symptom-free, and had her scratching her head. There was no fibromyalgia, just a strong suspicion I'd been drugged. When she offered to test my hair for traces of toxins, I wholeheartedly agreed, but then awaited the results with a cold, iron claw squeezing my heart.

If the test was positive, it could only mean one thing.

· · ·

I pull away from Adrian's chest slowly, confused, stunned as memories come into focus. The fine scent of spicy basil and suede fills my nostrils, now that my tears have dried, and I remember the first time I smelled it. In the producer's office, on location for *Summer Love,* on the first day of filming. The intrusive memory cascades over me but completes itself with the missing pieces of the puzzle at last, as I struggle to breathe.

"I won't do it," Adrian was shouting, glaring at his agent.

"Son, do you ever want to get laid again? Then sign the damn paper. It's your only chance."

Lyle stabbed Adrian's chest with his finger, but Adrian dismissed him with a hand gesture, seeming a little embarrassed. "I said no. It's not who I am." Then he started walking toward me with a shy smile.

Lyle had grabbed Adrian's sleeve and held him back. "Listen, no one can pronounce your name, kid; no one *wants* to. Let's ask that beautiful young woman who she'd rather date—the romantic chick-magnet Adrian Sera? Or the totally unappealing Adrian Sokolowski?"

Now I know what the fuss was all about. And why I had to remember it. My Adrian used to be Adrian Sokolowski.

The memory chills me to the bone.

I hadn't remembered that about him. Not until I raked my mind over and over to dig up this buried piece of information. It must've slipped my mind that day, a tidbit of irrelevant information about a man I was yet to meet. But I do recall that, later, when he shook my hand and introduced himself, he did it as Adrian Sera.

There's probably more I didn't know, starting with the fact

that he was a doctor who chose acting over practicing medicine. He never told me any of it.

Shaking, I pull away from him, walking backward until I hit the wall. "Why, Adrian? Why do this to me?" He doesn't speak, just looks at me. The warm glow in his eyes fades, leaving behind the chill of a deathly stare.

In that split second between my question and his answer, more forgotten memories come rushing into my mind, crashing into me.

FORTY-FOUR

It started with that damn stalker.

I was cooking dinner for myself, pushing myself to make more than a sandwich, a couple of months after Adrian and I broke up. For me, living alone tends to lead to microwave dinners in front of the TV and a waistline I couldn't afford in my chosen profession. I'd chopped all the components for a Greek salad, and I was waiting for some eggs to boil for an off-recipe addition to the old favorite. I peeked behind the closed curtains and saw him out there, by the aspen. It was the first time I'd seen the stalker since the night Adrian left me, in LA.

It was snowing lightly, and it wasn't too cold but still below freezing; the snow settled on the ground. He wore the gray hoodie I'd come to recognize and dread, with the hood up, eyes shaded underneath its edge. A black scarf covered his mouth and nose, wrapped around his neck under the hoodie. He kept his arms folded at his chest, and his feet, in heavy boots, were slightly apart, like a soldier or a cop.

The rage I'd felt back in LA resurged. This time, in my own backyard, I wanted him caught. I needed this to be over. Forever.

Despite my anger, I thought about it for a minute or two. I couldn't call the cops; I'd done that twice. Each time he heard them coming and disappeared, and I was left looking foolish. I wasn't going to shout at him from the doorway, like I'd done in LA, giving him ample time to vanish. No . . . I wanted to believe I could be smarter than that, learn from my mistakes.

First off, I opened the curtains just an inch, to keep his attention focused on that sliver of light, on the idea that he might catch a glimpse of me walking by. Then I walked through the house and snuck out the front door and inched along the wall until he came into view. I used the cover of the side hedge to get within a couple of yards of him.

The closer I got, the more I doubted that it was a great idea, but there was no turning back. I was done with being afraid. So, I left the cover of the hedge and tiptoed carefully, closing the distance until I could touch him.

I tapped him on the shoulder and said, "Looking for me?"

He whipped around, visibly startled. A gust of wind caught his hood and blew it back. The scarf fell loose, exposing his mouth.

Stunned, I faltered back. "Adrian? What the hell?"

He didn't say a word, his silence more threatening than anything he could've said. He walked toward me while I withdrew toward the back door, forgetting it was locked. When I remembered, I stopped. I turned on my heel and ran as fast as I could toward the front door.

I made it inside and had almost got the door closed when he put his foot inside and blocked me. He pushed the door open, and I let go, unable to resist his strength. I ran toward the living room, as he turned the deadbolt and locked the door behind me.

"Emma, stop," he called. "Let me explain."

I stumbled into the kitchen, my wet shoes slipping on the tiles. Grabbing the counter for support, I reached for my phone. "I'm calling the cops. Go away, Adrian, leave me alone."

He stood near the window, looking at me with an intensity I couldn't bear. It was as if his gaze drilled into my brain, draining my strength.

"I know what you did," I blurted in a short, breathless burst, as if trying to break the spell of that petrifying stare. "You poisoned me. The doctor said it was curare, a paralyzing agent. You gave me small amounts, small enough to only weaken me. Why, Adrian? Why stalk me, why do all this?"

"Because I love you, Emma. And because you're reckless and selfish and harebrained about your own safety. You eat what you want. Do what you want. Go out drinking with your so-called friends. Strut your stuff in front of drunks and perverts and all the scum littering the boulevards. That's why."

That again. I couldn't believe what I was hearing, but I didn't let it show. There was something about him that scared me out of my mind. "What do you mean?" I asked, just to keep him talking until I could figure out what to do, because I understood perfectly what his problem was. He couldn't handle a woman who had a mind of her own.

He raised his arms in the air then let them drop in an expression of frustration and disbelief. "Remember when you went out with Lisa and two other women? Girls' night out, I believe you called it, but it was just women dressed like whores, drinking. I watched you from across the street, so that I'd know you'd be safe. Then you hailed a cab." He scoffed and looked at me as if I were a toddler who spilled her milk. "A damn cab!" He paused for a beat. "You're a celebrity now, Emma. You don't ride alone in cars with strangers. Who knows what could happen. Men are not what you think."

His explanation fuels my rage. "You lied to me! You *knew* how afraid I was of this stalker. You *wanted* me scared, miserable, locked inside the house like a prisoner." I paced in place, desperate for a way out and not seeing it. "For crying out loud, you went with me to the cops when I filed the complaint against the stalker.

Against *you!*" I stabbed the air with my finger, but he didn't react, just stared at me.

His jaw was clenched, his muscles knotted under his skin. And his eyes were ice-cold, like a snake's. "I didn't have a choice. You're completely irresponsible. I thought if you'd be more cautious, it wouldn't hurt. All I wanted was for you to be cared for, protected, and safe. Was it really that bad?"

A surge of emotions made me stutter, at a loss for words. "I— is that right? I'm irresponsible? Well, then, I'm glad we're over. Now, get out. You're nothing but a sick, delusional, manipulative creep. You need help."

"Emma, no," he said, closing the distance between us with three large steps. I swung around the kitchen island and made for the door, running as fast as I could. When I looked over my shoulder, I saw him grabbing the fireplace poker and raising it, ready to strike.

He was going to kill me. I saw it in those terrifying eyes.

"Help! Someone, help me . . . Let me go!" I shrieked, still running, touching the wall for balance, faltering when I turned to look over my shoulder.

He was gaining on me, quickly. I couldn't see the poker, I didn't see his hands, or the expression on his face. Only the deathly stare in his eyes that seared its mark into my mind. It was an intense, unwavering, emotionless gaze. His eyes were fixed on me, as if looking through me, cold and piercing and final.

I reached the front door and tried to open it, but couldn't. Shrieking, I fumbled with the lock, pulled the door open, and turned to look behind me again, just in time to see the arm raised above my head starting to come down. Then I saw the asphalt of my own driveway rushing to slam against my face, before my entire world went dark in a burst of stars.

. . .

The flashback is still reverberating in my mind, when Adrian finally answers.

"Because I love you too damn much to sit idly by and watch you destroy yourself. Not when I can look after you."

My jaw drops in disbelief. I'm not going to rehash the same conversation we had that night. I already know how it ends, with my head split open, dying.

Instead, I swallow hard and force a smile on my lips. "Oh . . . I love you too, baby. I missed you so much."

The harsh line of his jaw softens a little, and his eyes warm up. I hold his gaze steadily—while my hand sneaks into my pocket and clasps the Versed syringe.

That moment, the back door swings open, and Jasmine comes in, stamping her boots against the doormat. "He's dead. I'm sorry—"

"Run," I shout, but she's not fast enough. For a precious moment, she stares at me, confused. Then she sees Adrian lunging and screams, but he's fast. He grabs her by the neck and slams her head against the wall with a sickening thud. Jasmine falls to the ground into a motionless heap.

Adrian kicks the door shut, then brushes his hands against one another. "She wasn't that good anyway. She can't follow a medication regimen to save her life." His short, maniacal laugh chills my blood.

I'm next.

There's nowhere to run. No escape. The two seconds I'd need to make a nine-one-one call are two seconds I don't have. I look at him, as warmly as I can manage, while my fingers, deep inside my pocket, struggle to take the needle cap off the syringe.

"I'm a little hungry," I say. "Let's make something."

He tilts his head almost imperceptibly, and a lopsided smile lands on his lips. "You must think I'm an idiot." His stare drills into me for a moment, then he lunges. He grabs my waist and lifts me in the air, my weak arms flailing against him.

"Please, put me down," I cry. "Please, Adrian, I'm begging you."

"I'll put you down, no worries." He takes me to the bedroom and drops me onto that dreadful bed.

He starts to move away but I put my hands behind his neck and intertwine my fingers. "No, don't go. I love you. I can prove it to you."

That gets his attention. "Really? Let's hear it."

Sitting upright against the pillows, I let go of his neck and slip my hand inside my pocket, then grab the syringe. "Even after the doctors told me I'd been poisoned, I never told anyone who it was. I never said a word, because I understood everything, Adrian. I understood *you*. What I meant to you."

He sits on the side of the bed and gives me a long, scrutinizing look. My heart is thumping in my chest. Sweat threatens my grip on the syringe.

"I don't believe you," he eventually says. "I know you didn't tell the cops about me. But I know you want me gone, out of your life."

"Why do you say that?"

"After Wyoming, you couldn't get away from me fast enough. You wanted to move back to Tahoe, remember? Don't tell me it's suddenly different now." He stands and walks over to the cart on wheels, the one with all the meds. "Now, it's time for bed, Emma. It's late. I have an early day tomorrow. We're kicking off season two in my TV series."

I get out of bed quietly and approach him, but he senses me and turns around. I grab his arm, but he pushes me away forcefully enough that I land on the floor, hard, the air knocked out of my lungs. It takes me a moment to fight the dizziness. I ache all over, and my head is throbbing so badly I don't see straight. Moaning in pain, I still manage to take the syringe out of my pocket and stab him in the calf with the needle, and push the plunger as hard as I can.

He screams and turns to look at the syringe, the needle still stuck in his calf to the hilt. He pulls it out and stares at it, while I wriggle backward on the floor, pushing myself as far from him as I can. He bellows in rage and comes after me, but I retreat under the bed. He swings a couple of times, but only gets my leg. Reaching further, he gets a grip on me and starts pulling me out.

But then he lets go, staring at me in disbelief and mumbling something I can't catch. Then he drops to his knees and falls on his side, breathing heavily.

I push myself away until I reach the wall.

After a while, I summon the courage to come near him. He's fighting the Versed drowsiness and losing, his eyelids heavy, his mouth slightly open.

I stare at the man I used to be in love with and shudder. I never saw it coming. Any of it.

"Why?" I ask softly, unsure if he can still hear me. Tears are flowing down my face, but I don't bother to wipe them away. "You blinded and paralyzed me . . . why torture me like that?"

He tries to smile as he's falling asleep. "My sweet Emma . . . you know I had to. I didn't have a choice. I couldn't let you die."

FORTY-FIVE

I couldn't stand there and watch Emma die. No matter the cost.

For a while, I paced near her, doing everything in my power to ignore the soft cries coming from her pale lips, when I wished I could pick her up and comfort her, hold her tight in my arms, carry her inside to warmth and safety. Instead, I trod the driveway like a caged animal, considering my limited options. What if I called for help, then destroyed my phone before they could track it? But they tracked those damned things in real time now. Then, what else could I do? What lie could I tell them to explain my presence there?

As I paced faster and faster, torn by my own indecision, I started to realize what I felt deep inside. How the metallic smell of her blood triggered an unclear yearning in me. How deeply troubled I was about the vulnerable body lying at my feet, the power of life and death I had over her.

That moment, on the serrated edge between life and death, she was completely and absolutely mine. And I liked it. The complete power I had over her, and I could keep having. From villain—the man who would haunt her nightmares forever— I could become her hero, the man she could fall in love with all over again. The people who visited her at first would stop coming, feeling too guilty about their own health and happiness to want to be in the same room with her. They'd abandon her, and I'd be the only one left by her side.

My sweet Emma.

Mine to have and hold.

Mine forever.

And so, the solution to my problem started forming in my mind, the way a simple idea can turn into a screenplay, and then into two hours of film. One scene at a time, polished, perfected, and seamlessly attached to the next scene. And the next after that, a journey of illusion and reality mixed and intertwined.

I took my phone out and checked the time. It gets dark early in November, but it was barely five thirty. I still had time.

Instead of nine-one-one, I called the largest supplier of in-home health supplies and equipment in the area.

"Heal Home Medical, *how may I assist you?" The voice on the other end of the call was sweet, eager, willing to please.*

"This is Dr. Adrian Sokolowski, license number A 054421. I have a patient discharged to home care after a head trauma. I need some equipment delivered tonight. Some supplies, too." *I give her the address.*

"Please hold, Dr. Sokolowski." *She took less than a minute to check my license.* "I see you're calling from the number registered with the Medical Board. What do you need?"

I looked at Emma's fingers. They were barely twitching anymore. I didn't have a moment to waste. "I need a full hospital room. Adjustable bed with mattress, cardiac monitor, fully stocked crash trauma supplies carts, the works."

"Got it. What else?"

"Trauma wound care basics, two weeks' worth. Gauze in rolls and pads, tape, hemostatic agents, suture kits with 3.0 absorbable and non-absorbable sutures. And add a couple of needle drivers."

"Noted." I could hear her typing quickly. She must be really good at her job.

I was thinking hard, pressed for time, afraid she might die right there, at my feet, while I was trying to save her life. And mine.

"IV fluids—lactated Ringer's and normal saline. I'd say about ten liters of each."

"What else?"

"Some pharmaceuticals and we're done. Midazolam—brand name Versed. Let's do 25 vials of the 2 mg concentration for procedural sedation. Add ten preloaded syringes. I need neuromuscular blocking agents, say, rocuronium bromide, 20 vials of the 10 mg/ml concentration. Add dexamethasone, brand name Decadron, in 4 mg/ml injectable vials, 20 of them, and fentanyl transdermal patches—we need them in 25 mcg/hr and 50 mcg/hr strengths, also 20 count. That's it for now."

I gave her a moment to finish typing. "When can I have it?"

"Tomorrow at—"

I looked at Emma and fear strangled me. "No. Not going to work. I need everything stat."

"Doctor, I'm sorry, but we can't—our people are leaving in ten minutes."

"Well, then, stop them. If the patient needs to pay extra, she will."

An endless moment of silence. "Let me see what I can do."

I waited impatiently, crouched near Emma, my fingers on her weak and thready pulse.

"All right, Doctor, you'll have everything within the hour. There will be a 15 percent surcharge on the entire order."

"You're amazing," I said, then ended the call.

I looked at the size of the dark puddle near Emma's head with a critical eye. She'd lost too much blood. I lifted her body off the ground and rushed inside the house. On the way to the guest bedroom, I pulled some towels off the bathroom rack. I laid her on the bed and started propping her up with pillows and towels. Then I moistened a towel and held it against the back of her head, applying pressure, hoping the bleeding would stop.

It didn't. I needed something to hold it in place while I ran outside and cleaned the blood off the driveway before the Heal Home delivery arrived. I didn't think they'd let a puddle of blood found at the site of an emergency delivery go unreported. Cops would be swarming the place within minutes, and I couldn't afford that.

I rummaged through Emma's closet drawers until I found something I could use to hold pressure on the wound: a white silk scarf. I tied it around her head, over the towel at the back of her head and on her forehead. I re-arranged the pillows, and the scarf slipped over her eyes.

That's how the idea came to me.

She could be blind for a while, giving the Versed the time to work its magic.

Versed works miracles for brain injury patients, to prevent seizures and keep them comfortable while they recover. But that's not why I ordered enough Versed to last me a month. It has an interesting side effect: anterograde amnesia. As long as Versed was dripping into Emma's veins, she wouldn't remember a thing. Not what happened, or how she came to be in that hospital bed. Not even my voice. Given enough Versed, she'd forget the incident completely, the memory permanently erased from her brain. Then she could fall in love with me all over again. She did it once before, didn't she?

I tightened the scarf over Emma's eyes and dimmed the lights. Then I went outside with the two bottles of peroxide I used to keep in the bathroom cabinets, thankful that Emma hadn't thrown them away since I left. I sprinkled them over the blood stain and let the oxygen work its magic. It took about thirty minutes of sprinkling and waiting and listening to the peroxide sizzling on the asphalt, but when it was finally done, all that was left was a faint pink hue on the accumulated snow at the edge of the lawn.

Next, I burned my bloodied clothes in the firepit, after changing into some of Emma's looser sweatpants and shirt. They were tight and short on me, but they weren't bloodstained, and that was all I needed.

Another half an hour or so passed, and I took delivery. The crew, professional and quick, installed and tested everything, and helped me move the king-sized bed that used to be ours into the small bedroom down the hall. I signed off the order after making sure I had everything, tipped them generously, and sent them on their way.

When the truck peeled off, I rushed back inside. There was a lot of work to do. I started by moving Emma into the master bedroom, where the new bed had been made with a new mattress and freshly unsealed hospital sheets. I washed my hands and slipped on surgical gloves, then hooked her up to a Ringer's IV, on the fastest drip rate, to help her replenish the lost blood volume. I cleaned her wound and stitched it up carefully. Finally, I applied eye lubricant and taped her eyelids shut, the way they do with patients undergoing surgery to prevent corneal damage from dryness.

The gauze wrapped tightly around her head was the final touch. Now, all I could do for her was sit and wait, letting her body do the heavy lifting. She was too weak to start her on the rocuronium, to further reduce her muscle tone; it could've triggered respiratory failure if done too soon. But I put the fentanyl patch on her arm. There was no point in having her endure the pain. Come morning, I'd add a tiny bit of the paralyzing agent, enough to keep her still. Finally, I added a vial of Versed to her IV.

She was resting comfortably, but I had a lot of work left to do. First, when I dared leave her alone for a little while, I snuck into Baldwin Medical Center wearing scrubs, a mask, and a stethoscope *around my neck. No one paid a flicker of attention to me as I went straight to the staff message board and pasted an ad there, offering trauma nurses some extra shift work in home care. "Call anytime," the ad said, and gave a burner number I had bought off the internet a while ago, when I started following Emma.*

Before I had to leave the next day, I had two nurses lined up, signing up for home care shifts. Both were told that the patient had suffered an assault in the home, and had recently been discharged. It would be in her best interest to not tell her she was no longer in the hospital. She had to believe she was safe. They bought it, with tears glistening in their eyes.

By 6 p.m., everything was ready for the first nurse to show up for work. A new lamp was installed in the master bedroom, to give the right light when I came to visit my sweet Emma. There were surveillance cameras already installed in the room and the corridor; I used to live there . . . I knew where things were. I added six monitors and connected them to the home's security system. I set everything up in the small bedroom, where I hunkered down, sleeping on the king-sized mattress that used to be our bed. The final touch: a couple of miniature speakers hidden in Emma's room, so I could play PA announcements I'd recorded with my phone in the hospital's emergency room the night before. I thought they'd soothe her when she was alone and seemed agitated.

"People see what they want to see" is the rule of motivated perception, or its close relative, confirmation bias. I knew what she'd think. I knew what everyone would think.

When Emma woke up, she'd feel much safer knowing she was in a hospital, cared for by a team of professionals, safe and secure. She'd expect that and nothing less, and I wanted her to have it, the hospital experience and the peace of mind it would give her, until I could figure out what she remembered—if anything at all.

I wasn't entirely selfless there. Orchestrating this for her benefit thrilled me, the sense of absolute power over her reality exhilarating. I was the ultimate illusionist, twisting realities and timelines, allowing everyone to see and feel exactly what I had scripted them to. There was no limit, because people see what they want to see. Always.

I wanted to have other people visit her, to put her mind at ease, and to make sure none of them would cause trouble. The same sob story worked for them too, and no one dared to tell Emma she was at home. Not before I told them it was okay to do so. When I lie, I make it a good one, half true, universally fitting, and with a thick layer of emotional glaze to make people buy into it quickly before they have a chance to think. It works every time.

My only problem was Lisa, who'd spent enough time with us to recognize me, even with the surgical mask I wore all the time and speaking with a softer, deeper voice as Dr. Sokolowski, with that Polish accent I do so well to match the name. But that was manageable. I simply let the nurses handle her. As for that self-absorbed, smug son of a bitch, Steve Wellington, he looked right through me and saw only what he wanted to see—some snotty doctor standing in his way. Even if he had directed two of the movies I played in.

The entire setup, the script that went with it, the scenography—everything was a masterpiece. And still, it wasn't good enough.

Emma should've welcomed me back into her life with open arms once she got better. But I failed to control her properly. I didn't anticipate how strong she was, or how determined to fight me. To fight the adversities of her reality. I didn't imagine that nurse would be so dumb as to forget to add the Versed to her IV.

Everything I did was well worth it, because it saved her life. She would've died that night if it weren't for me.

I could've made her so happy . . . if only she'd have let me take care of her.

My sweet Emma. Mine, forever.

FORTY-SIX

"It was rocuronium," Jasmine says. She's sitting on the leather chair behind the desk in my study, a bag of frozen peas held against her head. It's the closest I could come up with in lieu of an ice pack.

I struggle a little, but manage to pop open a can of Coke and down it thirstily. It's my second, and I can already feel the effects. My strength isn't what it used to be, but at least I can function.

"What was?" I ask, a little distracted, as I open the small closet where the security system is housed and take a seat on the three-legged stool.

"The vinegary smell on your patch. That was rocuronium, a paralyzing agent. It's a synthetic form of curare, did you know that?"

Curare again. Of course. "I had no idea."

"It had no business being given to you; it has different applications."

"Like what?" I fire up the screen and wait for it to load.

"General anesthesia, intubation, that kind of stuff. I guess I didn't want to believe it. Emma, I'm so sorry. I didn't smell it at first; only when I started to lift the patch. I was just curious if you could improve faster without the fentanyl. I didn't imagine anyone would do what he did."

"No one could." My mind is not on Jasmine; I don't hold any of what happened against her. If anything, I'm grateful. She peeled off the corner of my patch, helping me recover faster. Helping me see it was possible. "Are you still okay?"

"Yeah, hon, don't worry about me. He didn't crack this noggin, although he sure as hell tried." She laughs and turns the bag of peas over. "By the way, I just checked out his credentials online." She holds up her phone and waves it at me. "He went to med school in California, but failed his residency. Never practiced medicine after that—went into acting."

The acting part I knew. Everything else, I had no idea about.

It's as if that day, when Adrian agreed to sign those papers, he left behind an entire persona, not just a name.

I ask Jasmine if she can give me some time to look at the security feeds, before we call an ambulance for her. Before the entire world comes crashing in.

As the screen lights up, I'm cringing, afraid of what I'm about to see. I choose the outside view and go back to the moment Adrian tried to kill me. I see myself bursting through the open door, running. His hand raised, striking me down. Me, falling on the driveway and not moving anymore.

Then I see him pacing, checking on me, pacing some more, seemingly undecided. When he makes a call, I'm assuming he's calling nine-one-one. Later, he scoops me up and takes me inside. I flip through the security video feeds as things evolve, following the action from camera to camera. I see him laying me down on the guestroom bed, caring for me. I cry quietly as I watch, my hand over my mouth, tears streaming from my eyes until everything turns into a blur.

The hospital furniture is delivered, installed, then people

leave. I feel like screaming at them. "Stop! Ask questions, don't just walk away like that."

I was never in the hospital.

On the screen, he's cleaning my wound, suturing it, taping my eyes shut, wrapping my head in gauze. I see myself lying there, and I remember how terrified I was, how dark it was and how cold and scary and surreal.

I shift the viewing speed to 10x and keep watching. I see Isabella coming in, doing her work. I squeeze my eyes shut when she performs certain tasks, unable to handle seeing myself so vulnerable.

I don't realize I'm muttering, "No, no, no . . ." until I feel Jasmine's hand squeezing my shoulder.

"Maybe you shouldn't watch this," she says gently.

I put my hand on hers. "I have to." And I keep watching and remembering at the same time. What I felt. The thoughts that haunted me. The questions I had. The despair.

The second night of the stream, after Jasmine feeds me and changes the IV bags, she leaves the lights on when she leaves. Nothing happens for a while, but then, at about one in the morning, Adrian comes into the bedroom.

The first thing he does is to adjust the ceiling lights to the brightest setting.

He checks a few things, looks at the monitor, listens to my heart. He unwraps the head dressing and inspects the wound. Then he peels off the covers and removes my gown. I gasp and watch in disbelief as he combs my hair and washes my body with a washcloth, every inch of it. Then he starts speaking to me. I can see his lips moving but can't tell what he's saying, only that he's leaning close to my ear when he's saying it. He kisses my lips slowly, lightly, as I cringe and want to scream as I watch.

"Honey, that's enough," Jasmine says. She's standing by my chair and leans over, her hand hovering over the wheeled mouse to press Stop. "You don't need to see this. It doesn't matter any-more. It's over."

She's right.

Those images will haunt me for the rest of my life. I wasn't dreaming about that bright circle of lights; I was actually seeing it at night, drugged and traumatized, and didn't remember it. I remember hearing his voice in my dreams, my skin prickling as if touched by the wind on the lake shore. Now I know why.

Standing, I'm about to switch off the monitor, when I think of something else. I fast forward to the following night, and see the same thing. Bright lights shining over my naked body. Adrian touching me.

I feel sick.

Slowly, I walk into the master bedroom and turn on the lights, pushing the dimmer all the way up. Then I look at the man lying in the hospital bed. Wires are attached to his chest, leading to the heart monitor that beeps quietly. An IV is hanging from a stand, the tubing attached to his vein with an 18-gauge nee-dle. A spent vial of Versed and another one of rocuronium are abandoned on the tray, next to the syringe used to add it to the saline IV.

With a lopsided smile, I remove the needle from his arm.

Then I stare at the face of the man I used to love, and ask myself, again and again, how could I have not seen who he really was.

His handsome features are relaxed in deep sleep, but soon they start contorting when fear chases away the serenity of his slumber.

Then he awakes.

"Emma?" My name on his lips makes me want to scream. "Emma, I can't move. Baby, please. Let me go. You've forgiven me once before, remember?"

My stomach is riled up. I fight off my nausea with deep, sharp gulps of air. "Yes, I do remember, despite your best efforts. I believed all your lies, up to the very end. I didn't see the murderer that you are."

"Emma, please—"

"You have two options," I say coldly. "Stay here, paralyzed in this hospital bed, at my mercy for as long as I want. Or go to jail for the rest of your life. You get to choose, and in return, I get answers to all my questions."

"Please, don't call the cops. They'll lock me up. I'd rather be with you for the rest of my life. I know you'll forgive me someday."

The hell I will.

"Why me?" I ask. He doesn't reply, just stares at me, squinting. "Out of all the women out there, why did it have to be me?"

A smile flutters on his lips. "The moment I saw you, I knew how much you needed me. You seemed so lost, so shy and nervous and not prepared at all to face this world. I knew I could take care of you. Make you happy."

"The curare you used to poison me with, how did you give it to me?" I have to know. When I left for Wyoming, the improvement in my health had been immediate. But after he left me in LA, it didn't happen as fast. Not until after I moved to Lisa's apartment.

He presses his lips together for a moment. I glare at him, then show him the phone I'm holding in my hand.

"It was in the saltshaker. You like your food salty. I watch my salt intake."

I don't remember what I did with the saltshaker I had at that rental house in LA. I hope I threw it out with the rest of the stuff.

"Was there ever a Dr. Winslow? A neurology consult?" He doesn't reply immediately, and I'm short of patience. "Was there?"

"No." A beat of silence. "There is a neurologist by the name of Winslow, but he's never heard of you."

I breathe deeply to steady myself, to keep a lid on my intense anger. "All the lies you told, so smooth, so unbelievably real," I whisper, more to myself.

"We're actors, baby. We lie for a living, and we're good at it."

His arrogant reply exasperates me. "You were quite bold to assume you'd get away with this. What did you expect to happen?"

"Nothing, my sweet Emma. Only to save you. To make you love me again."

I look at him with pity. Somewhere inside that man is a fractured soul, a tormented personality, perhaps from some past trauma I never knew about. I almost ask, when I realize I don't really want to know.

A wave of bitterness surges over me and I let him have it. "You're nothing but one of those freaks who lock girls in basements. Only you use chemical restraints instead of chains and padlocks. You make me sick."

In the distance, police sirens are approaching. Fear lights his hazel eyes with shades of panic. "Emma? You promised!"

The smile blooming on my lips touches my eyes. "You don't get to call the shots anymore, Dr. Sokolowski."

A couple of hours later, they're almost done, and not a moment too soon, because I'm ready to collapse. Wrapped in a blanket, I'm shaking like a leaf in the brisk mountain wind. It's daylight, but barely, and the view is bleak.

In the back of an ambulance, an EMT is tending to Jasmine's head wound. Thankfully, he said it's not that bad, but she will still need a CT to be sure there's no concussion. She refuses and says she'll do that only if she's showing symptoms. They argue for a while, but they know each other, and the conversation is more friendly banter than quarrel.

Meanwhile, I'm watching Steve's body being loaded into the coroner's van, the black body bag strapped to the gurney depressing and spine-chilling. I came very close to the same fate. My eyes burn. I loved Steve . . . part of me still mourns him, and has done so since the day we got divorced. I'll always miss him—the Steve I used to know before her. Before Mikela.

I'm about to head inside, where I'm hoping to get some sleep. Without any drugs whatsoever. Alone in my house. Then I might grill a steak and have a beer by the firepit.

Jasmine walks over from the ambulance and gives me a hug.

"Will you be okay?" she asks, with an encouraging smile. I nod and squeeze her hand—my turn at last. "If not, you know you have friends at Baldwin, right? I'm a phone call away."

I place a smooch on her cheek, and watch her get behind the wheel of her car and drive off. Then I turn around and walk toward the door.

"Ms. Duncan?" An EMT is looking at me with professional concern. "From what I hear, you suffered a traumatic brain injury, but never had a CT scan done. We need to take you to the hospital."

I look him straight in the eye. "Oh, hell, no."

A LETTER FROM LESLIE

A big, heartfelt **thank you** for choosing to read *The Hospital*. If you did enjoy it and want to keep up to date with all my latest releases, just sign up at the following link. Your email address will never be shared, and you can unsubscribe at any time.

LeslieWolfe.com

When I write a new book I think of you, the reader—what you'd like to read next, how you'd like to spend your leisure time, and what you most appreciate from the time spent in the company of the characters I create, vicariously experiencing the challenges I lay in front of them. That's why I'd love to hear from you! Did you enjoy *The Hospital?* Your feedback is incredibly valuable to me, and I appreciate hearing your thoughts. Please contact me directly through one of the channels listed below. Email works best: LW@WolfeNovels.com. I will never share your email address with anyone, and I promise you'll receive an answer from me!

If you enjoyed my book and if it's not too much to ask, please take a moment and leave me a review, and maybe recommend *The Hospital* to other readers. Reviews and personal recommendations help readers discover new titles or new authors for the first time; it makes a huge difference, and it means the world to me.

Thank you for your support, and I hope to keep you entertained with my next story. See you soon!

Leslie

facebook.com/wolfenovels

amazon.com/stores/author/B00KR1QZ0G

bookbub.com/authors/leslie-wolfe

ACKNOWLEDGMENTS

A special, heartfelt thank you goes to the fantastic publishing team at Bookouture. They are a pleasure to work with, their enthusiasm contagious and their dedication inspiring.

A big thank you to Ruth Tross, who consistently makes the editing process smooth and engaging. She's been an incredible support and a true collaborator in all my publishing endeavors, always there to provide that much-needed creative push. I'm incredibly grateful for her assistance.

Thanks also to Kim Nash and Noelle Holten for their dedicated efforts in book promotion across various channels. Alba Proko deserves a shoutout for skillfully managing the audio versions of my books, ensuring they're produced to the highest standard. I'm deeply impressed with the work you all do.

Appreciation is due to the digital marketing team for their diligent work on every book launch, consistently raising the bar. You all do an exceptional job.

My warmest thanks to Richard King for his commitment to introducing my books to new audiences and markets, and perhaps, one day, to the screen. A heartfelt thank you for everything you do and for your keen interest in my work. It's much appreciated.